THE
POISON
GARDEN

Also by Sarah Singleton

CENTURY
Winner of the Booktrust Teenage Book Award
Highly Commended for the Branford Boase First Novel Award
Winner of the Dracula Society's Children of the Night Award

HERETIC

SACRIFICE

THE AMETHYST CHILD

SARAH SINGLETON

THE POISON GARDEN

SIMON AND SCHUSTER

For my godson, Ben Charlton-Fabian

First published in Great Britain in 2009 by
Simon and Schuster UK Ltd
A CBS COMPANY

Simon & Schuster UK Ltd
1st Floor
222 Gray's Inn Road
London WC1X 8HB

A CIP catalogue record for this book
is available from the British Library.

ISBN 978-1-84738-297-9

3 5 7 9 10 8 6 4 2

Printed by CPI Cox & Wyman, Reading, Berkshire RG1 8EX

www.simonandschuster.co.uk

www.crowmaiden.plus.com

BROCELIANDE

The Garden of Dreams

In and out the dusky bluebells,
In and out the dusky bluebells,
In and out the dusky bluebells,
Following the Master.

Traditional

One

High in the tower the bell tolled, counting out eleven hours. Spring fields spread away from the church. Bluebells swayed in the shadow of the graveyard wall and petals from the apple tree drifted over the heads of the mourners as the funeral procession moved along the narrow path.

Thomas was ten years old and walked behind his mother. She held his infant sister in one arm, his little brother with the other hand. His four elder siblings walked beside him, all in black. Ahead, his father helped carry the narrow coffin out of the church.

They were burying Thomas's grandmother, Augusta Jane Williams. His mother, pale and tired, wept intermittently while juggling the baby. Silky white petals clung to the brim of her black hat, with its mothy feathers.

'Man that is born of a woman hath but a short time to live, and is full of misery,' said the vicar.

'He cometh up, and is cut down, like a flower: he fleeth as it were a shadow, and never continueth in one stay . . .'

Another gust of wind tugged a cloud of petals from the apple tree and lifted the purple stole that hung around the vicar's neck. Thomas looked away, his attention snagged on the hawthorn hedge beyond the wall. He could see a shadow beneath the leaves and may blossom.

This piece of darkness, of indefinable shape, stuck out a black-gloved hand, flexed long fingers – and waved.

Thomas shook his head. Who was it, signalling to him? He looked again. The mysterious hand had disappeared. He wanted to run over and find out to whom the hand belonged – and why this person was hiding. But propriety held him in place. The mystery niggled, an itch he wanted to scratch.

After the burial, they returned to his grandmother's house. It was a dark, substantial building overlooking the village green. Inside, a meal of bread and cold meats awaited them on a table in the dining room.

'I am so sorry for your loss, Ellen.' An elderly and stooped great-aunt had taken his mother's hand between her own lace-mittened fingers and peered into her face. Ellen was an only child but Augusta had been one of twelve children – ten of whom had survived into old age. They hovered now, these survivors, in the gloomy dining room, a colony of gaunt old rooks contemplating the meal and eyeing up the silver.

Thomas tugged at his collar. He ached to leave the stuffy room and its cargo of elderly relatives. His brothers and sisters, bridled by their good manners, were also chomping at the bit for escape. Dieter, their father, pale and gaunt with a cap of dark, fur-like hair, frowned at his brood – the mass of little boys and girls doling out surreptitious kicks and silent gesticulated insults.

'Take them outside,' he said to his eldest daughter, under his breath. One of the crones glanced over and sniffed, doubtless thinking what ill-tempered children they were, to fret so at their grandmother's funeral.

'Take the baby,' he said. 'Let your mother have a rest.'

Christabel, just thirteen, was used to the mantle of responsibility. She took the baby with scarcely a sigh and signalled to the others. They followed her, a noisy herd rejoicing at their sudden liberation, into Grandmother's sumptuous garden.

Once outside, with one mind, the children started to run – ignoring Christabel's orders – away from the house and into the depths of the garden. It was a maze of paths and groves, dense flower beds and sheltered alcoves. Late tulips, the colour of claret and amber, burned in the shelter of the red brick wall. Thomas stretched out his arms, taking a deep breath of fresh air. His little brother galloped past, whooping.

The garden – his grandmother's passion. More than her dead husband, more than her family, Augusta had loved her garden. She had a study furnished with books and drawings about her plants and their uses. Often Thomas had spied her working in the kitchen with leaves, fruits and seeds – variously brewing and stewing, chopping, pulverising, steaming or steeping all manner of produce from the garden. A pantry in the kitchen, kept locked with a key Augusta stored in her pocket, contained bundles of dried herbs, tins of herbal tea and ranks of jars filled with curious pickles and jams each identified with a label written in Augusta's ornate hand. He had read one of the labels, when he was about seven or eight, sneaking in while his grandmother's back was turned. It said something very curious: Juniper Jam for Dreams of Remembered Sadness.

She had seemed a sour old woman, dressed in sable, an expression of grievance etched on her flour-white face – but this obsession with plants had intrigued him. For as long as he could remember, Thomas had followed her, shadowed her footsteps, peered into the study, picked up her books, glimpsed the contents of the pantry, wondering what she was doing, mesmerised by her devotion to her studies. Augusta, always, had shooed him away and shut the door. But his long enduring dedication had caught her notice. Once or twice, even as she scolded him for pushing his finger into a bowl of setting jam, he'd observed her calculating consideration of his persistent interest.

Standing in the garden, bereaved as the garden was also bereaved, Thomas felt the ache of an unexpected sadness, to think his grandmother was dead. Her absence was more real to him in the garden than it had been at the funeral. She would never walk here again. As soon as he could, Thomas broke away from the herd of sisters and brothers and headed off alone. He rarely had a moment to himself and he yearned for a silent space to consider his thoughts. And while he hadn't been exactly close to his grandmother, her garden was an entirely different matter.

She'd told him once, with a scowl, that the garden covered an acre of land. A wall, in a cloak of shining leaves, marked its boundary and joined the sides of the house. A single narrow iron gate to the east (often locked) opened from the front garden – the respectable neat-rows-of-flowers façade presented to the public. Thomas remembered staring through the gate when he was small, pressing his face between the wrought iron bars and gazing into the heart of the enclosed garden. How mysterious it had seemed to him – the hedges of thorns and roses, the gravelled paths leading off into shadowed groves, the perfume of musk and nectar drifting in almost tangible threads from the tangle of fruits and blooms.

Thomas stretched out his hand and touched a fat white blossom with the tips of his fingers. Fragile yellow veins flowed through the cool petals. Soft pollen dusted his skin. Inside the house his grandmother's solicitor would soon be reading the will. He had heard his parents whispering – understood how poor they were, how frequently his father's money-making ventures came to nothing. Everything should change, now his grandmother was dead. They had expectations and stood to inherit her house and fortune, and this, her astonishing garden. He stood up straight and thrust his hands in the pocket of his too-small jacket, looking to left and right, feeling, along with his sadness, an anticipatory sense of ownership.

He was standing on a diamond of untrimmed grass, with a sundial on a plinth in the centre. The grass was enclosed by dark shrubs and trellises upholstered with rambling rose bushes. Behind him the path led back to the bed of herbs at the rear of the house, where the maids cultivated rosemary, sage and coriander for the kitchen.

The sundial was made of a pale, silver metal, etched with Roman numerals and a mesh of circular and elliptical shapes. Although the sun was high, the curved pin rising from the centre didn't cast a shadow. Thomas pressed the palms of his hands on the face of the sundial. The metal sent a shock of cold through his bones, but he didn't move, feeling the etched patterns on his skin.

From here, paths led away: left, right and straight ahead. These paths branched, converged, doubled back, or came to dead ends, and en route offered other inviting side paths through little gates, under tunnels of greenery or over decorative garden stiles, opening on to lavish vegetable gardens, glasshouses for fruit and exotic flowers, elaborate and fragrant herb beds.

Beyond the shrubs he could hear the voices of his brothers and sisters. A game was in progress and if they found him, Thomas would be expected to join in. He looked back once towards the house, sensing movement, thinking one of his siblings was seeking him out. He couldn't see anyone, but he turned again, uneasily, remembering the hand that had waved at him from the hedge, during his grandmother's funeral.

'Christabel?' His voice had an edge – annoyance, and a note of apprehension. Something wasn't quite right. The garden seemed to shift around him.

'Come out, I can see you!' Still no response, though Thomas's sense of being observed intensified. He turned around again, trying to catch the watcher.

There – on the sundial – stood a wooden box with its lid open. Where had it come from? Thomas frowned. Someone had crept up on him and – he presumed – left it for him to find. Thomas stood tall, determined to look confident, and peered at this mysterious gift.

It was hard to see inside – the interior was dark and vague. He raised his hand, thinking to explore the contents but caution held him back. Then he heard a whistle. A jaunty, encouraging whistle – someone seeking his attention. Thomas looked up. A new path had materialised, leading away from the sundial.

Thomas stood and stared. He glanced back at the box, and the amorphous darkness it contained. Was there a connection between the box and this new path? How could a path just appear from nowhere? Perhaps he simply hadn't noticed it before. But how could that be?

The path beckoned. A gravel path, a tunnel of briars like the fabled passageway in a folk tale, it whispered and enticed. Thomas could not resist.

As soon as he passed beneath the roof of thorny stems, Thomas sensed he had moved into an entirely different space. He was in his grandmother's garden no longer – at least, not the garden he had known. Here the air was different – cool and strangely perfumed, the sky an unearthly turquoise.

The path veered one way, then another, before emerging at a cultivated patch edged by a low stone wall, where squashes and pumpkins, strangely shaped, grew in profusion. He saw a grove of willow trees by a pond where large golden flowers grew on sighing reeds. He was far away now, too far to hear the voices of his siblings. This part of the garden seemed largely untended. Rhododendron bushes created a jungle, narrow paths punctuated by natural caves among the twisted branches and leathery leaves.

Thomas pushed his way into this jungle. The stinging perfume of the flowers caught in his throat. Sometimes he found pathways. At other times, he had to force a way through densely growing stems. The roots reached out to trip him. Malicious clawed twigs poked his eyes and scratched his face. But Thomas, frustration chewing in his belly, was not deterred. He ground his teeth and slapped the leaves in a temper. At last he emerged on a narrow grass path. To the left – which Thomas surmised was vaguely the way he had come – the path ran downhill to a tall gate. To the right, the path rose to the crest of a hill. Hot now, he took off his jacket and dropped it on the floor and set off up the hill.

At the summit he stopped and shaded his eyes. Perhaps a storm was coming, because the turquoise sky was a pale green colour and the clouds huddled in an anxious circle. The path now dropped down to a marvellous orchard. How inviting it looked, a dozen fruit trees covered in blossom. Thomas felt his spirits lift. He set off at a gallop, down the hill to a narrow green gate through the broken fence.

'Make sure you close the gate – or the goat will get out.'

Thomas jumped. The voice came out of nowhere. He looked around, without result, for the speaker. He could see no goat either, though it seemed pointless to close the gate because the fence was so decayed it wouldn't prove an obstacle to any domestic animal. Still, he did as he was told.

'Over here,' the voice said. A man's voice, well spoken. It

possessed a pleasant musical quality, making Thomas wish to hear more. He stepped away from the gate and looked around the orchard. It was hard to make out what lay beyond the fence – the view was occluded by blossom or else seemed to melt into shade.

A loud bleat – and all of a sudden the animal was standing beside him, a tall black goat with long curved horns and cold yellow eyes. It pressed its bony body against his leg, jaws chomping on some mashed-up vegetable matter. It bleated again. Thomas was unnerved by the creature's grinding yellow teeth and the wicked horns, so he sidled away and peered into the heart of the orchard. The branches seemed to draw back, revealing a man in black who leaned against a stump of old stone.

'There you are,' Thomas said, without thinking. 'I mean, I'm sorry. I couldn't see you at first.'

He walked towards the man, intrigued by this stranger in his grandmother's garden. Presumably he was a mourner who, like Thomas, had wandered off into the garden.

'Here I am,' the man said. His prop, the stone, stuck up from the ground like a giant's thumb; a dull grey, with coins of lichen, and shaped by centuries of weather.

The man was tall and very thin, with coils of long and rather greasy hair. He wore a stained suit, a white shirt, an emerald waistcoat with a gold watch chain and a short top hat with half a dozen pheasant feathers in the brim. The suit, shiny at the knees and elbows, had a dried rose pinned to a lapel.

'And here you are,' the man mused, studying Thomas intently. 'Fancy that.' His face was narrow and bony, with a jutting chin and long slender nose. His pale, unlined skin made it hard for Thomas to assess how old the man might be. The same age as his father? Something suggested he might be much older than that.

'Did you go to the funeral?' Thomas said.

The man tipped his head to the side. 'Of course I did. I waved – don't you remember?'

It came to him in a flash, the black-gloved hand emerging from the hawthorn bush.

'But why did you hide? Why didn't you come into the church?'

'Ah well,' the man said. 'All those people, you see. All those relatives. If I turned up – well. They'd want to know how I knew her.' He looked away from Thomas, up to the blossom on the trees and his eyes glittered. Thomas chewed his lip and wished he had his jacket on, so he could thrust his hands into his pockets. But he couldn't resist the question.

'How *did* you know her?' he said.

The man looked down at his scuffed, pointed boots and smiled. He stretched out his fingers, still gloved, and pushed back his hat.

'Your grandmother? You look a little like her. Yes! Though I can see that doesn't much please you. I've known her a long time – since she was a beautiful girl. She had dark chestnut hair, you know – the colour of a ripe conker that first moment you open its case.'

Thomas tried – and failed – to imagine his grandmother with shining, conker-coloured hair.

'This garden,' he said, screwing up his eyes. 'I don't recognise it. Where am I? Everything changed after I looked in the box. Did you leave it for me to find?'

'I did,' the man said. 'And you're right. This is no ordinary garden. It is Broceliande, the Garden of Dreams, your grandmother's secret garden, Thomas Kurt Reiter.'

'A secret garden,' Thomas mused. 'How do you know my name?'

'Your grandmother told me, of course. Your father's German, I think.'

'My father's parents are German. My father was born in England,' Thomas said, very precisely. 'And, sir, what's your name?'

The man interlaced his fingers, and stretched them till the joints cracked.

'My name?' He considered Thomas, eyebrows lowered, evidently deep in thought. Then, coming to some decision, he said: 'Blake. Nehemiah Alfred Blake, in full. But you, Herr Reiter, may call me Blake.'

Two

Thomas stared into the trees. Oddly, fruit was growing alongside the blossom, as though spring and autumn had visited at once. The fruit was like nothing he had seen before – on one tree, fruit like long, golden fingers in clusters of two or three; on another, bunches of pert blue cherries. He reached out to pick one but Blake warned him to leave the fruit alone.

'Why did my grandmother have a secret garden? And how do I get back to the proper garden?' Thomas asked. 'Is there only one way in?'

Blake stood up straight and dusted off his jacket tails. He ignored the first question and said: 'There are other ways, into other secret gardens. I could show you, perhaps. Then, having had the pleasure of your acquaintance, I will take you home again. Will you remember this?'

'I never forget anything,' Thomas said bluntly. He tapped the side of his head with his fingertip. 'I have a good memory.'

Blake smiled again. 'I'm sure you have,' he said. 'Come along then.'

He led them out of the orchard. The goat followed them to the gate, but Blake was careful to tie it shut behind them. The goat stared through the wooden bars and gave one loud protesting bleat, though it didn't assay the broken fence.

'This way,' Blake said, turning sharp right. They walked along the front of the orchard and through a gap in a high hedge, beyond which stood a dozen elder trees shading damp, bare soil. They passed through shadow, weaving through the trees, until, without warning, they came up against a red brick wall and passed under an archway into beech woods drowning in bluebells. Sunlight pierced the fresh green canopy and illuminated the shimmering lilac sea of flowers. Thomas drew up short, staring in amazement at the bluebells spreading away in an unblemished, undulating lake, flowing between the trees. He couldn't see beyond the trees – the wood was enclosed, as though he were standing in the bottom of a green glass bottle. The sense of containment unsettled him.

Blake looked at him over his shoulder, amused. 'Come along,' he said. 'Keep up now.'

They wended their way, single file, along tiny pathways through the bluebells. Blake took long strides so Thomas had to jog to keep up. They moved quietly, but still the sound of their footsteps seemed to echo in the trees. Once Thomas saw movement in the distance; a deer perhaps. The faint, hazy bluebell perfume tickled his nose.

Once he stopped and look back the way they'd come – but the garden wall and the archway had been swallowed up by the beech trees.

'Where are we going?' he said, in a panic. What was he doing, running into the woods with a stranger?

'Come along,' Blake repeated, not looking round. 'You don't want to get lost.'

And Thomas, looking round, didn't trust himself to find the

way back despite the boast about his memory. What choice did he have? Ignoring the anxious clutch in the pit of his belly he hurried after Blake.

It wasn't far. They reached the edge of the wood. Lo and behold – they were standing by another wall and another gateway, offering an astonishing open view over smooth, swooping hills.

'We're at the edge of the garden!' Thomas exclaimed.

'Why – so we are!'

Thomas frowned. He didn't like to be made a fool of. Blake was beginning to get on his nerves, rubbing him up the wrong way.

He stared through the open gate. This view didn't make sense. Where was this expanse of grassy hills?

'Remember the way,' Blake said, with a gesture at the view. 'That is my garden.'

'*Your* garden? You're my grandmother's neighbour?' Nothing about the geography of the village suggested this could be possible. Thomas struggled to understand what he was seeing.

'Albion,' Blake said. 'My garden is Albion, the Garden of Love. Remember that too.' He sighed. 'You have a lot to learn. Your grandmother will have made arrangements but I promised her I'd keep an eye on you too.'

Thomas shook his head. 'What do you mean, sir? I don't understand what you're saying.'

Blake laughed, not unkindly. 'Come along,' he said. 'First we shall leave the garden and go back to the churchyard. I wish to pay my last respects, now everyone else will be feasting.'

Thomas was curious and annoyed at once. Blake was intriguing. But what did he want? What was he talking about?

Reluctantly he turned away from the vista over the green hills, the place Blake had called Albion. Blake led them back through

15

the bluebell wood, the orchard and the green path through the rhododendrons until they emerged – remarkably quickly – from the briar tunnel at the sundial.

Thomas blinked with surprise. Blake looked at him sideways. 'Going back,' he said, 'the path is always shorter.'

Blake scooped up the box from the sundial.

'This belonged to your grandmother. She asked me to show it to you one day, and I will show you much more. Just wait for me a minute, we'll talk about it further.'

Blake strode away, his coat-tails flapping, and disappeared through the back door into the house. When Thomas looked around, the path into the secret Garden of Dreams had vanished. He was standing once again in the beautiful but so much more ordinary garden in which his siblings were still playing.

His thoughts stewed. Who was this man? How did he know Thomas's grandmother? What was he talking about? Thomas thought about disappearing himself, finding his siblings and joining their game. But something about Blake held his attention. An aura of strangeness. The indefinable crackle of something entirely out of the ordinary. So he waited. He wanted to find out what would happen next.

Blake returned without the box and they walked through the village to the churchyard. The village was quiet now, the street abandoned except for a dusty black and white pig, scuffling through the gutter. The church loomed, a tall ship floating over the sea of houses.

'Wait!' Blake hissed, crouching down behind the churchyard wall. He gestured to Thomas and, still bent over, scuttled along the lee side of the wall. What had he seen? Thomas followed hard on his heels, till they came to a wooden kissing gate. Blake peered through, and Thomas crouched down so he too could stare through the bars of the gate at the fresh mound of brown soil, beneath which his grandmother lay.

'Who's that?' Thomas whispered.

The churchyard was empty – except for a solitary figure dressed in black standing at the head of the fresh grave. He was a short, stout man with mutton chop whiskers sprouting from a florid, jowly face. Like Blake, he wore a frock coat. In his left hand he held a violin, and in his right, a violin bow. As Thomas watched, the man raised the violin to his shoulder and began to play.

The music was sad and sweet, like the songs Thomas had heard a gypsy girl singing at the village fair the previous summer. The simple, haunting tune was played in endless circles, each time embellished and adorned in a new and unexpected way. The breeze snatched at the sound but still the music ran from the violin like a long, undulating ribbon that wove an ornate pattern around the churchyard.

'My God,' Blake said, in a hoarse voice. Thomas had been so caught up in the music he'd forgotten about his companion. He turned to him now. Blake was staring at the violinist, his mouth open, his face strangely wrung out.

'What? What is it?' Thomas was afraid now, seeing the shock in Blake's expression. He clutched at Blake's sleeve but Blake was oblivious. His attention was fixed on the violinist.

'What is it? Who is that man?' Thomas tugged at Blake. 'Why is he playing over my grandmother's grave?'

The tune reached a marvellous crescendo and the violinist played a series of long, melancholy chords. Petals drifted from the apple tree in a rain of white silk shreds, over the hat and shoulders of the player. How nimble his square, meaty fingers were on the slender neck of the violin.

The music stopped – though Thomas sensed it reverberating

around the churchyard, as though the pattern of notes still hung on the air. The violinist lowered his violin and tucked it into the same hand as his bow. Then he lifted his hat and bowed his head.

Blake growled. He stood up straight, leaped over the wall and threw himself at the musician. Suddenly they were rolling on the floor, the violin thrown away upon the grass. Thomas ran into the churchyard and grabbed the instrument. Despite the violinist's weight advantage Blake had speed and surprise on his side. In fact, the violinist didn't want to fight at all. He was shrieking and fending off the blows Blake rained on his face and upper body. Then Blake had him pinned down, sitting on his chest.

'Who sent you here?' Blake demanded. He slapped his victim again, across the face with the palm of his hand.

'Stop it! Stop it!' The man struggled without success. 'I don't know the name of the client. I can't tell you! I was sent here.'

Blake calmed a little. He folded his arms, still sitting on the violinist.

'How did you get the commission?' he said.

'A letter came, with the details of the funeral. I was instructed to come at the end of the ceremony when everyone had gone. I had no idea you were there. Please – will you let me free?' The man was breathless and panicky but Blake didn't relent.

'Where are you from? When did you receive the commission? Do you have the letter still?'

The violinist nodded: 'You can have it – but please – you'll have to release me to take it from my pocket.'

Blake rose to his feet and the stout, breathless man scrambled from the grass. He rummaged in his pocket and retrieved a folded letter. Blake grabbed the paper and scrutinised it briefly before stuffing it in his own pocket. Realising he was out of immediate danger of a throttling, the violinist looked around for his precious instrument. Thomas lifted it up. How lovely it was, so many elegant curves, the dark wood, smooth as satin. Instead of scrolls at the end of the neck, the violin had death's heads, left and right. The carvings were not grotesque but melancholy.

The man reached for his violin. He had a bruise ripening on his right cheekbone. 'Give me the violin, boy,' he said.

Thomas held it out, though he was reluctant to let it leave his possession. The violinist gave it a cursory check, straightened his cravat and brushed himself down in a bid to regain his dignity. He picked up his hat from the ground and scurried out of the churchyard through the main gate, leading to the village. Before he left, he turned and gave Blake one last frightened glance.

They watched him go. Blake was trembling with emotion. Was he angry or sad? Thomas couldn't read the expressions flickering across his face.

'What was he doing?' Thomas kept his voice low. He was a little afraid Blake might hit him too but he couldn't resist the question.

'Nothing,' Blake said. 'Nothing at all.' He stared at the violinist's retreating back, then he squeezed his eyes shut and sucked a deep breath through his aquiline nose. He held the breath for a moment then released with a long *paaah* through his mouth. Thus cleaned of his rage, he dropped into a squat and placed his hand on Thomas's shoulder.

'Did you love your grandmother, Thomas?' he said.

'I – well, I . . .' Thomas struggled. She had intrigued him, certainly. His fascination with her work, her determination to keep it a secret, had created a link between them. It had become a game of sorts.

'I think you should know more about her, Thomas. I think you're the one to do it.'

'What do you mean, Mister Blake?'

Blake sighed. 'She was a remarkable woman, Thomas. A strong, intelligent and resourceful woman. An inspiration!'

'She was mean!' he blurted. 'She never helped us, with money, that is. She didn't like my father.'

Blake smiled and he squeezed Thomas's shoulder. 'There is so much more to her. And it may surprise you to know she thought a great deal of you. She admired your tenacity, and your questions. She told me how you like to read, and that you were interested in her work.'

A small sense of pleasure blossomed inside the boy's heart. So he hadn't been deceived. His grandmother, despite her reticence, had approved of his curiosity about her hobby.

'I would like to see you later,' Blake said. 'We have a great deal to discuss. Will you meet me by the sundial at midnight? Could you sneak out?'

Thomas was reluctant to agree. Blake saw the doubt in his face.

'Please – it is important,' he said. Blake raised his hat in farewell as the boy ran away, following the path of the violinist away from the church and back to his grandmother's house.

Three

The children were sitting side by side at the long table in the kitchen, eating slices of white bread and butter.

'Thomas! Where have you been?' Christabel scolded. 'We couldn't find you. Lucky for you, Mother and Father are talking to the lawyer.'

The siblings stared at him, disapproving and curious, their eyes round and bright, fingers busy stuffing bread and butter into their mouths. Christabel joggled her tetchy baby sister on her lap. The infant had jam on her cheek and her white cotton bonnet was twisted to one side.

The elderly maid bustled into the room. She frowned at Thomas.

'So you've decided to come back, then. Wash your hands now, ready for your tea.'

Thomas did as he was told, then climbed onto a chair beside Christabel. He slid his hand around her arm and squeezed gently.

'Is there any news?' he whispered. 'How long have they been talking?'

The baby extended her fat, jammy hand and clutched at his nose. Christabel flicked the hair from her face and sighed.

'Nothing yet. Smith said they were called in to the drawing room an hour ago. It's taking a long time.'

The maid plonked a plate of bread and butter in front of Thomas, and poured thick, over-stewed tea into his cup. Pink roses adorned the porcelain on this, the second best china service. Smith's hand shook, slopping tea into the saucer. Thomas had no idea what age the maid might be, but he suspected she was even older than his grandmother. What would happen to her now? Had Augusta left provision for her? Would she find a new position? So many futures depended on his grandmother's last will and testament, on the words being read to the assembly in the drawing room.

When the bread and butter was eaten, Smith served scones with jam and cream, and cut huge slices of Dundee cake. The children ate voraciously, cleaning up the crumbs, licking butter and cream from their fingers. Thomas was just as industrious in his eating but his mind strayed to the wooden box, his adventure in the garden, to Blake and the funeral violinist.

At last they heard a door open, and the murmur of voices. Smith put the teapot down and stood up straight. She ran her hands over her white hair and down her apron, smoothing imaginary crumples.

'Smith – the lawyer wishes to speak with you now.' Thomas's father stood in the doorway. His face gave nothing away. 'And children – come along. The lawyer says you must listen too, so behave yourselves.'

A scramble from chairs, a wiping of fingers and faces as the herd of children left the kitchen and followed Smith out of the kitchen. Thomas had only ever glimpsed the drawing room through a half-open door. It had walls covered in a deep red paper, shelves of books, a low round table before the large marble fireplace and a dozen comfortable chairs in a semicircle. It seemed a room designed for cosy gatherings, for conversation among friends. Now the great-aunts and -uncles were ensconced in these chairs, or perched on dining room chairs brought in to make up the numbers. Smith had nowhere to sit, and neither did the children.

At the far end of the room, presiding over the gathering, the lawyer was sitting with a large bundle of yellow documents on an occasional table beside him. The lawyer was a huge man, barely contained by the armchair, a mighty belly spilling over his lap. An air of tense expectancy filled the room. If all was yet to be revealed, what had the lawyer been telling them, this last hour? Long legal preambles, perhaps, the lawyer enjoying his importance before an audience, discussing details regarding the laws surrounding inheritance.

'Smith,' the lawyer said abruptly. She stepped forward, as he took another swig of sherry from his glass.

'Smith,' he repeated. 'You are the oldest servant, and have served your late mistress faithfully for many decades. Consequently she has been most generous to you. You will receive fifty pounds a year for the rest of your life. There are also smaller payments for the other servants to tide them over while they seek new positions. I think you will be most satisfied, yes?'

The maid bobbed a curtsey. Emotions flickered across her elderly face and her eyes watered.

'Yes, thank you, sir. Thank you, Mrs Williams, God rest her soul.'

Smith left the room. Nobody said a word. The lawyer looked around at the circle of hungry faces, enjoying his moment of power. He took another gulp of sherry and smacked his lips.

'Next, Mr and Mrs Reiter,' he said. 'Mrs Ellen Reiter, you are the only child of the deceased, the widow Augusta Williams. Your mother had a number of valuable trusts and property holdings, from which you shall receive one hundred pounds a year. Mrs Williams has also made provision for your children; she will continue to pay for their education and each will receive a gift of five hundred pounds when they reach the age of twenty-one.'

Ellen was very pale. She looked at her husband and back to the lawyer, waiting for him to say more. Surely that wasn't everything? What about the house, the rest of the fortune?

The lawyer paused for a moment, and then called out: 'The boy – Thomas Reiter?'

Thomas didn't realise he had been summoned. He heard his name, hanging on the air, but it wasn't until Christabel jabbed him with her elbow that he pushed his way forward. All eyes were upon him.

'Thomas Reiter?' the lawyer repeated.

'Yes. Yes sir,' Thomas nodded. The lawyer referred back to his papers. 'There is a special provision for you.' He eyed the boy, as though Thomas had misbehaved in some way to deserve this singling out.

'Your grandmother wishes you to serve a particular apprenticeship, Thomas. When you are fourteen years old, you must leave school and travel to London, where you will be apprenticed to a distinguished chemist and herbalist, one Albert Constantine. Mr Constantine is an old friend of your grandmother's.'

Thomas didn't know what to say. He looked at his mother, who was twisting a handkerchief in her fingers.

'Go along now,' the lawyer admonished. He sat back in his chair and lifted yet another piece of paper. He flapped it in the direction of the audience.

'I have a list here – many specific personal items, pictures, jewellery, to be distributed to Mrs Williams' daughter, grandchildren, sisters and brothers. It is clearly written out so there can be no argument. That is the end of it.'

A silence descended on the room. They looked at one another, the great-aunts and -uncles, Thomas's parents. That was the end of it? So many dribs and drabs! What about the dead woman's fortune?

Ellen stood up. 'That isn't the end of it. What about the house? What about the other property, the investments?'

The lawyer, habitual bearer of bad news, smiled at Thomas's mother.

'The house and the bulk of your mother's fortune have been left to a third party, whose name I cannot disclose,' he said. *A third party:* he pronounced the words with particular deliberation.

A tumult broke out among the elderly relatives, each having hoped for a financial bequest. Shrill old voices demanded the name of the usurper.

The lawyer shook his head and bundled the papers. He ignored the questions, the expressions of outrage. Instead he gave an emotionless smile, picked up his hat, gave a quick bow and left the room.

Thomas glanced at his mother. She had her head in her hands. His father stood beside her, his face ashen. Thomas knew all too well how much they had relied on their expectations of a large inheritance. Ellen had grown up the only daughter of a wealthy family, always indulged. Then she had fallen in love with penniless Dieter Reiter, the son of German immigrants, and married him without her parents' approval. She had assumed they would forgive her but Mr and Mrs Williams had kept a distance: let her live the life she has chosen against our advice! Albert's many business ventures and money-making schemes had failed and so many children were born, needing food and shoes and clothing and schooling.

Augusta had relented a little when her husband died. She had wanted contact with her grandchildren. So she invited her daughter to move closer to home and bought them a cottage in the village. She also paid for the education of the older children. They would manage on a hundred pounds a year, and certainly they would be better off than many in the village. Still, Dieter's business debts weighed heavy and Ellen had been certain they would inherit the grand house where she had grown up, and the lifestyle she hadn't appreciated when she had it. How many times had she foolishly promised the children: one day, when we live in your grandmother's house; one day, when we are rich . . .?

The great-aunts and -uncles were bustling out of the room. Each had a copy of the list of bequests and, determined to ensure their entitlement, they were scurrying around the house to collect the jet necklace, landscape oil painting or small piece of furniture, all the while clucking about their dead sister's stinginess or quietly cursing the shadowy third party who had tricked them out of a proper and deserved inheritance. Then, once they had their claws on their treasure, they abandoned the house and departed in a host of black brougham carriages.

Finally only the servants remained, along with Thomas and his family.

'We shall stay here tonight,' Ellen said. 'We need to sort out the personal bequests, and besides, the baby is sleeping already.' Her voice was defiant, though her eyes were red from crying. Of course there was no need to stay – they only lived at the other end of the village – but Ellen, only daughter, was asserting her right to her mother's house one last time.

Smith softened a little that evening. Perhaps she felt sorry for Ellen, whom she had cared for throughout her childhood. She raised no objections to the staying over and helped ready the beds for the parents, six children and baby. Thomas followed his mother as she wandered from room to room, touching the furniture, gazing at the paintings, running her hand along the spines of books, picking up and putting down the gilded candelabra, marble ornaments, Indian antiquities. Every now and then she sighed or shook her head or clasped her hands to the sides of her head. Thomas knew what she was thinking – how much she believed this house was hers by right. How could her mother do this to her?

And he thought about his grandmother's curious gift to him – an apprenticeship in London with a chemist and herbalist. Why had she picked him out? Was this because of his interest in her work? He recalled his conversation with Blake, his enigmatic comments, the suggestion that Augusta would have made 'arrangements'. He had as yet no particular feeling about the destiny she had assigned him – except an anticipatory unease at the thought of leaving his family – because four years seemed such a long time away. Who knows what might have happened by then?

Later, over supper, his father quizzed Smith about the identity of the inheritor. Did she have any idea who it might be? What friends did the old woman have? Was there, heaven forbid, a *man* involved? When Smith shook her head and declared she knew nothing, Dieter disappeared to his mother-in-law's study and – without respect or restraint – rifled through her papers. Ellen remained at the table, cold meat and potatoes lying unwanted on her plate, a child on her lap. Her hair had come unpinned and locks hung, slatternly, around a tired face smudged with crying.

In her left hand she held the list of personal bequests. Thomas was keenly aware of the time. It was seven now, still sunny and light outside, the birds singing. Blake would be waiting for him in the orchard at midnight.

'It isn't so bad,' Ellen said at last, making the best of things for her children's benefit. They were not fooled. 'We have a home of our own, an income, and you will all be educated and provided for when you come to the age of majority,' she said. 'It is not what we expected – but it is enough.'

'What has she left for us?' Christabel asked.

'Haven't I just explained?' Ellen snapped, the strain showing.

'No – I mean—' Sensitive Christabel's eyes filled with tears. 'What little things – the personal bequests. I think there is something for each of us.'

Ellen pursed her lips. 'Yes. Yes she did. I haven't looked at it yet. Let me see.' She scanned the list. 'She has left me most of her jewellery. Well, that should amount to something. Christabel – you may have the fairy painting in her bedroom, the one you love so much, and any of Grandmother's poetry books.'

It took a moment for the news to sink in. Then a radiant smile filled the girl's face.

'Thank you,' she whispered, pushing a little brother from her lap so she could run up the stairs and retrieve her bequest.

Ellen continued her list. Various books, clocks, dresses, scarves and shawls were allotted to each child.

'Thomas,' she said. 'One carved oaken chest and contents.' Ellen raised her face. 'Do you know it? It's in her bedroom, I think. Fine brass hinges and a big lock. I've no idea what she keeps in it. The list says you will find the key in the drawer beside her bed.'

Thomas went upstairs to his grandmother's bedroom. It was

the largest room on the first floor, with a bay window and a view across the front garden and the village and another on the back wall overlooking the garden. It contained a huge mahogany bedstead, two heavy wardrobes and a dressing table. The old woman's peculiar odour still permeated the room – a mixture of Parma violets and starched cloth and confined, elderly flesh. This intimate perfume confused his senses, as though some mistake had been made and his grandmother wasn't dead at all. He worried, unreasonably, that she might still be in the room and caught himself looking over his shoulder or sensing movement where there was none.

The chest rested at the foot of the bed. The large brass key, however, was not in the drawer but jutting from the lock. Thomas took it out, still nervous, and stared at it lying on the flat of his palm, brightly polished and burning with potential.

The clock on the mantelpiece ticked loudly and declared it was half past seven. Thomas knelt before the chest, slid the key back into the lock and turned it to the left. Then he lifted the lid.

The strange wooden box Thomas had seen on the sundial perched on top of a mound of books and papers, some tied with string or ribbon. Thomas picked it up. The lid was still open, revealing again the uncanny pocket of darkness inside it. The box was made of a beautiful reddish bird's-eye maple with an attractive swirling grain. The lid was hinged, a complex pattern adorned its surface – golden threads, mother-of-pearl, and various dark and light woods inlaid in the surface of the maple to create a complex maze which appeared to shift and transform as Thomas stared at it, trying to make it out. He lowered and raised the lid, but didn't entirely close it – afraid it might not open again. He turned the box over, looking for a lock, but found none.

The papers held less immediate interest. He registered documents about plants, bundles of letters, drawings – but it was the box that held his attention.

He was conscious of the ticking clock and the minutes passing by. He wanted to talk to Nehemiah Blake. His feet itched to run out into the garden, to see him again. The encounter, the visit to the Garden of Dreams, seemed not entirely real to him now, just a couple of hours later. And the box was so deliciously lovely. Thomas ran his fingertips over the inlaid pattern, the glimmering mother-of-pearl and the smooth woods. His grandmother had valued him. What a gift she had given him.

At eight his parents told him to go to bed, and settled him in a back room with his two brothers. But Thomas didn't sleep. He ached to be out in the garden, eager for the midnight appointment. So he lay awake, heard his parents go to bed, and the servants. Thoughts turned over and over in his head.

At night the joints of the house creaked and curious draughts moved through the rooms, carrying the perfume of fresh grass, apple blossom and some other more musky pollen. Thomas hadn't slept in his grandmother's house for years, not since he was a very small boy. The bedroom windows were open. The questing breeze pushed at the drapes. The draughts whispered to him, needling him with half-heard words. He sensed voices, speaking from a distance, as though the walls reflected conversations from a lost past or perhaps a time to come. He thought about the garden that had appeared and disappeared. *Broceliande.* The word echoed in his mind, rich and exotic. Why had Blake called it the Garden of Dreams? Because it arose and vanished like a dream? He remembered something else – the special jam his grandmother had made last summer, the time he had stuck his finger in the copper pan, and licked the tart, greenish preserve.

His grandmother had been furious, scolding him, trying to work out how much he had eaten. Very little, he told her truthfully. She had warned him the jam might give him bad dreams. Had the fruit perhaps come from the orchard in the Garden of Dreams?

At last, sleepless, Thomas got out of bed and went to his grandmother's room. It was too dark to see much so he picked up the open box and placed it on the windowsill, to see it better. The mother-of-pearl glimmered in the moonlight. It was past eleven, but the sky was not entirely black. Thin films of grey and silver cloud rose over the horizon. The moon was almost full, bright as a new coin. Thomas realised, with a mixture of shock and excitement, that the view was not of his grandmother's familiar garden, but instead revealed Broceliande, the Garden of Dreams. It seemed to curve, like the view through a fish bowl. He could see the forest of rhododendrons, and the long path up the hill, and the orchard too. It was strange, very strange, because looking at the whole garden the shapes were indistinct but when he focused on a particular part the details resolved. Why, if he stared at the orchard hard enough he could even see the goat, curled up by the gate, its head cushioned on its flank.

Thomas frowned. It wasn't only the garden that curved. Now he came to think about it, wasn't the sky distorted? As though the whole scene were contained within a huge glass ball – or maybe even a small glass ball that he had his eye pressed up to. The thought made him shiver and he drew away from the window for a moment, back behind the curtains into the safety of the room. Then he looked out again, unable to resist the garden's siren call. The moon flickered and the stars blinked. Had something passed in front of them? A bird perhaps, or a flock of birds. Then movement on the ground, creeping from the trees and bushes, as though the shadows had congealed and gained a life of their own. Thomas strained his eyes to see. Were they rats? The shadows poured over the grass like water, gaining speed as they approached the house. Then they disappeared into the walls, fluid as ghosts. Thomas was gripped by an instinctive dread. His body quivered, resonating to a supernatural note.

He waited a moment, conscious of the silence in the house. Who was coming? Was it Blake? Thomas opened the bedroom door and looked across the landing. Everything was still. He stepped inside again, closed the door behind him. He took the open box from the window, thrust it into his grandmother's wooden chest and locked it. Then he sat on the chest. His grandmother's perfume was stronger than ever – almost a physical presence. A dark shape slid under the door into the room – a mobile shadow. Thomas watched it flow across the floorboards and onto the ornate rug by his grandmother's bed. He didn't feel afraid, though the tiny hairs on arms stood up and tingled.

'What are you?' he said, in a cold, clear voice.

The shadow stopped. Could it hear him? It contracted, and formed itself into an hourglass shape on the floor. A second shadow crawled under the door, and a third. Perhaps some mysterious communication passed between them because as one they moved towards the oak chest, where Thomas was sitting. They slid up the sides of the chest, now long and thin like snakes. Thomas felt his heartbeat accelerate. What should he do? And then a shadow passed over him, on his nightshirt and over his thighs. He couldn't feel it, but panic balled in his stomach. In a frenzy, he tried to brush it off, but the shadow couldn't be touched. It rose over his belly and chest towards his face. Thomas jumped to his feet, fruitlessly clawing at the shadow. And there were quiet footsteps on the landing outside the door. His eyes widening, his hands clutching his throat, Thomas watched as the handle turned and the door swung slowly open.

A large, massed darkness stood in the doorway, in the shape of a man. A shadow with substance, stepping into the room's faint light, and revealed – tall, gaunt and top-hatted – to be Nehemiah Blake. His eyes glittered turquoise-blue, like gems, as though a light burned inside his face. He raised his head and peered down at Thomas beneath lowered eyelids. Then he put his hand into his pocket and drew out a small glass bottle. A light flared inside the bottle's round belly and the shadows on the chest stopped still. Then, slowly, reluctantly, they were drawn away from their quarry backwards over the floor, up the long legs of the man with the bottle, along his arm and down into the bottle. Blake stuck a cork in the bottle mouth. The light burned brightly then went out, and Blake dropped the bottle in his pocket again.

'There is someone else here, Thomas,' Blake said. 'I was afraid for you.'

'What are they – the shadows?' Thomas struggled to steady his voice.

'I know what they are – but where they've come from? That's a much more worrying matter.'

Frustrated, Thomas tugged at Blake's sleeve.

'What are they?' he demanded. 'What's happening?' His first instinct was to call out to his parents for help but he sensed the encounter, like the orchard in the garden, was entirely out of his parents' reach. Like in a dream in which you are obliged to outrun unseen monsters, there was no help to hand – no appealing to outside agencies.

'What's in the wooden box?' Thomas persisted. 'You put it back in the chest, didn't you? What's inside it? What does it do?'

33

Unconsciously, his hand had strayed to his pocket and gripped the key to the oak chest.

Blake shook his head. He paid Thomas little attention, ignoring his string of questions, lost in thoughts of his own.

'Come along,' Blake said abruptly. He raised the bottle from his pocket and waggled it from side to side.

Thomas said: 'They were yours. Your creatures.'

Blake shook his head. 'Not mine. Someone else's. Someone knows. Someone wants.'

'Wants what?'

'Wants the box, of course.' Something caught Blake's attention because suddenly he turned to the front window.

'What is it?'

Blake flapped his hand, to silence Thomas. He appeared to be listening intently but Thomas couldn't hear a sound. If Blake were telling the truth and the shadows did not originate from him, presumably their master was also nearby?

'Who is it?' Thomas whispered.

Blake frowned, grabbed Thomas by the scruff of his neck and hauled him over to the window. 'Look!' he hissed. 'See for yourself.'

A man stood on the road, outside the house. It was hard to make him out clearly, in the moonlight, except that he was young, with short flaxen hair and a long coat. A host of shadow creatures – presumably all those which Blake hadn't sealed in his bottle – flowed from the house across the lawn towards the man. He held out his hands to them and they climbed over his body, across his face and were absorbed through his eyes into his head. The man staggered as the last one was melted into his face. Thomas was appalled.

'They went – went *inside* him,' he said. 'Through his eyes! What are they? Who is he?'

34

'I don't know who he is,' Blake said. 'But the shadows? They are thought forms. It is simple enough. But where did he get the herb? Who is helping him? He's looking for the box, and he'll know some of his creatures are missing. I have to go now. Quickly – give me the box.'

Thomas shook his head. 'I won't give it to you,' he said. 'Why should I? It's mine.'

'There is no time for this,' Blake said. He seized Thomas, wrapping his right arm around him and digging in the boy's pocket with his left. As Thomas struggled, he fished out the key.

'We are not enemies!' Blake whispered. 'God's blood, stop fighting me! I want to protect you.' Once in possession of the key he pushed Thomas across the room and dived towards the chest. As he unlocked it, Thomas jumped on Blake's back and tried to pull him away. Blake cursed quietly, and batted at the boy with his spare hand even as he retrieved the box. Then he stood up, thrust Thomas out of his way and strode out of the bedroom.

Thomas was sitting on his rump beside his grandmother's bed, the wind knocked out of him, but his blood was up so he struggled to his feet and set off in pursuit. He ran downstairs and through the tiled hallway to the kitchen. The back door was wide open and, without a thought for his safety, Thomas launched himself into the garden and after the retreating form of Nehemiah Blake, as the old man's long, narrow body stalked through the silvered flower beds and into the shadowed lanes.

Four

The sky was an ocean of deepest blue, awash with stars. The moon blazed, creating a world painted in shades of silver, blue and grey. The trees were very still. Leaves glittered.

When he ran barefoot over the chilly grass into the garden, Thomas realised how foolish he'd been to go out without any shoes on. But it was too late now – if he turned back, how would he find Blake again? He had no plan. He was a small boy in pursuit of a strong man. What could he do even if he caught up with him? But the sensible words in his mind made no impression on the cauldron of anger boiling inside his ribs. This sense of outrage compelled him to follow. It was a stupid endeavour, he knew, but his blood was up. He wanted his box back.

At the sundial, the path into the Garden of Dreams had reappeared. Thomas could see Blake walking away from him, the thin black figure curiously elongated, as though he were watching him through a piece of thick, warped glass. Thomas ran after him, sensing he had to seize the moment and afraid the path might close, taking Blake, the box and the garden with him.

The path stretched away. Blake disappeared, one more shadow among the stripes cast by the moon and the trees. Thomas swiftly lost any sense of the geography of the garden. Which way to go? He could see no sign of Blake, and no immediate clue about the direction he had taken. Thomas didn't fancy his chances pushing a path through the bushes in the dark. Surely Blake hadn't done so either? He paused for a moment, sweating and out of breath, looking to left and right, straining his ears for the sound of Blake's flight.

Then, beside him, a man emerged from the dark leaves with his arm raised. The figure loomed large, blocking out the moonlight as he strode forward. Thomas tried to dash away but he wasn't quick enough. The arm came down from on high, striking Thomas hard across the top of his head. The night-time garden reeled and the strength left his legs. As he tottered Thomas caught a glimpse of the side of the man's face in the moonlight – enough to reveal this wasn't Blake but the man who had stood at the front of the house. Then his joints loosened and his body gave way. His mind folded up and disappeared.

He lay in a faint for perhaps a few seconds. Dimly he sensed strong hands pulling him upright. Thomas opened his eyes. He was stupefied, the sky swimming and his pulse beating painfully against the walls of his skull. The man squatted beside him, patting at his clothing.

'Where is it?' the man said. His voice was low and calm.

Thomas tried to assemble his thoughts. 'What?'

'Where is it?' the man repeated, in the same measured tone.

'Where's what?' Thomas found it hard to speak. His mouth tasted of blood. Perhaps he had bitten his tongue when he fell. The night went out of focus – all he could see was the pale, intent face in front of his own.

'The box,' the man said. 'Where have you put it?'

'It's mine,' Thomas protested. 'My grandmother gave it to me.'

The man paid no attention to this. He continued to stare at Thomas, and seeing his shining eyes Thomas remembered the shadows – the thought forms – and the way they had slithered through the man's eyes into his head. Were they inside him now, swimming like fish through his brain?

'Who are you?' Thomas croaked, playing for time.

'Where is it?' The man raised his hand to strike again, and Thomas cowered in fear. The pain already resident flared up, reminding Thomas he didn't want to be hit again.

'I haven't got it!' he cried out, all bravery abandoned. 'You're too late. Someone's already taken it from me – some other filthy robber!'

The man lowered his hand. 'Blake,' he said. 'Blake has the box. Where is he?'

'I don't know – I was chasing him. He's somewhere in the garden.'

The man let Thomas go and stood up straight. 'Do you know which way he went?'

Thomas shook his head. His face was sticky with dirt and tears. He wiped it fruitlessly with his hand and struggled to his feet.

The man frowned. He looked one way and another. Despite the setback he seemed remarkably calm, considering carefully before taking his next step. He looked back at Thomas and away again.

Then he said: 'You'll have to come with me.'

Thomas shook his head and began to back away but quick as a shot the man grabbed him by the wrist.

'Come along,' the man said. 'We'll have to be quick.' And he turned to the right, dragging Thomas behind him.

The garden passed in a blur. The man moved fast, and he wasn't considerate of Thomas's bare feet or his hurting head. Thomas soon lost track of their route and the man didn't seem sure of the path to take. Often he stopped abruptly, to double back or else take a new direction. From time to time Thomas pleaded to be released, but the man didn't take the slightest bit of notice. Then, at last, they reached the crest of a hill and a wide moonlit vista opened up in front of them. It was the orchard, and beyond it the dark treetops of the bluebell wood. Perhaps it was an effect of the darkness, but the orchard looked so much bigger now. The moon was very low, rolling above the tops of the trees, and the horizon gently curved, reminding Thomas of his view through the window and his perverse fancy that the garden was actually very small.

They began to walk down the hill, Thomas still captive. Moonlight dusted the crowns of the fruit trees and the blossom glowed. The man pushed the gate open and the black goat came trotting towards them, bleating loudly. The man strode through the long grass, to the piece of stone like a giant's thumb. Here, at last, he let Thomas go. The boy slumped on the ground, nursing the bruises on his wrist. His feet were numb. The goat came to him, and snuffed his face.

The man stood up straight and rested his hands on the small of his back.

'Blake!' he called. His voice was loud and alien in the silent, grey and silver orchard.

'Blake!' he called a second time. The sound created a ripple of disturbance. The trees moved, though there wasn't a breeze. The long moon-shadows weaved together on the grass.

'I have the boy, Blake. The old woman's grandson – I have him here! Show yourself. Show yourself now!'

The goat bleated again, butting Thomas's shoulder with its hard head. Where was Blake? And why should he bother coming back for Thomas? After all, he had what he wanted.

The man waited, his body tense and alert, his face raised as he looked to left and right, waiting for Blake to show himself.

Then, to the west, a shape emerged from the trees.

'Here I am.' Blake looked almost jaunty, stepping out into the open. He stalked towards Thomas and his captor, his hands in the pockets of his waistcoat.

'Here I am,' he repeated, taking out his hands and extending his arms, palms up, in front of him. 'Let the boy go. He doesn't know anything,' Blake said. Then: 'Goodness me! This is all a little unnecessary, isn't it?' He gave a wry, mocking smile, his hands still open in a gesture demonstrating how defenceless he was.

'I want the box,' the man said.

'Ah, the box. And to whom do I have the pleasure of speaking?'

'Where is it?'

'Now, there are only seven people who know about the box and one of them was buried this afternoon. If we exclude her, and subtract me of course, that leaves five. Did one of those five people send you here? How did you learn about the thought forms? Who supplied you with the herbs?'

Thomas observed that Blake was edging closer, slowly, slowly.

But his opponent noticed too. He thrust his hand in his pocket and drew out a small revolver.

'Stay back,' he said. 'Just tell me what I want to know.'

Blake jumped back with his hands in the air, over-dramatic, in a show of alarm.

'A gun? Isn't that a little crude – a little clumsy – for a man of your obvious talents?' Blake said.

But the man didn't answer. Instead he swung the gun to his left so it pointed directly at Thomas. His gaze, however, was still levelled at Blake.

'Tell me now, or I shoot the boy.'

Thomas felt the ground lurch beneath him.

'It's in the wood,' Blake said. 'I dropped it in the wood. Let the boy go and I'll take you there.' His voice was even but Thomas sensed a change in his posture – an increased alertness in the face of this new threat.

But the man swung the gun away from Thomas and pointed it, his arm straight, at Blake instead.

'Lead the way,' he said.

Blake glanced once at Thomas before he strode out of the orchard to the gateway in the garden wall. The blond man followed close behind Blake, not once taking his eyes off him, the revolver gripped tight in his hand. They moved away and the shadows weaved around them till the two men entirely disappeared into the forest of the night. Everything was silent. The moon loomed over the trees, impossibly large and bright. If you climbed a tree, you could reach out a hand from the treetop and touch it.

'*Bleeah*,' the goat said, loudly, in his ear. It tore up a wad of grass and began to chew noisily, its nose just inches from the boy's face.

'Get away!' Thomas said, flapping his arm to drive the beast away. His heart was thumping hard in his chest, but his mind was unexpectedly clear. He should try to run back to the house as fast as he could. But still he wanted the box – wanted it more than anything. If the two men were occupied with each other, couldn't he perhaps sneak along and outwit them?

'*Bleeah*!' the goat said again, puffing a grassy breath in his face. It wasn't perturbed by his flapping. In fact, its strange slotted pupils seemed to consider him almost sensibly.

'I want to go after them. I want my box,' Thomas said aloud. The goat stopped chewing and stared. Thomas nodded. He climbed to his feet and ran across the orchard.

It was easy to follow. They had left a path through the long

41

grass, which led to the gap in the high hedge, the elder trees and the iron gate. He stepped into the bluebell wood.

The moon was obscured by the delicate roof of lime green beech leaves but blades of silver moonlight pierced the canopy over and over. In this multitude of beams, raining into the woodland, motes of dust glittered and bleached moths fluttered. The bluebells merged into overlapping sheets of glowing silken lilac. Long ripples passed over the surface, though Thomas could feel no breeze.

He walked forwards, his hands touching the tops of the cool bluebells. The place filled his mind, more strange and beautiful than anything he had ever seen or imagined. Perfume rose from the flowers in a low, undulating mist, visible in the moonlight. A single moth, with huge pale wings, fluttered in front of his face. It seemed to leave a sparkling trail behind it, on the air. This thread of phosphorescence faded slowly, as the moth danced away from the boy. Thomas gasped. He realised he'd been holding his breath. All thought had fallen away – all sense of purpose dissolved.

But he did have a purpose. Blake and his captor were in the wood, and he had to find them. Thomas looked around him. It seemed impossible anyone else could be here – the scene was so complete and undisturbed. But they were here, somewhere. They couldn't be so far ahead. The men hadn't ploughed a path through the bluebells, so must have headed along the narrow dirt track. Thomas began to run.

The path wove from left to right, threading between trees, plunging into shadowed caves and then, when the leaf canopy opened, into pools of light where the sky overhead burned with stars. From time to time the path forked and Thomas chose left or right without thinking, relying on his instinct to tell him the way to go. Once he nearly ran into a badger, making its way towards him on the path. The creature's pied face lifted in alarm when it encountered the boy, and it dived off into the bluebells.

Still Thomas ran. He lost all sense of time and distance. Perhaps he had run for an hour or more. Perhaps only a minute or two. And the woodland offered no identifiable landmarks. Maybe it knitted itself around him as he ran, changing shape, cradling him in its silver heart. He remembered the white pet mouse his sister Christabel had kept, and how it ran across her hands, over and over as she placed one palm next to the other again and again. Was the wood playing with him too?

Then he stopped, out of breath and disorientated. He had no idea where he was, which way to go forward or to retrace his steps. And still not the slightest sign of Blake or the blond man. He hadn't thought of his bare feet as he ran, but now they throbbed, bruised by stones, soles stinging from scratches and splinters.

A sound, like a slow sigh, passed through the trees.

Thomas looked up, alert for another presence in the woodland. The sound came again, passing from left to right, almost a whisper.

The hairs on the boy's skin stood on end. He felt a chill ripple over him, from his scalp right the way to his toes. It was an ancient animal warning, a primordial reaction from the deepest, oldest part of his brain.

The whisper came again, floating from tree to tree. A hint of words, but nothing he could make out, though he strained his ears to hear.

'Who's there?' he shouted out, in a show of bravado. 'Blake, is it you?' His voice was huge and crude. He sensed his clumsy words crashing over the bluebells.

The whisper, circling, closer all the time.

'Where are you? Show yourself!' He wished he had a stick to hold, or a stone to throw.

A long, sibilant sound – to his left, to his right. Thomas thrashed out with his hands in a panic but there was nothing to touch. The hiss resolved itself into a voice, a word. A girl's voice, eerie and unformed: it pronounced his name, in two long, slow syllables.

'T h o   m a sssssss . . .'

Almost a song, a teasing call. Thomas shivered. He was breathing fast; his lips and tongue were strangely cold. He turned around, and around, trying to catch the source of the voice.

'T h o   m a sssss . . .' The call came a second time, a little louder and clearer this time.

'Who are you?' Thomas demanded. He was almost in tears and his voice trembled.

Suddenly he saw her. Far away, in an opening among the trees so the moonlight shone on the top of her head. She was dressed in a long, simple gown of the palest violet. Bluebells rose to her knees. Her long, dark hair hung over her shoulders and her face was a narrow, white smudge in the twilight.

'T h o   m a ssss . . .' The voice again, whispering through the wood. The girl didn't move. Her hands hung by her sides.

'Who are you? What do you want?' Thomas was desperate. His voice was pleading. Tears leaked over his cheeks.

Then she was beside him – close enough to touch. He hadn't seen her move, neither had she time to walk the distance between them. Nonetheless, now she was standing an arm's length away. Her head was tipped forward so curtains of glossy chestnut hair hung over her cheeks. Only the central part of her face was visible and her eyes were partly obscured. Thomas could see only a small nose and a perfect chiselled mouth. Her skin was an unnatural matt white, like paper.

Gently, hesitant, Thomas lifted his hand to touch her. But

when he blinked she disappeared – and reappeared standing, motionless, in another part of the wood twenty strides away. He sobbed with fear and frustration.

'What do you want?' he repeated. She shifted again, far away among the sheets of lilac blue, so he could see her only vaguely – a pale shape in the shadows. Then she was standing in front of him, just out of reach. This time Thomas waited. He didn't try to touch her; neither did he accost her with questions. He was aware of how noisily he breathed, of his sweating face and bloody feet. The girl was so entirely perfect, so perfectly unreal. What was she? A fairy? A phantom?

The moment stretched. Moonlight punctured the cavern of the wood, making silver stripes in the dusk. Moths flittered, the haze of perfume roiled over the bluebells.

The girl lifted her face. Slowly, so slowly, till the hair fell back from her cheeks. She raised her eyes – entirely, deeply black, without white or pupil – and stared at Thomas.

'Thomas,' she said, though her lips didn't move. 'Do you know who I am?'

He shook his head. The girl looked about the same age as his sister Christabel, and in some indefinable way there was a resemblance too.

'You don't recognise me.' A ghost of a smile on the still face of the girl. 'I don't suppose you do.'

'How can I hear you? You're not talking – your lips don't move.' Thomas was too loud, and stumbled over his words. He was afraid she might disappear again, but the girl remained where she was. In any case, she ignored his question.

'My name's Augusta Jane,' she said. 'I am – I was – your grandmother.' The suggestion of a smile again. Thomas gaped. His thoughts tumbled over one another.

'Yes,' she said. 'A ghost. It is as you're thinking. Though the term revenant would be more apt. I have – returned.'

'My grandmother?' Thomas could hardly countenance the possibility. Nothing about this girl accorded with his memory of the thin, gnarled, scowling old woman. Had this beautiful creature been buried beneath his grandmother's forbidding exterior? Blake's words drifted into his mind, how remarkable Augusta had been.

'So why have you returned?' Thomas ventured.

'Where is the box I gave you?' the girl said.

'It's – well, Blake – he took it. He stole it from me,' Thomas said. 'But another man came after him, trying to steal it for himself. They're in the wood somewhere. The other man has a gun and he's making Blake tell him where he hid the box. I followed them – that's why I'm here.'

The girl froze for a moment, as though the animating presence absented itself from the puppet form. Then, after a second or two, the voice came back.

'I know where they are,' she said. 'Consider Blake a friend, Thomas. I told him the box would come to you. If he decided it would be safer in his keeping, he must have had good reason, doubtless because of this new threat.'

'So why have you returned?' Thomas repeated. 'Why are you here?'

The girl didn't speak, but she opened her mouth revealing teeth covered in blood. A shocking red, like holly berries, and thick as syrup, the blood welled over her lower lip and trickled onto her chin.

'I was poisoned, Thomas,' the voice said. 'I was poisoned.'

The girl lifted her arm and stretched out a hand. Her narrow fingers brushed against his forehead and the entire woodland scene blinked out. Trees, moon, bluebells, girl – all gone – leaving only darkness.

Glimpses of dreams, colours, voices. Now he saw another place – his grandmother's bedroom. The old woman (could he detect the girl in the raddled face?) was lying in bed. She was sitting up, in her nightgown, while Smith the maid brought in a tray bearing breakfast. A teapot, plate, cup and saucer decorated with pink roses. A rack with three slices of white toast, sugar, butter and honey. The tray was placed on a low table beside the bed. They chatted easily, the two old women. Smith drew the curtains, letting in the bright sunshine. Augusta helped herself to toast and honey, while the tea brewed. Somehow Thomas could smell the tea. It was tart and herbal. His grandmother medicated herself (and the rest of the family) with all sorts of special teas which she cultivated in the garden, to promote their health and help them sleep well.

Smith left the room, and Augusta ate a slice of toast. She poured the tea, added a spoonful of sugar, and sipped at the brew. When the cup was empty, she put it on the tray and sank back on her pillows. Time passed; how much it was hard for Thomas to tell. His grandmother was asleep when Smith came back for the tray. Smith was clearly surprised by this – and gently touched the old woman's forehead with the palm of her hand. Then she jumped back in shock, her face pale. Augusta's lips parted, revealing a mouth full of blood.

Smith clapped her hands to her cheeks, staring in disbelief. She took two, three, deep breaths and stared at the dead woman lying in the bed. Then she stepped towards her again and dropped to her knees. The maid clutched Augusta's still, cool hand, pressed her face into the bedcover and began to sob.

The scene dissolved. A host of images flew through Thomas's mind: voices, places, recollected dreams. Then he was folded in darkness, locked in and covered up. Far away he heard a familiar tune being played on a violin, a sweet, melancholy music. He tried to move – a terrible panic overcame him. He had to get out – had to escape. He thrashed helplessly, kicked out, shouted . . .

He opened his eyes. He was standing in the wood and the girl Augusta was in front of him still. The blood had gone.

'They're over there,' she said, raising her arm and pointing over his shoulder. Thomas turned around. Yes, he could see them – Blake walking ahead of the younger man.

'What should I do?' Thomas said.

'Help Blake. You can trust him, Thomas. He'll help you.'

'But who – who poisoned you? Why did they do it?' Thomas was beginning to panic.

'I don't know who it was,' Augusta said. 'I need you to find out because the threat will certainly follow you, if you have the box. I want to protect you.'

Thomas took a deep breath. He nodded to his girl-grandmother, and set off in pursuit of Blake. He tried to hide himself, darting from tree to shadow to tree in the hope the two men wouldn't notice his approach. Soon he was close enough to hear them speaking. Blake had stopped and was striding up and down in a circular glade with a standing stone, the twin of the stone in the orchard.

'I left it here,' Blake said. He threw up his arms in a theatrical gesture of dismay.

The man with the gun said: 'Then it must still be here. Stop playing the fool.'

Blake wandered about, pushing the bluebells aside with his

booted foot, looking for the box. The other man stood and watched him.

'It's gone,' Blake said. 'It's disappeared.' His voice was cool and sarcastic.

The man drew back the hammer on the revolver.

'There's nothing to stop me killing you,' he said. 'No-one will find you here. I think you should stop playing games and give me the box.'

Blake stood still. He stared at his opponent, as though daring him to carry out the threat. Thomas could see him squeezing the trigger. Then – *she* appeared. The ghost girl – the revenant: Augusta with her black eyes and dead white skin. She was standing in the moonlit glade, one hand resting on the stone.

The man stepped back in alarm. The gun twitched in his hand but he didn't shoot. He made a noise – a choked cry of shock. Thomas stepped out from his hiding place. When he moved, he couldn't see Augusta, though the man was still staring at her. He skirted the glade towards him and Augusta reappeared. The revenant was paper-thin – a trick of the light, like a shadow – existing in two dimensions. You could only see her from the front. So what about Blake, standing behind her? What did he see?

Augusta moved forwards. She didn't step – she drifted, making no impression on the bluebells in her path. The man gave a peculiar snort and stepped back. Then he fired the revolver. The shot went through her, making no impression, and before the man could fire the gun again, Blake hurled himself through the air, pushing through Augusta and landing on top of the intruder. The man shouted out, and for the second time within a day Thomas witnessed Blake engaged in a heated fight, rolling on the ground, fists flying with a horrible abandon. It was not so different to the skirmishes he'd witnessed or engaged in at school, in the playground, except that the men were so much more physically powerful. He ran closer, wondering if he might help Blake. It was hard to see who had the upper hand – so much grasping and scrabbling and cursing and kicking. Probably the fight went on for a minute or two, but to Thomas it seemed a very long time. He stepped from one foot to another. How could he intervene?

He glanced back at Augusta, but her face was very still. Was she watching the fracas? Perhaps her attention was elsewhere.

The gun fired. Blake was lying on top of his opponent. Long and narrow, except for the widening at the shoulders, Blake looked like a coffin. For a moment Thomas couldn't be sure who had fired the gun. Blake rolled off the other man, his clothes covered with blood. The other man didn't move at all. He lay in the bluebells on his back, a knife protruding from his chest.

Thomas stepped back. He couldn't believe it. How had this happened? Why did he have to be a part of it? The revenant didn't move, but her face contained a kind of cold triumph.

'You killed him,' Thomas said, in a small voice.

Blake struggled to his feet. He was breathing heavily. Bruises flowered in his face. He clutched his left side, where quantities of dark blood seeped.

'He shot you,' Thomas said.

Blake didn't stand for long. He half collapsed, and propped himself against the standing stone. Thomas hurried over and peered at the man's wound, the blood all black in the pool of shadow behind the stone.

'You're bleeding,' he said, in tears again. 'What can I do? Shall I run back to the house and get someone? Shall I find a doctor?'

Blake shook his head. 'There isn't time,' he said. 'Just sit down, Thomas. Sit by me. I don't want to be alone.'

Blake's face had turned a bleached fish-belly white. His lips were pale and bloodless, all colour leaking away.

'Where's Augusta?' The voice was thin and hard to hear. His hands were shaking.

'Here I am.' The cool voice of the revenant, standing in front of them. Blake gazed up at her.

'Augusta,' he whispered. Blake took his hands away from his wound and offered them to her, inky blood up to the elbows. 'This is the end of it.'

'Oh no, Nehemiah,' she answered. 'It isn't the end of anything.' The revenant was beginning to fade. The moonlight shone through her now, the uprights of the trees visible through her face and lilac dress. Blake let out a sound like a sob and stretched his hands out further.

'Goodbye, Nehemiah.' The words drew out, like a sigh through the wood, and the ghost girl was soon no more than a suggestion, a hint of colour hanging on the air. Then she was gone.

When she disappeared, Blake seemed to dwindle. He was struggling to draw breath. Thomas knelt on the ground beside him. He didn't know what to do or how he could help.

'Please let me get help,' he appealed, longing to be away from here, to pass on the responsibility to someone else, to a competent adult.

'No!' Blake hissed. He grabbed Thomas's arm, dirtying his sleeve.

'I have to talk to you, Thomas. You must take the box.'

Thomas didn't answer right away. He considered the dead man lying in the bluebells with a knife in his chest, and Blake bleeding beside him. Then he said: 'What's in the box?'

Blake stared into his face. 'You have to keep it safe,' he said. 'One of the others wants it. There are five of them left now – only five who know. Now you are the guardian of this box. Haven't you guessed what's in it? Well then, remain in ignorance. You will find out soon enough. Simply – keep it safe.'

'Where is it?' Thomas said.

Blake was growing weaker by the second but he gestured to the other side of the glade. 'You see the beech tree there – with the forked trunk? Look behind it, in the bluebells. Go now – so I know you have it. And when you leave the garden, close the lid. That is most important. Promise me you will close the lid.'

Thomas got to his feet and ran to the tree. Sure enough, the box lay behind it. The lid was open still but now the box seemed ordinarily empty, with a smooth, varnished wooden inside. He picked it up and hugged it to his chest. Then he hurried back to Blake.

'I have it,' he said. But Blake didn't hear. He was dead, though his eyes were open and the whites glittered eerily in the moonlight.

Afterwards Thomas couldn't remember how he found his way out of the garden. Perhaps it was the shock of witnessing the fight, of seeing the blond man die, and then watching Blake's life seeping away. He ran away, as fast as he could, through the bluebells and the orchard, along the paths through the rhododendrons, unthinking, only hoping his body would carry him safely. So it did. He emerged at the sundial, still clutching the box, out of breath, his mind reeling. Now he was outside of the Garden of Dreams, the box seemed full again – but full of what? A dense ball of darkness, which he found daunting and fascinating in equal measure. Why had Blake insisted he close it? Why had the blond man wanted it so much? Thomas took a deep breath. He was too tired to think about it now so he did as Blake had told him, and closed the lid. It sealed, the smooth, perfectly crafted wood sliding into place. As it did so, a thread of white light glittered at its edges, miniature veins of lightning, and Thomas was so alarmed he dropped the box on the grass. The pattern on the lid began to glow, the box jumped once, and three white sparks spilled from its sides. Then it was still. The glow faded away. Thomas waited for several moments, stunned by what he had seen and half afraid to pick up the box again. The path into the Garden of Dreams had disappeared. The night gathered around him.

The following morning, the entire adventure had the quality of a dream. Except that his feet were bruised and broken, and bloody handprints patterned his shirt sleeves. He stuffed the soiled shirt under the mattress of his bed, hoping no-one would find it, and told no-one what had happened

That morning the family left the house for the last time. They tried to find out who the new owners were, the upstarts responsible for stealing the house and the fortune, but all investigations proved fruitless. The beneficiary organisation was very private, the solicitor said. Nothing would be revealed.

The house was shut up for several months, and then the undisclosed inheritor rented it out.

Thomas found his memories of the night in the Garden of Dreams faded very fast. Within a day or two he could only recall fleeting details. Soon, like a dream, only isolated images remained – the moths in the moonlight, the revenant, the man with a knife in his chest. It stopped being real to him. He doubted it had happened at all. Thomas took the box home but never managed to open it. Sometimes he dreamed about his grandmother and remembered the revenant's story of murder and poisoning but in the morning he would brush the dream away.

Four Years Later . . .

The day before Thomas was due to travel to the city for his apprenticeship, curiosity drove him back to the old place.

It was Midsummer's Eve, the day was long and golden. Since the current tenants were away in town he chanced his luck that the servants wouldn't notice him and sneaked through the side gate into the garden.

It hadn't changed greatly – still the herbs near the kitchen and the sundial. Life for his family had changed a great deal, of course. Christabel was married now, with a baby of her own. One of his older brothers lived in the town and had a job as a clerk in a bank. Another two children had been born. The family wasn't rich, but they had managed well enough. Now he was to leave them, to fulfil the terms of his grandmother's will. He had mixed feelings about the impending adventure. Excitement, of course – he was longing for adventure and novelty after a childhood in a small village. He was anxious about leaving his loved ones too, but he sensed something important awaited him – that he possessed talents his grandmother had recognised and which might now be brought out and nurtured.

He wandered in the garden, remembering the times he had played here. Of course it looked smaller. He had grown. He was fourteen now. The current tenants didn't care for it as his grandmother had done, judging by the weeds and overgrowth. The kitchen garden still looked productive, though.

He mooched about, unsettled and nervous. On the eve of his taking up an adult life he was nostalgic, looking back to his childhood. He wanted something from the garden, but couldn't decide what it was.

The following morning he packed his clothes and books in a tin trunk, along with the wooden box his grandmother had given him, and took the train to the city.

ARCADIA

The Poison Garden

*Arcadians skilled in song will sing my woes upon
the hills. Softly shall my bones repose, if you in
future sing my loves upon your pipe.*

Virgil

One

November sunshine, deceitfully bright, slanted through Albert Constantine's plate-glass window. Above, a sign in gold paint declared: Constantine & Blacklow – and beneath this in smaller letters: Pharmaceutical Chemists. It was a large establishment. The window framed a magnificent display of the products and accoutrements of the chemist's trade – glass storage jars, bottles for oils and syrups, and boldly labelled salt-glazed stoneware jars containing Constantine's own patented ointments. In the smaller window to the right of the door, Mrs Constantine had what she called her Ladies' Window – an artful display of lavender and rosewater soaps, smelling salts, skin tonics and perfumes, framed by loops of blue and white silk and posies of fresh flowers which she replaced every other day.

Constantine's (as everyone called it – the titular Blacklow having retired long ago) was a very successful chemist, and customers travelled to it from all over London. They weren't in the heart of the city – the shop stood halfway along a street of shops in one of London's more prosperous districts, amid long roads of semi-detached villas, where stockbrokers and businessmen made their homes with their families of half a dozen children and a cook and a housemaid and a nanny.

Thomas pulled his scarf tight around his neck and pulled his cap over his brow. It was five o'clock, the sun crouching over the rooftops and casting precious little heat. A bitter breeze nipped at his exposed skin.

He'd lived with the Constantines for five months now. Thomas had quickly made the city his home – at least, this part of it. He enjoyed its size and bustle, the cosmopolitan crowd even here, in this respectable quarter. He had missed his family at first, but he was always so busy and the Constantines were so kind, that the pain of separation had eased. Now he was on an errand to deliver an order to an address in Quaker Street, some half an hour's walk away. He passed the park at the end of the road, where in the mornings the nannies wheeled their charges in beetle-black prams to give them some air, while the little children played on the grass beneath the ornamental trees. These trees were almost bare, just the last drab rags of leaves clinging here and there. It made him think of his grandmother's garden, which he missed.

Mr Constantine had written complicated directions for Thomas to follow. Usually he despatched Billy, the youngest of the three apprentices, a skinny London boy with vivid red hair and endless energy who knew the city inside out, but from time to time, the job fell to Thomas. He didn't mind. It was a pleasure to leave the shop, even in this biting cold. They worked six days a week and the shop stayed open till ten o'clock at night. It was interesting enough, and there was so much to learn, but it was still a treat to get away on his own.

The streets were busy – hansom cabs, carriers' wagons, horse-drawn trade vans. Mud and horse muck spotted the surface of the roads. The pervading winter perfume of coal smoke hovered in the air, mingling with the mist rising from the river. Yet above the fog of horse sweat, smoke and manure, over the houses, the first star burned in the clear sky and banners of burning orange blazed on the horizon. Thomas smiled. He was warm now, walking swiftly through the pedestrians. On a street corner a girl with chilly blue hands offered roses for sale to the passers-by. An old man with a barrow full of fruit bargained away the last of the day's bruised Kentish apples.

He turned left along a narrow street walled with tenements of the poorer sort and the crowd died away. The street closed to an alleyway, mud and rubbish underfoot, and then opened onto another row of dingy homes. Light blazed from a grocer's shop and, further along, a junk shop selling old barrels and coils of rope. In the gathering darkness, Thomas lost sense of himself – he was simply a pair of eyes, observing all, soaking up the spectacle as he passed. In the pool of light before the junk shop three tiny children played on the pavement. The baby girl looked up at him, smiled and waved her hand. From the doorway, the fat-bellied shopkeeper stared out and scowled. But Thomas hurried on and they were gone, all of them, shop, baby, man, swallowed up in the night as he moved to the next scene, and the next.

Quaker Street ran along the north side of a small square, a grassy park in the middle. Thomas saw a row of grand terraced houses, now coming down in the world. The limestone façades, adorned with columns in the classical style, were soot-blackened. Rubbish congealed in the gutters. He took out his directions and peered at Mr Constantine's opaque handwriting. Apparently the house didn't have a number. It was called simply: Arcadia.

He mooched along the pavement, glancing through illuminated ground-floor and basement windows, into furnished rooms and busy kitchens. One of these old places was a boarding house. Another was a small private school, according to the flaking board outside. The last house in the row looked entirely uninhabited. The windows were dark. But the name Arcadia was carved in the lintel above the door.

Thomas pushed open the iron gate, climbed the three steps and knocked on the door. It didn't look as though anyone was at home, but he waited a minute or two. Finally he heard a key turning in the lock and the heavy door opened – just enough to reveal an elderly female face with a pursed, toothless mouth.

'I have a delivery from Constantine's,' Thomas said, holding out the parcel with its brown paper wrapping and string.

The old woman stared. Thomas expected her to take the box but she twitched her head and said: 'Come in. Mrs Lawrence wants to speak with you. I expect she has another order for Mr Constantine.' She backed away and held the door open just wide enough for Thomas to squeeze inside. Tiny, with hunched shoulders and black mittens on her hands, the old woman raised an oil lamp in her left hand, so shadows raced along the hall.

'This way.' She shuffled down the long red-tiled hall to a staircase. They ascended, Thomas towering over his guide but caught, as she was, in the pool of light from the lamp. At the top of the stairs they turned right along a red-carpeted landing. Then the old woman opened a door and led him into a parlour.

'Ernestina, the lad from Constantine's is here,' the old woman said. Thomas couldn't see who she was talking to at first. Mrs Lawrence was sitting in a large winged armchair, its back to the door, close beside the fire. He heard a voice say: 'Come along, Thomas – sit over here.'

He glanced at the old woman. How did she know his name? She ushered him to an armchair the other side of the fire, where he sat nervously. He cleared his throat.

'Good evening, Mrs Lawrence,' he said, looking at an elderly lady, very thin and straight as a rod, with long white hair pinned in a bun. She wore a tight black dress and a wealth of jewellery – huge, jet earrings, a necklace of silver and pearl, a black brooch, rings stuck with giant stones that glimmered in the low light of the gas lamp hanging from the ceiling.

She considered him, hands folded in her lap.

'Thomas Reiter,' she said at last. 'Augusta's grandson.'

'You knew my grandmother?'

'Yes, we were friends.'

'But I didn't see you at . . .'

'At the funeral? No. I didn't go. The funeral was a family affair, I think. None of them would have known about me.' The hint of a smile crossed her face. 'How do you like it at Constantine's?'

'I like it well enough,' Thomas said. 'It's hard work, but very interesting. Mr Constantine and his family have been very kind to me. I find myself quite at home.'

'I am happy to hear it,' Mrs Lawrence said. Her voice was very cool and haughty, but Thomas detected something unexpected in the modulation. He hadn't been in London long, but he had a keen ear and had already learned a little of the geography of the city's accents. Ernestina Lawrence had a distinct flavour of the East End in her speaking. And the armour of jewellery – perhaps a little vulgar for a lady? She had come up in the world. Still, he thought she had the bearing of a queen – a queen in exile, perhaps.

It was a comfortable room. Painted peacocks glowed on the tiles around the fireplace, where the lively fire burned. The armchairs were upholstered in dense red velvet. A mirror hung on the wall over the marble mantelpiece, cherubs and scrolls carved into the golden frame. Pictures covered the walls, huge oil paintings depicting appropriately Arcadian English rural landscapes. On the mantelpiece an ornate clock, fancifully held aloft by golden nymphs, gave six tinkling chimes.

Thomas tried to hand over the delivery from Constantine's, but Mrs Lawrence waved it away.

'Put it on the table,' she said. 'Are you hungry? My ward will be having her tea in the nursery. Why don't you join her? She would enjoy some company.'

'I think I should return to the shop. Mr Constantine will need me – but thank you,' he said, rising to his feet.

But Mrs Lawrence was implacable. She raised her hand.

'Albert Constantine can spare you a short while,' she insisted. 'He and I are also good friends, and I shall write a note when I return you to explain your delay.'

Thomas, still standing, fidgeted with his cap. He wanted to leave but didn't dare risk offending one of Constantine's customers – especially if she was a friend, as she said.

'Then I shall stay – and thank you,' he said, placing the package on a table by his chair.

The old woman (a servant, presumably, though she wore no cap or apron) had been waiting by the door all through this conversation and now she gestured for Thomas to follow her. She guided him up a further flight of stairs.

'The day nursery's here,' she said, opening a door. 'Maud? I have a visitor for you.' Then, to Thomas: 'You go inside. I'll bring up your tea on a tray.'

The old woman stepped back, allowing Thomas through. He noticed that she, too, had an accent from the East End – less suppressed than Mrs Lawrence's.

A girl was sitting on a cream-coloured rug in front of the fire. She looked up and stared at Thomas.

'Hello,' he said. The girl scrambled to her feet but didn't say a word. Thomas guessed her age at ten, though it was hard to tell. She was small and slight, with a wide forehead and narrow chin, large, broad-set eyes and long black hair tied with two blue ribbons. She wore a long white dress and looked uncannily like a doll. In fact she dangled a doll, a facsimile of herself, in her left hand.

'My name's Maud,' she said. 'I'm Mrs Lawrence's ward. I'm thirteen. How old are you?'

'Fourteen,' Thomas said, surprised she was only a year younger than he was. Then again, he lived and worked in the adult world. Maud's life, it seemed, was limited to the house and the two old women.

'What would you like to play?' she said. The room was a treasure trove of toys and games. It would have been a slice of heaven for Thomas three years before. Even now, though he had left his childhood behind, he felt a moment of excitement to see it all laid out for his enjoyment. A dappled rocking horse with a long black tail stood in the corner of the room, harnessed in red leather with glittering silver stirrups. An elaborate doll's house stood on a table in the middle of the room, and up against the wall, a large cardboard theatre kitted out with cut-out figures all ready to perform *A Midsummer Night's Dream*. Wooden toys, paints and an easel, skittles, a wooden hoop, board games in boxes – where to start?

'I've never seen so many toys,' he said.

Maud shrugged. 'It's hard to play on your own, however many toys you have.'

'You're not alone now. What would you like to play?'

Maud went to a chest of drawers and took out – simply – a pack of cards.

'Aunt Ernestina never has the patience to play cards with me for long.'

Thomas nodded and they sat side by side on the rug, basking

63

in the heat from the fire as Maud shuffled the cards. He grasped her narrow wrist and opened her hand.

'What cards are those? I've never seen ones like that before.'

Maud raised her haughty little face. 'They're German cards. See? The suits are hearts, leaves, bells and acorns. I know lots of games. I'll teach you how to play Sedma.'

'My father's German,' Thomas said. "Why do you have German cards?'

Maud shrugged. "I don't know. I found them in the nursery. I think my aunt bought them.'

She dealt them eight cards each.

'You want to win aces and tens in tricks,' she said. 'And since you're the elder you may play first.'

At first Thomas had no idea what he was doing, and she beat him outright. Slowly, though, the rules began to make sense and he began to offer some creditable opposition. He loved the cards – each of the numbers had a little picture on the bottom. The nine of acorns showed a piggy bear cub riding a dog and blowing a horn. Beneath the nine of hearts curled a cheeky unicorn. The atmosphere grew tense as they concentrated on the game. The glossy cards glinted in the low light. Their conversation shrank to nothing as they played. Maud beat him again – narrowly this time.

'Why do you live with Mrs Lawrence?' Thomas ventured, as Maud picked up the cards and shuffled them again. She glanced at him, pressing her lips together.

'My mother died,' she said. 'I don't know what happened to my father.'

'I'm sorry,' Thomas said.

Maud looked up at Thomas and gave him a smile that transformed her quirky little face. 'That's kind – but truly, I haven't anything to complain about. My aunt is very generous. I want for nothing. Except, maybe,' and she smiled again, 'a little company from time to time.'

The door opened and the old woman stepped in with a large wooden tray. Maud jumped to her feet and cleared a space on the table so the tea could be laid out – bread and butter, biscuits, elegant cakes iced in pink and white.

'Sit down, Thomas.' Maud gestured to a chair at one end of the table. She set out the plates, cups and saucers.

'Thank you, Aunt Lucy,' she said.

'Do you have everything you need?' the old woman said.

'Yes, thank you. Everything.' Maud squeezed her hand. So Lucy was not a servant but a sister. A very plainly dressed and unadorned sister, who answered the door, who fetched and carried.

As she left the room, Thomas glanced at Maud, the question on his lips. But Maud anticipated him. She said: 'Lucy never married and she has no income of any kind. She has lived on Ernestina's charity since their parents died, thirty years ago.'

Thomas frowned. 'They have no servants?'

'There's a girl who comes in every day but Ernestina won't have anyone living in. She doesn't allow it.' Maud picked up a slice of bread and butter and took a bite. She passed the plate to Thomas. Her skin was so pale he could see the veins running blue in her wrist. Did the old women keep her locked up in the house, out of the sunshine?

'So Mrs Lawrence is a widow? Why doesn't she allow servants to live in?' He had so many questions.

'Mr Lawrence died twenty years ago, and as for the servants, well, the fewer people in the house, the fewer eyes there are to see, or mouths to tell,' Maud said. 'Now, eat up – we have plenty.'

She poured the tea, offered milk and sugar. Tangles of faded violets decorated the china service, and fragrant steam rose from the teacups.

'To see and tell what?' Thomas said.

Maud smiled annoyingly. 'As you have probably worked out, my aunt wasn't born to this kind of life. She and her late husband made their money by rather dubious means. I only know a little, but I gather Mr Lawrence was, for a time, notorious in some parts of London, for getting what he wanted.'

'What do you mean? He was a criminal?'

Maud smiled and shrugged her shoulders. She wasn't going to tell him any more. Instead she asked him about his own family, about his apprenticeship and life at Constantine's. He talked for ages, and she listened eagerly, drinking up tales of his brothers and sisters, begging for more details about his long working day, the habits of Mr and Mrs Constantine, the foibles of the other apprentices. She laughed out loud at some of his stories, bringing colour to her pale cheeks.

The time passed quickly. Aunt Lucy returned to clear the table and told Thomas it was time to leave. Maud frowned.

'Already? Why does he have to go?'

'It's getting very late, Maud. The boy has to walk all the way home and your Aunt Ernestina wants to talk to him before he goes. Be a good girl now – perhaps he will come again.'

Maud pushed her hair behind her shoulders and turned to Thomas.

'Will you? Will you come again?'

Thomas didn't know how to answer. His time wasn't his own. Maud's face pleaded.

'I hope so,' he said. 'I do hope so.'

Lucy led him back to Mrs Lawrence's parlour. She was still

sitting in her chair by the fire, though she had a book closed on her lap.

She looked up and smiled at Thomas.

'What do you think of my ward, Master Reiter?'

Thomas swallowed. How to answer such a question?

'I like her very much,' he said.

'Perhaps she could be a new sister to you – since you've left your sisters behind. Is she as pretty as your sisters?'

Thomas frowned. He had never formed a judgement about the prettiness or otherwise of his sisters. It had never crossed his mind to consider it. His sisters were his sisters, just as the dog was the dog and the cook was the cook. And as for Maud? She was too strange – too black and white. Prettiness, for Thomas, invoked vague images of honey-blonde ringlets and dimpled cheeks.

'I don't know,' he said. 'I've never wondered if my sisters were pretty.'

Mrs Lawrence smiled. 'I suppose not. But if you like Maud, perhaps you might come and see her another day.'

'I should like to. However that's for Mr Constantine to decide. He has a deal of work for me to do.'

Mrs Lawrence clapped her hands together in satisfaction. 'You leave Mr Constantine to me, Thomas. I shall manage him. You see the paper on the table? Bring it to me. I shall write a note for Constantine and you shall take it to him.'

His gaze strayed to the little table beside her chair. He took an involuntary step back.

'What is it?' The widow looked up, with a knowing smile on her face.

Thomas swallowed and tugged at his jacket. He felt very hot. There on the table (had it been there before? Surely not – she had placed it here now, to trap him) was a smooth, inlaid wooden box without a lock. At first glance, Thomas was certain this was his box – the one still locked in the wooden chest he had inherited from his grandmother, now resting under his bed at Constantine's. The box he had never found a way to open again.

Now he saw this was *not* his box – but a brother to it. The size was the same, and so was the style of its making and decoration. Only the pattern on its lid was different. How many times over these last four years had he traced the inlaid lid of his own box with his fingers? Somewhere, in the convoluted patterning, lay a way to open it, he was certain. This method had so far eluded him.

'Your box,' Thomas said.

'What about it?' Her voice was chilly. He realised she was playing with him – and had done so since his arrival. He reined himself in.

'I was just . . .' he said. 'I was just admiring it. So beautifully carved.'

'Isn't it?' the widow said, passing her hand over the lid. Then, her voice crafty: 'You have one very like it, I think. Your grandmother's box. Is it here, in London?'

'No, I left it at home,' he lied.

'Have you opened it yet?'

'Not yet.'

'Perhaps you could bring it to me, and I could show you how it's done.'

Thomas bit his bottom lip. 'Perhaps you could show me how you open yours, so I could try the same on my own – when next I visit my parents.'

Mrs Lawrence laughed. She had a hearty, unaffected laugh, in which the East End expressed itself with greater colour. 'A good answer, Master Reiter. A very good answer.'

Questions burned in his mind. Where did the boxes come from? What was inside them? Why did Mrs Lawrence have one too? She was staring at him with narrowed eyes, her face a web of wrinkles. She would tell him nothing. Instead she asked him again for the paper, then scribbled a note for Constantine.

Thomas picked up the letter, said his goodbye and found his way out of the house. The walk home was bitterly cold and he hurried as much as he could to keep warm.

It was after nine by the time he returned to the premises of Constantine & Blacklow. The shop front glowed, warm and golden, in the cold November night. The bell rang as Thomas pushed his way through the door. Billy was standing behind the counter, dusting a tray full of empty dispensing bottles.

'You're late, Tom. You'll catch it,' Billy warned, with a grin. 'Where've you been? We was expecting you back hours ago.'

'The customer kept me waiting,' Thomas said, too shy to explain he'd spent the evening playing cards with a girl. 'Where's Mr Constantine?'

'He's upstairs. He'll be down when it's closing time.' Billy yawned. It had been a long day and once the shop was closed he would have to sweep the floor before turning in for the night. Then Thomas would have to scrub the doorstep before eight the following morning, when the shop would be open again. Mr Constantine was a genial employer but he didn't want to miss a single customer. He was perfectly prepared to get up himself in the middle of the night if a doctor called by for an emergency remedy.

'Sickness doesn't know the hour of the day or night,' he opined to the boys. 'We have to be prepared to serve at any time – it's part of our calling.'

Billy sniffed. 'Well, you can give me an 'and now you're 'ere. See the syrup bottles? They'll want a polishing too.'

Thomas tied on a long apron and took down the tray containing Constantine's patented blackcurrant cough and throat syrup. Mrs Constantine was most particular about the appearance of the shop and expected every bottle to gleam. Since the place was constantly under assault from the dust on the street and, in winter, smoke and dust from the fire, the battle to keep the place up to standard was constant and unremitting.

Billy chatted on, but Thomas found it hard to concentrate on what he was saying. He was tired and hungry, despite the tea and cake, and he couldn't stop wondering about Maud and Mrs Lawrence, and the widow's desire to see his grandmother's box. Perhaps she had used Maud to win him over and gain his trust.

At ten o'clock Mr Constantine came down the stairs to the shop. He was a plump, good-natured man with a red face, bristly white hair and bushy whiskers. He dressed very well, in tailored suits and starched white shirts, a gold watch chain twinkling from his pocket. He rubbed his hands together and gave the boys a broad smile. His sharp eyes scrutinised the rows of bottles, and a large hand stretched out to turn a bottle more exactly label-out. Then he ran the tips of his fingers along the counter top, looking for stray specks of dust and dirt.

'It's looking marvellous,' he said. 'Well done, lads, well done.'

'I done most of it, Mr Constantine, sir,' Billy piped up. He fairly jumped up and down on the spot, like a terrier hungry for a treat.

'It's true, sir,' Thomas said. 'I only got back from the delivery a few minutes ago. Mrs Lawrence gave me a note for you, sir – another delivery.'

Mr Constantine's eyes fastened on Thomas. 'Mrs Lawrence, yes,' he said. 'We'll talk about her later.'

Thomas had been resident long enough to know that beneath

the exterior of hearty bonhomie Albert Constantine was a very shrewd man. Doubtless there was a method in his sending Thomas to the old woman's house, and perhaps he might tell more about her. Mr Constantine, his grandmother and the widow Lawrence all knew each other and now had drawn him, the unwitting fool, into their circle. Constantine was friendly enough but still Thomas knew he was out of his depth; he sensed he was a little mouse caught in the middle of the floor between grinning cats.

James, the third and eldest apprentice, stepped off the street and into the shop just before Mr Constantine locked up. He had accompanied a doctor on a call, armed with a case full of tinctures, ointments and potions. James was nearly twenty and would soon complete his apprenticeship, when he hoped to leave and set up shop on his own, back in Leeds where his family lived. He was a long, lean and rather humourless young man, who wore a moustache and kept his hair slicked back against his head. He had little time for the younger apprentices, though it was part of his job to supervise them.

'Time for supper,' Mr Constantine beamed, staring from one young man to another. 'Billy – you sweep the floor. Be quick about it. Then come up at once. I'm sure you are all very hungry. I am fairly worn away myself – perfectly famished.'

And he turned on his heel and walked smartly up the stairs, James and Thomas behind him, leaving Billy alone with the broom and an expanse of tiled floor.

Two

The Constantines' dining room was wallpapered a dark mossy green. Long velvet curtains were drawn across the windows and a gas lamp glowed above the table. The fire burned merrily in the large hearth, so the room was altogether warm and cosy, the chill November night shut out.

They were a friendly, informal family: the three apprentices dined every night with Mr and Mrs Constantine and the pair of daughters, Agatha and Amy. Mrs Constantine and her daughters were very clearly cast from the same mould, being tall, bony people with rather horsey faces. And all three were similarly good-natured and easy to get on with, generous with their friendship and prone to fits of laughter. Altogether it was a very pleasant place to live.

The maid brought in dishes of lamb chops, mashed potato and carrots, all served with lakes of savoury gravy. Mr Constantine quizzed his daughters about their day and regaled his wife with his latest thoughts on a new perfumed soap. The boys were too much focused on their dinner to contribute much to the conversation. Once the chops were eaten and the plates cleared away, the maid carried in a bowl a-brim with stewed plums and a jug of double cream. Then it was time for coffee, and unusually Mr Constantine asked Thomas if he would take his cup and join him in his study, as he had a matter he wished to discuss.

The study was a huge room sprawling over the second floor. Here Mr Constantine kept his book collection as well as numerous drawers of botanical samples, endless notebooks full of drawings, jars of herbs, pressed flowers and various pieces of scattered equipment for his various experiments into the properties of herbs.

'Sit down, Thomas,' he said, gesturing to a chair by the desk. Mr Constantine pushed aside a pile of papers to clear a space for their coffee cups. He fussed with the tail of his jacket as he sat himself down upon his well-upholstered posterior, tugged at his whiskers and sniffed loudly.

'Well then,' he said. 'What did you make of Mrs Lawrence?'

It was a tricky question to answer, since the widow claimed Constantine was a friend.

'She was very generous,' Thomas said. 'She invited me to stay for tea with her ward.'

'Ah yes, Miss Maud.' Mr Constantine pressed his lips together and puffed out his cheeks. 'She must be a similar age to you, I think?'

'A year younger.'

'Well, that's near enough.'

Thomas took a deep breath and said: 'I understand Mrs Lawrence hasn't always been a lady – that she has come up in the world.'

Constantine laughed. 'Come up in the world? Yes, that is one way of describing it. This information shall be kept between the two of us, Thomas, but it is fair to say her late husband had quite a name in the darker side of London. Charlie Lawrence wasn't a man anyone would cross lightly; except in the end of course.

Someone got the upper hand. Still, he'd left his widow plenty to live on. And I strongly suspect she still has her hand in the criminal world. Be careful of her, Thomas.'

'So how do you and Mrs Lawrence and my grandmother know each other? Is it something to do with the wooden box? You see, Mrs Lawrence has one too. She showed it to me. Well, I think she wanted me to see it.'

Mr Constantine considered his apprentice. 'We do know each other, yes we do,' he said. 'We have – or had in your grandmother's case – an interest in common.'

Thomas glanced around the room. 'Of course,' he said. 'Plants. Herbs and medicines. Is this an interest Mrs Lawrence shares too?'

'Yes,' Mr Constantine nodded. 'Just so. It is a long story, our coming together, but I can tell you we created a Guild of Medical Herbalists. A very select guild it is – admitting only those with the highest qualifications. There were seven members, until your grandmother died. Perhaps one day, if you have the inclination and the ability, you might take her place. That was her intention.'

'That's why she sent me here,' Thomas wondered. 'She wanted you to teach me. But why me? I've plenty of brothers and sisters she might have chosen.'

Mr Constantine gave a sad half-smile. 'Clearly she saw something in you the others didn't possess. We spoke about you a number of times, Thomas, and she told me how intriguing you found her work, even as a little boy.'

'So what is in the box?'

'Artefacts relating to the guild. It won't be of use until you're older. In the meantime, take good care of it.'

'So why did Mrs Lawrence want to see it?'

'We are all curious,' Mr Constantine said. 'We each have a box, you see. I expect she wanted to see what Augusta had done with hers.' He looked away, a shadow on his face, leading Thomas to suspect the story was more complex and that perhaps the remaining members of the guild did not entirely trust each other. He perceived he had been given a partial truth.

'So,' Thomas said. 'What next? Mrs Lawrence wants me to visit her again.'

'Certainly. By all means. Be a friend for Maud. But pay attention. You're a bright boy Thomas – I have seen that for myself over these last few months. You learn fast.'

Then, after a moment's hesitation: 'You understand you can never speak of this with anyone else? The guild is secret.'

'Why is it secret? Who are the other members?'

Mr Constantine's face twitched. He tugged his whiskers.

'I wonder . . .' He scrutinised Thomas, staring into his face. He put a hand on Thomas' shoulder and peered into his eyes. Thomas could smell the port and coffee on his breath.

'I can't help thinking – perhaps you have seen another of our members,' Mr Constantine said. 'He disappeared four years ago, at the time of your grandmother's funeral.' He dropped to his knees in front of Thomas, who was still sitting on the chair, so their eyes were level.

'What's the matter? What are you doing?' Thomas said.

But Constantine ignored him. He said: 'Do you remember him? Did you meet Nehemiah Blake?'

The name banged in Thomas's head, like a door blown open by a sudden breeze. Curious scenes rose in his mind, like animals woken from sleep. Hidden, camouflaged, now they stepped out and stalked into the boy's conscious mind.

Constantine's eyes widened. He stared into Thomas's face.

'There is something!' he said. 'When I mentioned the name, I could see it stirring!'

He raised his hand, palm towards Thomas's face, and made a curious gesture with his fingers.

Fear rose up inside Thomas, like black water, cold and choking. Darkness filled his mind, and his eyes, blotting out sight. He felt something moving inside his skull, tearing through the fibres of his thoughts. The darkness, the presence – whatever it was – clung on tight, embedded itself in the corners of his skull. But it was leaking away, slowly, slowly, drawn through his eyes. Then the shadow was gone. Instead Thomas saw a dark shape held in Constantine's hand.

Thomas batted Constantine's other hand from his shoulders. He stood up and pressed his hands against his eyes. Memories burned through his brain, flashing bright before his mind's eye. The shadow – he remembered now, the shadows leaking into the house.

'A thought form,' Thomas said, words tumbling over each other. 'He told me, Blake told me – he's dead. He was killed.'

Constantine, still on his knees, impossibly grasped the shadow in the palm of his hand. He had it pinned in place with the force of his attention.

'See the jar on the back of the desk,' he whispered. 'The cloudy jar with the glass stopper. Bring it – quickly. Take out the stopper.'

Thomas ran round the table, seized the bottle and plucked out the stopper. Slowly Constantine raised his hand, pursed his lips, and sucked the shadow into his mouth. His face grew bloated and grey; his eyes shrank into his head and seemed to fill with blood. Thomas wanted to recoil and turn away but he screwed his courage to the sticking point and held out the cloudy jar. With shaking hands, Constantine took it from him and pressed his lips to the opening. Slowly, carefully, he exhaled the shadow into the bottle and jammed in the stopper.

They were silent for a moment. Constantine reached for his pocket and drew out a handkerchief, which he dabbed on his face. His usual florid colouring had returned, though his eyes still looked bloodshot. His hands were shaking as he reached for a glass and poured a dash of whisky. The glass clinked against his teeth, and he swallowed with a grimace before pouring a second shot and passing it to Thomas.

'Takes away the bad taste,' Constantine said. 'I haven't had to do that for a long time.'

Thomas was still disorientated. The shadow, like a dirty curtain, had been torn away to reveal a room in his mind he had only glimpsed before.

'I thought it was a dream,' he said. 'But it was real! I can remember it all now – as though it were last night! The shadow – it was in my mind all this time? For four years?'

He was appalled now; repulsed to think of it – the parasite hidden away inside of him, like a tapeworm in the gut. He thought Blake had caught all the thought forms but this one had stolen inside his mind and wrapped itself around his memory of the garden and the revenant, of Nehemiah Blake and the murder in the wood.

Questions piled up and spilled over.

'She was poisoned!' he cried out. 'My grandmother. The revenant came back to show me. Her tea was poisoned; and a man came after the box and fought with Blake in the wood. Blake stuck a knife in him, but he was killed too.'

Constantine stared at Thomas, his eyes beady, his face calculating.

'My dear boy,' he said. 'Sit down. Sit down, please. Now tell me everything.'

Thomas opened his mouth to speak then closed it again. He

restrained himself. He had to think quickly. After all, what kind of medical herbalist commanded shadows that crawled inside a mind and occluded memories? What manner of man was Constantine?

The older man nodded. Perhaps he had detected the boy's reservations.

'You're afraid now,' Constantine said. 'You're wondering what I am – *who we are*. Well, I can't blame you for that.'

'So – who are you?' Thomas said.

'Medical herbalists.' This with the shrewd smile. 'Of course, as you have seen, we have acquired considerable powers.'

'Who are the others?'

'Well, if Blake is dead that leaves only five of us. Mrs Lawrence, myself, and three more. In the light of what you have told me, we shall have to meet and consider what has to be done. On that occasion you can meet them all.'

Then, more gently, he added: 'You needn't be afraid of me, Thomas. I'm still the same man. Do you think your grandmother would have entrusted you to anyone wicked?'

Thomas shook his head but he wasn't convinced. Perhaps Augusta had been wicked too. She had been poisoned after all.

'Perhaps you had better understand the need for secrecy,' Constantine added, tipping his head to one side. 'Nobody else knows anything of this – not Mrs Constantine, or the daughters, or the apprentices. You are bound to silence.'

Thomas nodded. His head ached and he had a shrill ringing in his ears. He was dead tired and wrung out. All he wanted now was to lie down in the dark, to be still and silent.

'Go to bed,' Constantine said. 'We'll speak further.' He also looked exhausted. The flesh on his face seemed to weigh more heavily than usual. He rubbed his eyes with his knuckles.

The following two days, life was outwardly as normal. Thomas got up early with the other apprentices. He scrubbed the doorstep and opened the shop. He made up prescriptions, sold medicines, ground ingredients, advised callers on face creams and hand lotions. Between them the boys kept the fire burning and the dust at bay. They braved the winter cold to make deliveries. At lunchtime and at night he sat down to eat with Billy and James and the Constantine family, and made conversation with Amy and Agatha. But these two days his ordinary life was like a shadow play, so much movement without substance, because his thoughts were bound up tight with the events in Constantine's study. The memory of the exorcism filled him with dread and revulsion; Constantine's story about the Guild of Medical Herbalists intrigued and infuriated in equal measure. And of course, his memories jarred against each other. He remembered – as though it were last night – his adventure in the garden at his grandmother's house. It hadn't been a dream.

He wanted to talk with Constantine again, to press more answers from him. But Constantine was very busy. He went out early every morning and came home late at night. He seemed distracted and a little restless, failing to join the usual banter at the supper table and telling Thomas – abruptly and more than once – that he didn't have time to talk to him.

Early the third day a note arrived at the shop, addressed to Thomas and requesting his presence at Arcadia with a delivery of cough syrup. The letter was written on a piece of yellowed paper and the handwriting was crabbed and awkward. It weighed in his hand like a stone. His instinct told him to stuff the note in his pocket and forget it – but Mrs Constantine was supervising the shop and insisted on seeing the message.

'Of course you must go, and at once,' she admonished. 'Come

along, Thomas.' She handed him the appropriate bottle from the shelves. 'Here's your scarf,' she said, wrapping it around his neck as though he were six years old. 'Take your hat and gloves too. It's cold out, and I don't want you to be falling ill. We promised to take good care of you.'

She herded him out of the door and into the sunshine, where hansom cabs and tradesmen's wagons jostled in the road, and he set off at once for Mrs Lawrence's house.

Arcadia looked no less dingy in the daylight though it was tall and imposing. The house was soot-blackened and the windows dirty. The light picked out flaws in the stonework and the flaking mortar. Thomas pushed his hat back on his head. He felt a reluctance to knock on the door. The first visit had been curious enough. He shrank from the prospect of putting himself in range of Ernestina Lawrence's sheathed claws again.

Still, what choice did he have? He couldn't linger all morning on her doorstep. The Constantines would find out soon enough if he didn't make the delivery. Shivering despite the brisk walk, he climbed the steps and knocked on the front door. Dowdy Lucy opened the door without a word and ushered him to the parlour. Mrs Lawrence was sitting in the chair by the fire, just as before, her jewellery glittering in the firelight so she appeared also to be covered in tiny flames, a blaze of jet and silver and pearl.

'Good morning, Thomas,' she said. 'Sit down, please. Maud would so like to see you again but I would like to talk to you first.' She picked up a cup and saucer from the little table beside her and slowly stirred the teaspoon in her tea, staring at Thomas all the while.

'I've received a letter from Mr Constantine,' she said, as the steam rose from the teacup in front of her face. 'He has hinted that your grandmother's death should be of concern to us.' Her words were slow and measured. She placed the teaspoon on the saucer and took a sip from the cup.

Thomas didn't respond. He had no idea how much Mr Constantine had told her. He saw the box stood on the table by the teacup – and the lid was open.

'Well,' she said, a little sharply. 'Has the cat got your tongue Thomas? What do you have to say?'

Thomas flinched. 'What do you want me to say?'

'What happened to Augusta?'

Thomas didn't answer right away. He thought fast, wondering what he should reveal, and what it would be prudent to conceal. Then Mrs Lawrence laughed.

'Look at you. I'm not going to eat you. What are you afraid of?' she teased, eyes shining like the pearls at her ears. 'I shall find out soon enough. Mr Constantine has called for a meeting – did he tell you?'

Thomas shook his head. 'No, he didn't.' Inside his belly a kind of feverish fury brewed.

'Well, ask him about it. You will be attending, I think. The others will be curious to meet you.'

Thomas felt the heat rising to his face. What were they up to, these crones, talking about him, wishing to paw over his memories? He screwed his hands into tight fists and glowered at the floor.

'Here's what you wanted,' he said, casting the packet on the old woman's lap. 'Can I leave now?'

'Oh, Thomas Reiter,' the widow scolded. 'Don't be so cross. You're just as fierce and twice as touchy as your grandmother. Do you know how rarely I get visitors? Can't you allow me a little game? Anyway, don't you want to see Maud again? She would be so upset if you went without speaking to her.'

'Then I will see her,' Thomas said hotly. 'If that's what she wants.'

Aunt Lucy, wordless, escorted him not to the nursery but downstairs to a basement kitchen. There Maud was sitting by the table, swinging her legs. She gave him a dazzling smile.

'Oh there you are!' she said. 'I've been waiting for ages.'

Two men were standing in the shabby, old fashioned kitchen. They were an odd pair, one very tall and thin, the other stout and unshaven, his chin melting into his neck. The shorter man eyed the children and grinned. Aunt Lucy handed him money and the two men shuffled off, back through the house to the front door. Maud glanced at Thomas, raised her eyebrows and smiled.

The kitchen table was scrubbed clean but high up on the ceiling dusty cobwebs looped in the corners and across the tops of the shelves and dressers. A film of grease veiled the copper pans hanging from a rack. At one time the house would have had half a dozen servants. Now it was evidently all too much for the two elderly women.

'We're going out in the garden,' Maud said, jumping to her feet. This morning her black hair, glossy as a rook's wing, was tied in a long plait. Aunt Lucy shuffled towards her, a woollen hat and coat in her arms. Very tenderly she placed the hat on Maud's head and held open the coat for Maud to slip inside.

'This way,' Maud said, scooping up her doll from the table. She half walked, half skipped across the kitchen to the back door and unlocked it using a huge black key. Then she danced up the steps to a patch of raggedy grass. Thomas hurried after.

The back garden was enclosed by a high hedge, bare and black and thorned in the winter sunlight. Ice spangled the grass: shadowed by the tall house, the garden was a pocket of frost. A few straggly rose bushes poked up from a weedy border.

'Come on,' Maud said, catching the sleeve of Thomas's jacket. She pulled him through a passageway in the hedge. Coils of rusty bramble arched over them, clawed and vicious, but Maud ducked and scrambled her way through with Thomas close behind.

And then . . . they emerged into a wide open space, a vast necropolis spilling over a hill, down and down, with a path winding like a river and clumps of winter trees. At the bottom lay a grey lake and beyond that, a blur of woodland.

The air was fresh and clear, reminding him of walks at home. No sooty smoke, no grit. The view filled him with a peculiar excitement, a thrill he felt physically from the soles of his feet to the roots of his hair. A sense of anticipation – a tingling in the blood. And it was familiar, yes. He'd felt this before, though perhaps as a child he hadn't recognised it in the same way. The view was utterly different but it reminded him of the mysterious garden he had visited years before, his grandmother's Garden of Dreams.

Maud was smiling. The breeze whipped threads of black hair from her plait so they blew around her face.

'Do you like it?' she said. 'The garden's called Arcadia. Its other name is the Poison Garden. I play here often. You think it's a strange place to play? It's safe enough, as long as you don't touch or eat anything, at least without my say-so. No-one else ever comes here, except for Aunt Ernestina.'

Without waiting for a reply she set off at a run down the hill, through the tottering headstones and long, dead grass. The Poison Garden? The name was a shock. Why fill a garden with poisons? Thomas thought of his grandmother and the tea that had killed her. If Mrs Lawrence grew poisons, did that mean she murdered Augusta?

Thomas wasn't as sure-footed as Maud and quickly fell behind.

The dark slate headstones were edged and tooled in gold. Many tilted downwards, succumbing to relentless gravity. Some leaned together, like lovers. So many hundreds in this city of the dead. But the necropolis was a garden too – a multitude of shrubs and herbs grew around the graves, or crawled over them. Purple ivies with berries, pale, creeping plants that grew up from the graves; tall crimson flowers, like poppies. Thomas steered clear.

He lost sight of Maud for a minute, as she weaved to left and right. Near the bottom of the hill the funerary architecture altered. The forest of headstones gave way to larger monuments, angels on columns, curious pillars and sarcophagi swarming with ivy. Then he saw her, standing at the gate of a huge tomb. She waved: 'Over here!'

He was out of breath. 'I lost you for a minute. This place is so big.'

The tomb was perhaps the resting place of some wealthy family. It was built of dark, grainy granite and the lock on the iron gateway was broken. Maud pushed the gate open and stepped down two small steps into the dim interior.

'What are you doing?' Thomas was uneasy. Outside it was bright and clear. Soft pearl and ivory clouds massed in the sky, and the sunlight burst through clear and gold as the champagne Agatha had drunk on her birthday. To the west of the tomb, in a patch of cultivated soil, a dozen trimmed shrubs carried a weight of translucent red berries. Something about the berries filled him with revulsion – the fruit like bloody frogspawn.

'Come along,' Maud scolded, poking her face through the doorway. 'Are you afraid?'

So he stepped inside, into the twilight of the tomb. To left and right, dusty old coffins rested on stone couches, both pushed carelessly to the side so that Maud could perch on the edge. Her doll was sitting on the stone-flagged floor, presiding over a makeshift tea party. Three cracked and mismatched cups and saucers lay on a soiled red silk scarf. Half a dozen stones, grey and black and white, waited in a ring on a plate.

'Sit down,' Maud said. Then, with utter seriousness: 'Would you like some tea?'

It was a fine porcelain teapot painted with lilies and roses, though the spout was partly broken. It poured, leaking, a soil-brown liquid into Thomas's cup.

'A cake?' She offered the plate of stones. Thomas had played similar games, more or less willingly, with his sisters over the years. This time he should have been self-conscious, to act the part of a child again. But he wasn't. It was something to do with Maud's complete self-possession. She was acting out some kind of ritual and had invited him to be part of it. So he took a stone (was that a finger bone, among the cakes?) and placed it on his knee. There they sat, Thomas, Maud and the doll, at their tea party among the coffins in the tomb.

'We only pretend to eat, of course,' Maud said primly. 'You must never eat anything in the garden of the dead.'

Thomas frowned, thinking of the red berries outside the tomb.

'I would never eat anything I picked in a graveyard,' he said, picking up his cup. 'But you play here.'

'I've played here hundreds of times. This is the first time we've had a guest, though.'

'Thank you. I feel honoured.' Fat red roses were painted on the cup. Grime coated its interior and three tiny pebbles lurked in the bottom of the murky water it contained.

'Doesn't your Aunt Lucy play here with you? Or your guardian?'

Maud wrinkled her nose. 'Sometimes,' she said. Then, fixing

85

Thomas with an acute stare: 'So, have you come to any conclusions about them yet?'

'About who?'

'Aunt Ernestina, Mr Constantine and the others.'

Now Thomas looked at her. How much did Maud know? Would he be breaking a confidence if he mentioned the Guild of Medical Herbalists? It was also possible Mrs Lawrence had primed her ward to ask these questions. They stared at one another, Maud and Thomas.

Maud broke away first, plopping her cup back into its saucer and sniffing loudly. 'They are a bunch of old witches,' she said, all matter-of-fact. 'You know that already.'

Thomas opened and closed his mouth, the cup still suspended in his hand. He felt a plummeting inside, as though the tomb floor was falling away underneath him.

'Witches,' he repeated.

Maud pursed her lips. 'Well, they give themselves another fancy name, but I think that's what they are.' She busied herself with the crockery, placing a cup and cake before the silent doll.

'The Guild of Medical Herbalists,' Thomas said.

Maud laughed. She had a bright, lovely laugh. 'Medical herbalists, yes. So what do you know?'

Thomas frowned.

'You don't trust me?' Maud said.

'I don't know if I trust you or not.'

She quirked her mouth into an odd half-smile, revealing a dimple in her cheek. 'Do you know,' she said, leaning towards him, 'that you must be a witch-in-training too?'

Thomas drew away with a start, which knocked his cup and sent pebbles and mud water spilling over the scarf. Maud laughed, a little maliciously perhaps, revealing white, white teeth.

'What do you mean?'

'It's so simple, I can't believe you haven't worked it out for yourself.'

Thomas felt the falling again, the tomb dropping away into a dark space deep beneath the earth.

'I'm not a witch, don't be stupid,' he said.

'Don't be scared, Thomas. That's why my aunt is interested in you – why she let me take you into her garden. You're a witch in training.'

'What d'you mean?'

'You have a box, don't you? Mr Constantine's teaching you how to be a witch, even if you don't know it.'

Thomas folded his arms and glowered. He could feel his temper rising and didn't want it to get the better of him. He had to think.

'So you are a witch?' he said.

Maud lowered her eyelids and, from her sitting position, gave a mock bow.

'Of course,' she said. 'Well, I shall be one day. At first I thought I would inherit Aunt Ernestina's box, but the situation has changed now.'

'How can I be a witch? What does it mean?'

'You have one of seven boxes,' she said. 'There are seven witches. Two of the old ones have died, and we two young ones step into their place.'

'That's absurd,' Thomas said hotly. 'I don't know anything about it.' But images rose up in his mind: the revenant in the bluebells, the thought forms crawling over his grandmother's house, the shadow Constantine had drawn out of his mind to expose his memories . . .

'Nehemiah Blake's box will come to me. Aunt Ernestina is

taking care of it,' Maud said. 'I haven't opened it yet and I haven't been initiated into the guild. We are both in the same position. Your grandmother sent you to live with Constantine. She wanted him to teach you and take care of you.'

'Nehemiah Blake. I saw him killed,' Thomas said.

Maud nodded. 'My aunt told me. Constantine sent a letter to the others to share what you told him. They will be meeting soon, the five old ones, to work out what to do. They'll want you to join them.'

Thomas looked up at Maud. Her face was gentle now, showing sympathy for his confusion.

'Why are *you* telling me? Why didn't Constantine?'

Maud smiled. 'They are tricksy people. None of them really trusts the other. They've always had little alliances and arguments and fallings-out. So many cloak-and-dagger games. But nothing's happened like this before. Two of them dead – and who's to blame? It has to be one of the five, but no-one knows which one it is and they're all afraid. Perhaps Constantine wanted to be sure of you first.'

'If your guardian has a Poison Garden, surely she must be the guilty one?' Thomas said. 'Isn't it obvious?'

'It isn't so simple,' Maud said. 'Mr Constantine has a Garden of Healing, and in it he grows a special variety of digitalis – the foxglove. In small doses it stimulates a weak heart. In a large dose, it is poisonous. You see? Yes, my guardian specialises in the cultivation of poisons, but the others have access to poisons too.'

Thomas stood up, as far as the low ceiling of the tomb would allow.

'I'm going outside. I want to breathe the fresh air. Will you come with me, Maud?'

She nodded, and picked up the doll, leaving the tea party spread out on the floor.

They joined the weaving path through the cemetery and walked side by side in the sunlight. A rook on an obelisk cawed as they passed. Otherwise it was entirely silent. No single sound of the city reached them, not the trains or the factories or the din of the ceaseless horse traffic. They reached the sombre lake and sat on a bench beneath a yew tree. Thomas shaded his eyes and strained to see the far side of the water, where a skein of trees shaded into the distance. Strange purple reeds grew in the shallows.

'This place is like my grandmother's garden,' he said. 'It doesn't truly exist.'

'Of course it exists,' Maud said. 'Otherwise how could we be here?'

So Thomas explained about his discovery of the Garden of Dreams within his grandmother's garden, the bluebell wood, the orchard with the black goat. He explained how the path into this garden had appeared and disappeared.

'Isn't this place the same?' he said. 'Another day, I might come back to your house and find only the grass patch behind and a wall enclosing it, and dustbins and alleys behind. This,' he indicated the wide necropolis with a sweep of his arm, 'this isn't London.'

Explaining to Maud, allowing himself to understand and believe it, Thomas felt a huge relief and a curious sense of expansion in his mind. Some clinging, fearful part of him let go the safe certainties of the past and opened to the possibility that the world he inhabited was much stranger than he had thought.

Maud smiled. 'Come on. We'd better go back to the house now. We've been gone a long time.'

They wended their way uphill, through the garden of headstones, tombs and marble angels.

'What happens now?' Thomas asked, as they pushed their way through the brambles and back to the house.

'The meeting,' Maud said. 'They'll have dinner together, the five of them. I shall be there too. Keep your eyes and ears open. One of them is killing the others, don't forget. And who's to say they wouldn't kill us, too?' She reached out her hand and squeezed Thomas's fingers.

'Thank you for this morning,' she said. 'Don't forget I'm your friend. The others are so much older and stronger than we are, so we should be close, don't you think?'

Thomas nodded. 'Yes,' he said. Maud ran into the house, into the arms of her Aunt Lucy, and Thomas hurried home to Constantine's without another word to Mrs Lawrence.

Three

Fog smoked from the wet, muddy roads. Evening was drawing on, although it was only four in the afternoon. The windows gave on views across murky fields and patches of bare, straggling woodland. Thomas and Mr Constantine had been travelling in the brougham since first light and both were cold and tired. At the edge of London, they had stopped at the city's market gardens where Mr Constantine negotiated with growers over stocks of dried lavender and roses for the shop's soaps and lotions. Later they pulled up at the Red Dog for a midday meal of steak pie and potatoes, and changed horses for the remainder of the journey. But it was bitterly cold, despite hats, coats and blankets. Draughts whipped through the carriage as it bumped and lurched along the country lanes, further from London and deeper into the wintry countryside. Water sprayed from flooded ruts, splattering the sleek wooden sides of the brougham. The horse too was up to his belly in thick, clay mud and the driver, perched on the box seat, must have been coldest of all.

The sun declined over low hills in the distance, and the water lying on the fields burned orange with its reflected light. The carriage passed dank, black ponds and ploughed land full of stones. The driver lit the lamps but the road became more difficult, the weary horse struggling to make his way through the mud and potholes. Then, at last, they turned through two high stone pillars and up a long gravel drive towards a large country house surrounded by woodland.

The house stood in a saucer of low land, trees rising from the higher ground behind it creating the impression, from a distance, that the building was sunk into the ground. The drive went gently downhill and the driver pulled up in front of the porch. Stiff and achingly cold, Thomas climbed down from the carriage. A servant in black stood at the open door of the house and without a word indicated that he and Mr Constantine should step inside, leaving the driver to struggle with the luggage and take the horse to the stable-yard.

Huntington Hall appeared to be a grim place, despite its majestic exterior. As soon as Thomas stepped into the hall, a clammy draught insinuated its way through his clothing and against his shivering body. The house had been built perhaps a hundreds years before and had enjoyed few improvements since. No gas lighting at all, only oil lamps and candles, and everywhere dark, old-fashioned wooden panelling behind which the mice rattled. Walking through the corridor behind the silent servant, Constantine gave Thomas's shoulder a comforting squeeze.

'I can't wait to be by the fire, Thomas,' he said. 'There isn't a single part of me that isn't cold.'

The servant, raising his lamp aloft, opened a door and ushered the two guests into a parlour where a huge fire blazed in a stone fireplace. Candles flickered from sconces in the wall when the door closed; Constantine and Thomas were left on their own.

'Sit down; take your coat off,' Constantine said. 'Pull a seat by the fire and warm up a little. We shan't have to wait long. Once the luggage has been brought in we can change our clothes.'

'Are the others here yet?' Thomas asked.

'I don't know. Everyone will be here by eight when the dinner begins.'

So it proved. The wordless servant returned and escorted them to a large bedroom, where their cases awaited. Another good fire sparked and cracked in the grate, throwing violent shadows on the curtains of two old four-poster beds. An oil lamp glowed from a table between the beds, and a second from a chest by the window.

Despite the fire, the room was chilly and smelled of damp. A bowl of hot water had been placed on the table so the guests might wash their hands and faces before changing from their travel-stained clothes into something clean, dry and appropriate for the dinner to come. Thomas felt deadly tired and, though Constantine chattered on making unimportant observations about the room and their journey, Thomas sensed his avuncular guardian was agitated and attempting to soothe them both. He had said precious little about the dinner and meeting but on the journey that day Thomas had sensed Constantine's mind had been entirely preoccupied by thoughts of the Guild and the events Thomas had revealed.

As the clock on the mantelpiece chimed seven, a maid knocked on the door and indicated they should follow her downstairs. She led them to a huge dining room, filled with yellow light from dozens of candles. A long table had been spread for dinner, covered in white cloth and polished silver, embellished with glossy ivy. Half a dozen people were milling around the fire, and others had arrived behind them. Thomas crossed the threshold and saw, with huge relief, a face he recognised.

'Maud!' he called. She turned to him with a happy smile and a wave. Thomas took a step towards her but Constantine grabbed him by the shoulder.

'Wait, Thomas,' he said, in a low voice. 'Be discreet. Let me introduce you to everyone first.'

They took their places at the table, seven in total; the five older members and the two young people, Maud and Thomas. An elderly woman dressed in dark purple silk stood at the end of the table. She had long white hair tied up in an elaborate coil, full of glittering pins.

'That is Miss Louisa Hudson,' Constantine whispered. 'Huntington Hall belongs to her. She's our host.'

Miss Hudson had a plump figure, a bosom like a soft bolster and amply cushioned hips. Her cheeks were plump, so even her face seemed well padded. She clapped her hands together, gazed along the table and gave her guests a twinkling smile.

'Oh good evening everyone,' she said. 'I can't tell you how glad I am to see you again – together after so long! It does my heart so much good to see you.' She pressed a hand to her chest. 'I am sorry, however, that we meet in the shadow of death, and under such trying circumstances. There is not one of us, I am sure, who doesn't feel – keenly feel – the loss of two of our number. Augusta and Nehemiah have been dead four years now, ladies and gentlemen. To have lost them is bad enough but it is the manner of this loss we meet to discuss tonight.

'But let me set this sad matter to one side for the moment. I wish to welcome two young people. I hope they will be members of our guild one day. Here they are – Maud Lawrence – and Thomas Reiter.'

Nods and murmured greetings. Miss Hudson sat down and the servants began to move around the room, taking lids from steaming silver bowls, serving soup to the guests at the table. Thomas felt uneasy, seeing the soup, remembering how his grandmother had died, and thinking of the Poison Garden. He glanced at Mr Constantine, wondering if he was entertaining the same worry. It was true that Constantine checked that the others were eating before he took up his spoon. Only then did Thomas follow his example.

He took a moment to observe everyone. Maud was dressed in a long and ornate black dress with ropes of pearls around her neck. This rather absurd outfit made her look very young – like a child dressing up in her mother's clothes. Mrs Lawrence was much as always, in her jewellery and funerary black. On the other side of Maud was a tall, slender man with short blond hair and two long, thin scars on his right cheek. Then, last to take a seat, the biggest man Thomas had ever seen. Powerfully built, with huge shoulders, he towered over Constantine, his extraordinarily long glossy black hair falling halfway down his back.

So this was the guild. Maud had called them witches.

Maud was slowly stirring her soup with her spoon, and staring all the while at the blond man's scars with big, round eyes. Her attention seemed to agitate him, because he cleared his throat and his shoulders gave a curious, irritated wriggle. Nothing deterred, Maud said: 'What happened to your face?'

The man turned to her abruptly. The scars ran diagonally, straight across his cheek, from just below the temple. One stretched right to his mouth. The wound, when it had been afflicted, had cut through his top lip.

'They are duelling scars,' he said.

Maud continued to stare. 'You're German.'

'Yes little girl, I am German.'

Thomas could see she was itching to ask more questions, but Mrs Lawrence put her hand on the girl's arm and said: 'Forgive her curiosity, please. She leads a very sheltered life and I'm afraid we haven't taught her proper manners. That will need to be changed. Let me introduce you. Maud, this is Rupert Hegel.'

'Hello, Mr Hegel,' Maud said, arching her eyebrows, her voice saucy. Rupert Hegel wore a very smart, closely-fitted suit. Everything about him was fastidious, from his manicured fingernails to his immaculate clothes. His pale hair was closely cut, except that his fringe was long and swept in a neat curve above his high, forehead. And he ate fussily, frowning at some perceived deficiency in the soup, taking a sip before putting the spoon back on the plate and leaving the rest untouched. Thomas was utterly intrigued.

Beside him, Constantine now had no qualms about the quality of the soup. He was quaffing it noisily, a napkin tucked in the front of his jacket. He tugged at Thomas's sleeve.

'This is Robert Lee,' he said, gesturing with his spoon to the tall man sitting beside him. 'He's a damn good chap, Thomas – even if he is an American – and I want you to be friends with him.'

Robert Lee had smooth, tawny skin and clear, dark eyes. He smiled at Thomas and, reaching over Constantine, shook Thomas's hand.

'It's a pleasure to meet you,' he said. 'Your grandmother was very kind to me and I admired her greatly.' Something about Lee reminded Thomas of Nehemiah Blake, as though Lee, like Blake, was a walker and a wanderer.

After the soup came a huge roast beef in gravy, with roast potatoes and copious bowls of vegetables. Cold and tired after the long journey, Thomas was ravenous and had his plate piled high. Hegel, on the other hand, declined all but the vegetables. When he saw Thomas staring at his plate he said: 'Are you German, Thomas Reiter?'

'No,' Thomas blurted, his mouth full of hot potato. 'My father's parents are German and they moved here to England.'

Hegel nodded. 'Do you know which part of Germany they came from?' His English was slow and precise.

'Saxony,' Thomas said, glad he knew this one small nugget of his paternal family history.

'Saxony, yes. I come from Berlin but I attended the university in Gottingen, in Lower Saxony. Do you speak German, Thomas?' His eyes glinted.

Thomas shook his head and Hegel gave a quick, disappointed tut. Across the table, Maud offered a small, secret smile.

When the dinner was eaten, the servants brought in a pudding of stewed fruit and cream and then a platter of dried fruit and cheese. Finally, the plates were cleared away leaving only the bottle of port on the table. Miss Hudson dismissed the servants and the doors were closed. Thomas felt a tightening in the atmosphere, as though everyone, finally, was focused on the task at hand – the reason for their visit to far-flung Huntington Hall.

Constantine stood up and cleared his throat. The conversation halted.

'Guild members, welcome,' he said. 'Thank you for making this journey to be here today – I understand how little some of you like to leave home at all.' This with a glance at Mrs Lawrence and Rupert Hegel.

'But the meeting is vital. Absolutely vital. We all received news of Augusta's death a long time ago. Then Nehemiah disappeared. I must confess I didn't let his absence worry me. We knew what manner of man he was. He had disappeared before, for months, years, at a time travelling who knows where. Travelling as I have done. Now, however, we know he was killed and we have evidence suggesting Augusta, also, was murdered.'

Constantine turned to Thomas. 'Stand up, Thomas,' he said. 'Now, you must tell us all everything that happened on the day of your grandmother's funeral. Don't leave out a single detail, do you understand? Everything you can remember, all that you saw, all that was said.'

Thomas rose to his feet. So many eyes on him – the American Lee, Hegel with his duelling scars, Constantine, the widow Lawrence, plump Miss Hudson and Maud. He licked his lips and swallowed. Constantine gave him a reassuring pat on the back.

'Go on, boy,' he whispered. 'Tell them.'

So Thomas told it all: the funeral and the reading of the will; the discovery of the Garden of Dreams and his meeting with Nehemiah Blake; the walk to the graveyard and Blake's attack on the violinist; the gift of the box, the thought forms sliding into the house and the words of the revenant telling him his grandmother had been poisoned; finally, Blake's fight with the young man in the bluebells, a fight that killed them both.

He spoke for a long time, the memories of that long-ago night shining bright in his memory. And they stared at him, the six, drinking in the details, turning over the implications, looking surreptitiously at the others, doubtless wondering, which of their number had turned against the rest?

When the story was over, Thomas dropped heavily back into his chair. The room was silent for a moment, as the guild members weighed his words. No-one knew where to start – or what to say. One of those present had evidently recruited an assassin – the young blond man – so how could they trust each other now?

Lee leaned forward, his elbows resting on the table. 'There are two possibilities,' he said. 'The guild's secret history has been uncovered by an outsider – or secondly, that one of us sitting here has betrayed the others.' He looked from one person to the next, all around the table. How to read them? Hegel responded with an icy stare. Mrs Lawrence plucked at the jet and pearl pendant hanging around her neck.

'It has to be the first,' Miss Hudson jumped in. 'How can we suspect each other? What would be gained by it?'

Again they looked, one to another.

'If the man who killed Nehemiah used thought forms, we must wonder where he obtained the necessary herbal ingredients,' Lee said. 'Which one of us supplied him and taught him?'

'If that is the case, then one of you has let our secret slip,' Hegel said. 'One of you has passed on a confidence.'

'One of *you*? How can we be sure it wasn't you, Rupert?' Mrs Lawrence said.

Hegel gave a little shudder of distaste and ran his fingers over his perfectly-aligned fringe. How old was he? Thomas found it hard to say. Younger than some of the others, certainly, though he looked very well preserved.

Constantine stepped in: 'Isn't it likely this problem is already over? Doesn't it seem to be the case that whoever was trying to take Augusta's box is already dead and no longer a problem for us? Whoever he was, however he found out, this man was killed by Blake. Don't forget, nothing more's happened in four years.'

Some murmured agreement, others shook their heads. Thomas glanced at Maud. Her face was intent, drinking up the conversation.

'The boy tells us this young man used thought forms,' Hegel said. His pale face was angry now, impatient with the perceived stupidity of his colleagues. The thin scars flushed red. 'He must have an ally here. It is the only logical explanation.'

All the voices rose at once, in a tide of denial and recriminations. Lee stood up, a dominating presence, and held up his hand to silence the others.

'Something strikes me about Thomas's account, something we need to consider very carefully,' he said. 'After the funeral, a violinist played over Augusta's grave. This so infuriated Nehemiah he jumped on the man. Why should that be so? Who paid the violinist?'

As one, the guild members looked to Hegel. His lips were pressed into a thin line and his blue eyes blazed.

'It has nothing to do with me,' he said.

'You are the only one of us who plays the violin,' Mrs Lawrence said.

'So I am. That tells you nothing. I wasn't the man playing at the funeral.'

Lee was impatient, breaking into their conversation. 'Don't you see?' he said. 'This is important. Why pay someone to play over a grave?'

'You're quite right,' Constantine nodded. 'I see precisely what you're saying. Someone had Augusta poisoned and then celebrated their victory in this grotesque manner with the funerary violinist.'

But Thomas piped up: 'How do you know it was the killer who commissioned the violinist? Mightn't it have been a long-lost friend?'

Constantine considered. 'A friend? It is a good question, Thomas, but we must wonder why Nehemiah was so enraged. What was it about the man that prompted him to attack? Will you describe him to us again, in as much detail as you can? Perhaps that is where the clue lies. Maybe Nehemiah knew who the man was.'

The discussion went on. It moved in circles, never seeming to make any clear headway. The port was consumed and the voices became louder. The guild members began dragging out recollections of the historic slights and annoyances they had suffered at each other's hands. Recriminations filled the air. Tired and well-fed, bored by the pointless arguing, Thomas grew drowsy and yearned for bed.

Finally Lee stood up again, his hands clenched into fists, anger shadowing his face.

'This is getting us nowhere!' he shouted. The strength of his voice quelled the squabbling in an instant. Mrs Lawrence patted her face with a lace handkerchief. Hegel abruptly shook his head.

'Then what can we do?' Constantine said. 'None of us will admit they instigated this, so we can no longer trust each other.'

'Perhaps it was a personal matter, between Augusta and one of us. A feud of some kind. That would explain why nothing has happened since,' Hegel mused.

'The violinist,' Miss Hudson said, flapping her hand. 'He is our only connection. Whether this villain was an outsider, or one of us, the violinist is the only way to find out.'

Hegel nodded slowly. 'The Guild of Funerary Violinists, yes. Perhaps they will remember.'

'Do you know them? Do you have contacts with this guild, Rupert?' Constantine asked.

'Yes,' Hegel said abruptly. They all stared at him. The admission was faintly incriminating, of course. There was a further question in the air. Since they could no longer trust each other, how could they be sure Hegel would make thorough investigations?

Hegel threw his hands in the air, in a gesture of frustration. 'We can't all go,' he said. 'Let me take the boy with me.' – this looking at Thomas – 'Maybe he can identify the man who played at the funeral and he can act as your ears and eyes also.'

Thomas sat up straight and rubbed his eyes. 'Me?' he said. 'You want me to go with you?'

Then they were all staring at him. Constantine looked

troubled. He said: 'What do you think, Thomas? Would you go with Herr Hegel?'

Thomas glanced across the table to Maud. She gave the faintest nod.

'Of course,' he said.

The following morning, Constantine and Thomas climbed back into the brougham and began the journey back to London. Thomas had slept very heavily the night before, worn out by the long cold day and stupefied by his enormous dinner. Constantine didn't look as though he'd fared so well. His face was pale and pouchy in the morning's grey light and he had little appetite for the breakfast they were given in a basket to take for the journey.

Two hours passed and muddy lanes joined wider thoroughfares. In the middle of the day they stopped again at the Red Dog for a meal and to change the horse. The inn was quiet. Constantine and Thomas sat by the fire for their pork chops and potatoes with only one other solitary drinker in the room. It was a dark place, the wind whistling in the chimney and the gloom relieved only by the fire and the cheerful voice of the young woman singing to herself behind the bar.

At last Constantine spoke up: 'So, Thomas, how much did you understand of last night's discussion?'

'I think I understood the argument well enough, Mr Constantine. But I am still very much in the dark about everything else.' He glanced at the other drinker, too far away to overhear them, though he lowered his voice in any case.

'Who are you all? Maud told me you were all witches and that I would be one too. What does that mean?'

Constantine sighed. 'I'm sorry. I had hoped this could wait

until you were a little older. I had no wish to burden you with any knowledge of the guild while you were growing up. That was not my intention at all.'

'So you *are* a witch.' Thomas was feeling itchy and antagonistic. He was tired of secrets and evasions. He needed to know.

Constantine shook his head slowly. 'That isn't the word I would use.'

'But you use magic.'

'Magic? Again that wouldn't be the word I'd use.'

'So what *would* you use?'

'You must understand, the Guild of Medical Herbalists is very old indeed. Its history stretches back over centuries. We have archives dating back to medieval times and some from earlier still. It was a guild of healers who had an accumulated knowledge of the properties and uses of plants, a wealth of information passed from generation to generation. But a century ago, in the so-called Age of Reason, the guild went into decline. The members drifted apart and the library was all but forgotten. Books were sold or lost or destroyed. Documents were taken away, passed from hand to hand. Then thirty years ago a group of disparate people began, each on their own account, to gather clues of its existence.

'Miss Hudson and your grandmother were botanists first and foremost. Mrs Lawrence, well,' he gave a grim laugh, 'remember what I told you about her connections. She was famous in the East End among certain circles. Rupert Hegel was a university student researching rare manuscripts and forgotten books. It was my profession as a chemist that drew me in. Blake and Lee – well, it is hard to know how precisely they came to this particular path. They are both remarkable men, and each was looking for something. Blake – it's hard to describe him – a wanderer, an actor, a street magician, a hustler. I don't think it's fanciful to say he had a very old soul. Perhaps he was Merlin in an earlier life.' Constantine gave a small, sad smile. 'I can't believe he's dead.'

He glanced at Thomas. 'And he had a passion for your grandmother.'

'But she didn't care for him?'

'I think she did. I think she loved him deeply, but she was married, don't forget.'

'What is your garden called, Mr Constantine?'

'It is Tadmor, the Garden of Healing. I have devoted my life to the care of the sick and suffering. It was this quest that led me to the guild, and through it I have achieved so much, and hope to do more.'

'So how did the guild come to be?'

'Slowly, over a number of years, as often happens when people share an interest, these diverse people came into contact with one another. Each had a piece of information or a document or an old book. We wrote notices in various papers and journals, looking for clues and contacts. Then we exchanged letters, pooling what information we had. At last, working together, we discovered the guild's lost archives, locked away and forgotten in the cellar of an old house in London. Books on shelves, documents baled up in chests. Some were lost or decayed beyond repair but most had survived. What a discovery that was – so much for us to learn.'

'Where's the guild's library now?'

'At Huntington Hall. In truth, the house belongs to us all – to the guild itself. Miss Hudson takes care of it for us.'

Something turned over in Thomas's mind. 'My grandmother's bequest,' he wondered. 'Was the guild the third party? Did she leave everything to you?'

Constantine nodded. 'Yes, she did. The guild owns her house.

It is rented out, as you know, and this, along with the revenues from her fortune, is used to finance the upkeep of the guild's library and the purchase of rare books and documents. We agreed, all of us, that although we would provide for the future of our families we would pool any remaining resources for the good of the guild. We are, all of us, wealthy people as a result of our discoveries. That surprises you? We don't make it obvious. And in any case Blake had no interest in money.'

Constantine sat back in his chair. 'It's time we returned to the brougham, if we want to be home before dark.'

Their own little bay horse, which had been stabled overnight at the inn when they borrowed a fresh replacement, now stood in harness between the shafts of the carriage. He whinnied a welcome when Constantine stepped out and the driver, climbing up to his box, laughed and said: 'He recognises you, sir.'

'Cupboard love only,' Constantine replied. He dug in his coat pocket for a crust of bread and held it on the palm of his hand for the horse to eat. It was starting to rain again, a thin, chilly drizzle. Constantine climbed into the carriage with Thomas, the driver cracked his whip and the journey resumed.

'So you found a library,' Thomas said. 'What about the boxes? What about the things I've seen you do?'

Constantine sighed and rubbed his face with his hands. 'Patience, Thomas. Haven't I given you enough for now? The boxes came many years later. I have so much to think about.' He lapsed into silence, staring out of the window, but Thomas – like a terrier on a rat – did not relent.

'What about Hegel?' he demanded. 'You're sending me off with him. What might happen?'

Constantine shook his head. 'Am I? Am I going to send you? That is precisely what's troubling me now. Should I have agreed? Am I putting you in needless danger? I am having second thoughts about the idea. I am having very serious doubts.'

'No, don't have second thoughts,' Thomas jumped in.

Constantine looked up, surprised by the boy's assertive response. 'You want to go?'

'Yes, yes I do. I want to know what's happening.' An image of the revenant rose in the forest of Thomas's mind. 'But how can I be safe if you don't tell me everything?'

Constantine wrinkled his face.

'You think it might be Hegel,' Thomas said. 'Is that why you're worrying? You think it was Hegel who sent his assassin after my grandmother. Or perhaps it was Mrs Lawrence, with her poisons. And all her questions . . . that's what you think?'

'Did I say that?' Constantine said abruptly. 'Did I say so, Thomas? Did I even hint at it?'

Thomas shook his head. 'No. No, you didn't. I was just . . . wondering.'

They were both quiet for a time. Questions buzzed in Thomas's head but he didn't dare ask again. He bided his time.

Despite the rain they made good progress. The roads were much better this second half of the journey. As they drew into London's endless suburbs the houses closed in around them and the roads grew hectic with horse-drawn traffic. They drew up outside the premises of Constantine & Blacklow as dusk was falling and removed their cold, aching bodies from the carriage and into the welcoming family home.

Everyone was pleased to see them. Agatha and Amy shrieked with delight to see their father returned safe and sound. They buried him in hugs and hung upon him all evening. Even James seemed glad to have his second-in-command back and rewarded him with a punch of the arm and a list of evening jobs to complete before they closed up shop.

After their expedition, Thomas felt the pleasure of this homecoming very keenly. They were a good-hearted family and the house was full of warmth and colour and delight in each other's company. The place was a comfortable bastion against the darkness and unknown. He thought of his own mother and father, of the little house in the village where they too would be sitting around the fire together. He was very fond of the Constantine family, but he missed his own people too.

Then, at ten o'clock, a young man arrived with a message for Mr Constantine from a doctor. A medical preparation was urgently needed: could the chemist make a preparation and bring it to the given address? The girls moaned and groaned, unwilling to let their father go, and he looked none too happy to leave them. But duty called. Constantine and James went down to the shop to sort out various potions and ingredients and then Constantine left with the young man – promising to be as quick as possible.

An hour passed and Mrs Constantine sent everyone to bed. She looked tired and worn by then and Thomas wondered how much – if anything – she knew about the guild and her husband's secret activities. Constantine said he kept it secret from her but the couple seemed perfectly devoted so perhaps she simply trusted him to do what was right. Thomas was the last to be shooed from the drawing room and when he departed he left her sitting at the window looking out into the street with a single candle burning by her side.

The three apprentices shared a bedroom behind the shop. By the time Thomas went downstairs Billy was already asleep, sprawled on his back across his bed and snoring gently. James was on his knees, his eyes closed, whispering his prayers. Thomas jumped under his covers, eager to be warm.

'So where did he take you?' said James, as he slid into his own narrow bed, across the room from Thomas.

'To see a client – miles away. Out in the country.'

'Was it interesting?'

Thomas lay in the dark and considered. 'Yes, it was very interesting. Has he not taken you out of town before?'

'Oh yes, many times,' James asserted, not wanting to be outdone. Distantly they could hear the rumble of carriages passing in the street and the faraway thunder of a train. Despite the stream of questions in his mind, Thomas drifted into sleep. He dreamed of the bluebell wood and of Blake leaking blood into the soil. He dreamed of his grandmother, young and pretty, sitting in her bed drinking poisoned tea. And he dreamed of Maud, lying in a stone coffin with her doll while dirt was shovelled over her face and she began to cry and scream . . .

. . . and scream. He woke up in a sweat. The noise had leaked from his dream into his waking. Or had it been the other way round?

'What is it?' James was awake too. Dimly Thomas could see him sitting up in his bed. 'I heard a huge crash,' James said. 'I thought it was a dream.'

'Who's screaming? Someone in the street. Has there been an accident?' Thomas jumped out of bed, James close behind him. They ran into the shop. Just outside they saw a confusion of images – people rushing about, a horse struggling on the ground. James fumbled with the lock on the door and opened it just as Mrs Constantine arrived from upstairs, her hair in a long plait dangling from her nightcap.

'What is it? What's happened?' she demanded. 'Open the door. Let me out! I had a terrible dream – let me pass!'

She ran out, barefoot, into the cold night with the apprentices just behind her. It was hard to see what was happening. A hansom cab had overturned and a horse lay groaning in the road, its chest all torn open and blood spilling into the gutter. Another dark shape lay on the pavement – a man with his head cushioned on a folded coat, while two people fussed about him, all in a panic.

'Albert? Albert?' Mrs Constantine bent over the man on the pavement. 'Albert, wake up, Albert!' she repeated. Thomas felt the cold creeping into his body, running up his hands, over his throat and face and inside to his heart and lungs and entrails. Nowhere was safe. He was on his own.

The cab driver was down on his knees beside his horse, running his hands over the animal's heaving sides, whispering to it, trying to coax it to its feet.

'You'll be all right boy,' he pleaded. 'It isn't so bad, you'll see. You'll be all right,' he said hopelessly, over and over again.

NINEVEH

The Perfume Garden

*Knowing well that you are mortal,
lift up your heart and take delight in feasts.
You will have no more pleasure when dead.
For I am dust who once ruled great Nineveh —
and these things I had which gave me joy —
what I ate, my desires and what I
found through passion.
But many happy things are left behind.*

Diodorus

One

All through the night the snow fell, obliterating London, briefly covering the ubiquitous soot and filth, and making the city perfect. Then dawn came, a burning cauldron, pouring light over spires and rooftops.

Thomas stood inside the shop by the door, staring out at the street. Already footprints pocked the snow. The milk van was making its way along the houses, drawn by a patient, whiskery horse. The driver sat up on the van, swathed in coat, hat and scarf, while a boy darted back and forth with the requisite cans of milk.

Now the boy was hurrying to the chemist's. He was a skinny London sparrow, thin legged, his face nipped pink by the cold. Thomas opened the door.

'It's the funeral today, isn't it?' the boy asked, handing over the milk can.

Thomas nodded.

'Going to be a grand affair, so I hear.'

'Yes,' Thomas said. 'Very grand.'

'Well say one for me.' The boy touched the front of his cap. 'He was always very kind to me, Mr Constantine.'

From the van, the driver made some indistinct but irritated sound, indicating the boy's talking time was over. He turned away and hopped back to the milk van, leaving Thomas in the doorway. The frigid air swirled into the shop and Thomas shivered.

He took the milk to the kitchen where Mrs Constantine was sitting with her daughters. She had aged since the accident a week ago, as though Constantine's death had sapped all the strength and will from her body. The flesh on her face had begun to sag and her hair seemed, suddenly, to be grey. They were very pale, the three women, trying to drink their tea, the girls trying to take care of their mother.

The funeral procession began at eleven, outside the shop. The three apprentices, Thomas, Billy and James, top-hatted and dressed in black, walked ahead of this grandiose ship of death. Behind them stood the hearse, furnished with glossy black ebony and elaborate silver adornments. Six statuesque horses stood in harness, ink-coloured, brandishing black feathered plumes on their heads. The coffin was visible through the polished glass sides of the hearse, swathed in white hot-house lilies, cold ferns and sprays of ivy.

Four coaches followed the hearse, bearing the chief mourners. Mrs Constantine, Agatha and Amy travelled in the first. The blinds were drawn down as the procession moved along the street at a steady walking pace. No-one spoke. The snow muted the sound of the horses' hooves but the clink of their bits, the creaking of the harness, seemed loud in the aura of silence and regret. As the funeral wound its circuitous path from the shop to the cemetery, passers-by stopped what they were doing and removed their hats. Children stared, open-mouthed.

It had been an unspeakably difficult week. Albert Constantine had died on the pavement, his skull shattered, without ever recovering consciousness. The scene had stained Thomas's memory – Mrs Constantine standing in the street, broken by grief, the front of her white nightgown red with her husband's blood. It seemed as though the world had stopped, then. The following days had no substance, revolving around the single fact of Constantine's impossible, incomprehensible absence. In the mourning house, the curtains drawn, the mirrors covered, the inhabitants moved about in silence as though they were the ghosts – as though they, and not Albert Constantine, had passed away.

Before the funeral came the inquest, examining the circumstances of the death. It was a terrible ordeal for Mrs Constantine. They gathered in the gloomy coroner's court, just one in a queue of suffering families obliged to undergo this process of inquisition. The coroner was a short, toad-like old man, with a beef-coloured face and no neck to speak of. From his seat on high he stared down at Mrs Constantine and her daughters when they shuffled into the dark, wood-panelled room. Thomas was questioned, and Constantine's cab driver.

'I dropped him off outside the shop, sir, and he went to see Tom and give him a slice of apple he had in his pocket,' the cabbie said. He was a gaunt, long-boned man who twisted his hands together nervously as he spoke.

'He was a kind gentleman, Mr Constantine. Always had time for me and the horse. Not like some of them – those that treat you like you're not flesh and blood and keep you waiting all night in the cold, as though you haven't any kind of human feeling.'

The coroner frowned and signalled for the cabbie to get on with his story. The man wrung his hands.

'Well, he was standing at Tom's head, when another cab comes tearing along the street. It had no lamps on, and the horse was sliding over the road. The driver was laying into the beast with his whip and hauling it round. The horse came straight towards us –

runs into Mr Constantine and knocks him off his feet – and though the cab turns away the right shaft runs into Tom's chest, right deep.'

The cabbie flushed, deeply distressed, and rubbed his hands across his face.

'There was nothing I could do,' he said. 'He just bled to death, there in the road. And he was such a good horse – the best I've had. Never let me down, he didn't.'

The coroner frowned again. 'Mr Little, I am not interested in the horse. Please tell me what happened to the other cab.'

The cabbie struggled to master his feelings.

'The other cab didn't stop,' he said. 'The end of the shaft broke off and the horse stumbled on its feet. Then it was off again, at a hell of a pace.'

'Did you see the driver?'

'I didn't see anything. It had no lights, and the driver was all muffled up. It all happened so fast and I had my eyes on poor Tom, and Mr Constantine lying on the pavement, and then his wife came out. What could I do?'

The police had investigated, of course. They had no way of identifying the other cab and their inquiries came to nothing. At the end of the inquest the coroner concluded the death was an accident. They had no reason to think otherwise. While the other driver should have stopped, no criminal proceedings could be brought against him because they had no idea who he was. The process was over. Mrs Constantine was free to bury her husband.

Of course Thomas didn't believe the death was an accident. As soon as it happened he had known and understood. Constantine, his friend and protector, had been killed, just like Blake and his grandmother.

And so Thomas plodded through the snow, at the prow of the

funerary ship. His feet were cold and, despite the black gloves, his fingers were numb. Clouds massed over the city and its endless streamers of chimney smoke. A first few flakes began to fall, settling on the apprentices' top hats. At last the cemetery hove into view, and the seemingly interminable death march reached its end. The procession made its way along the wrought iron railings and through the grand gateway, along an avenue of cypress trees to the white marble chapel at the heart of the cemetery.

After the service, the mourners stood by the open grave as the snow continued to fall, clouds of flakes like fat white bees. Mrs Constantine and her daughters were standing on the opposite side of the grave, dressed in black crepe gowns with long smoky veils blowing over their faces. The vicar read from his prayer book, as his white surplice billowed in a gust of wind and locks of grey hair fluttered over his shoulders.

'Yet oh Lord God most holy, O Lord most mighty, O Holy most merciful saviour, deliver us not into the bitter pains of eternal death,' he cried out, battling with the storm. He raised his hand, as though to stay the elements. 'The days of man are but as grass; for he flourisheth as a flower of the field. For as soon as the wind goeth over it, it is gone; and the place thereof shall know it no more . . .'

A swirl of snow filled the air, almost obliterating the Constantine women from Thomas's view. They were swallowed up in the cloud of whiteness, briefly reappearing like ghostly negatives. Snow settled on the top hats and shoulders of the men, and the wind tugged at the tails of their mourning suits. The weather, capricious, oblivious, seemed to dance around the funeral.

After the interment the mourners returned to the Constantines' home where the fires blazed and a sumptuous meal awaited the guests. Mrs Constantine was pale and dignified, leaving her daughters to take care of the mourners. So many offered their condolences, expressed their disbelief, their sense of loss. The day dragged on, each slow hour painfully plodding until at last all had been endured and the mourners departed one by one. By then night had closed in, blacking out the windows. The servants drew the curtains and fed the fires. At five o'clock the family lawyer called Mrs Constantine and her daughters into the drawing room. The apprentices retired to the kitchen, where the other servants were busy cleaning up.

James was lost in thought, his lips moving silently, screwing up his face from time to time, evidently rehearsing some conversation in his head. Billy, elbow on the table, his cheek propped on his hand, stared and grinned. He looked across to Thomas.

'I know what he's thinking,' he said, all chirpy. 'I know what you're thinking, Jimmy boy.'

James looked up and flushed. He glared at the junior apprentice.

'You don't know anything,' he said. 'Watch your mouth, Billy.'

Nothing deterred, Billy persisted. 'You're going to ask Miss Agatha to marry you, that's what you're going to do. Then you're thinking you'll help Mrs Constantine run the shop. Isn't that right?'

James flushed a deeper crimson. He jumped to his feet and slapped Billy on the head so the boy was knocked sideways. Billy just laughed, straightening himself after the blow. James marched out of the room. The housekeeper tutted as she bustled past, unimpressed by the boys' disrespect on this day, of all days.

'Is it true? What you said?' Thomas asked.

Billy grinned and nodded. 'I overheard him, sweet-talking with

Miss Agatha yesterday. She told him it was too soon, but I don't think he can wait.'

Thomas sighed. So life went on. What about *his* life, now? Constantine, his guide, had been taken away. Now it was time to start finding out the truth for himself. He went to the room he shared with the two other apprentices. At the end of his bed stood the chest he had inherited from his grandmother, inside of which the sealed box nested on piles of papers and letters. The other boys were absent, so Thomas took out the key from its hiding place, a gap under the skirting board behind his bed, and unlocked the chest. There it was – the wooden box. He felt a tremor to see it – anxiety or excitement? A mixture of both. What was it about the box, and its fellows, that would incite to murder? The box seemed to glow in the evening gloom, as though it contained some interior illumination. How smooth and beautiful it was, the polished wood glistening like water beneath his fingertips. In the low light, the pattern on the lid seemed to move, as though the inlaid woods were liquid and able to flow. He hugged the box to him, loving it, relieved to know it was safe and still in his possession. It thrummed in his arms, charged with energy, and seemed to flex with a peculiar muscular life. He placed it on the floor beside him. It was time to take a closer look at the documents, papers and letters his grandmother had gifted him.

Thomas had only given these papers a cursory inspection before. They had appeared dull and daunting – correspondence written in his grandmother's dense hand, long lists of plants, botanical drawings. Now Constantine had whetted his interest with his talk of the guild and Thomas wanted to find out more. He picked up a tight bundle of letters tied both ways with a piece of string. The knot had pulled tight so he took out his penknife and cut the string, so the letters, released, spilled over his lap and onto the floor. He picked up a letter at random and unfolded it. The brittle paper cracked as he did so. Writing covered the page – hard to read in the low light, but still he could identify this was not his grandmother's handwriting. Thomas took it to the gas lamp on the table, to see better. The letter opened: 'My dear Augusta . . .' and concluded: 'With my deepest affection, Nehemiah Blake.' It was dated some ten years previously. Thomas took a deep breath and began to read. The first letters he read were accounts of travels, descriptions of plants Blake had cultivated, warm enquiries about Augusta. Then Thomas picked up a letter which took a more interesting track.

'. . . Of course the revived guild is still in its infancy, but I fear for its survival, Augusta. We are a diverse group and we have yet to agree on a firm purpose and a path for our future work. I have grave concerns about the decision we made, when the garden was divided. No longer do we work together for the common good, to expand human knowledge and share the fruits of our discoveries for the benefit of all. That was my wish – my dream. Instead certain individuals are using the gift to indulge their own interests and accumulate power over their fellow human beings . . .'

Thomas pondered. Which garden was Blake talking about? The Garden of Dreams? The Poison Garden? It was hard to imagine that a poison garden could be used for the benefit of humankind. Was it Mrs Lawrence Blake was referring to, when he suggested guild members were indulging their own interests?

The oil lamp guttered and went out. Thomas folded the letter and placed it back in the chest, along with all the others. He was very tired and lay on his bed, in the dark, aching for sleep to take him. But his mind refused to be still, turning over the events of the day and speculating about the guild.

Later, unable to rest, he crept downstairs to the dark, quiet shop with the intention of sweeping the already spotless floor. It was very peaceful, after the stress of the day, to stand in the gloom with a broom in his hand. The clouds had cleared away, and the moon shone through gaps in the ragged cloud. He walked to the door and pressed his face to the glass, staring out at the night. Stars glittered. A horse and carriage plodded by. Minutes passed as Thomas waited. Something would happen. He sensed it, the web of movement beyond the glass, the manoeuvring. He was part of a larger pattern. A game – a deadly game – was proceeding move by move. What hand would come, to manipulate him again, in this chess game of impossible magic? What would it be? He stood till his body grew numb. In the rest of the house, the family were settling down for the night. The servants would be heading for bed. His mind went blank and heavy, charged with the strain of the funeral. The clouds swallowed the moon, spat it out again.

Thomas drifted into a kind of sleep on his feet, though his eyes were open. He found himself walking along a shadowed corridor in a great house, where doors opened to left and right. He followed a presence, wrapped in darkness, and always moving ahead of him, just out of sight. He knew it was important not to fall behind but dreaded the prospect of catching up, and finding out what this presence might be.

A sharp, knuckled rap on the door. Thomas came to with a start. A small boy stood outside, gesticulating at him to open up. Was this the call? Was this what he'd been waiting for? Thomas unlocked the door.

'Thomas Reiter?' said the boy. He was wrapped in several ragged coats, the rents in each revealing snippets of the one beneath. On his feet were odd shoes and his trousers were tied with string above one knee.

121

'What do you want?' Thomas said. 'D'you have a message for me?'

'You've got to come with me,' the boy said. 'I'll show you where to go.'

'Who sent you?'

'A big man. The biggest I've ever seen.'

So, it was Lee. 'Where is he?' Thomas asked.

'I'll show you,' the boy repeated, heading out of the door. 'Come on – hurry up.'

'Let me get my coat,' Thomas said. He ran to the apprentices' room, grabbed his coat and hat, and ran back into the shop where the little boy waited.

'Come on!' the boy urged. 'He said to hurry! Be quick, he told me.' The boy dashed out into the snow, Thomas struggling to keep up with him as he wove away from the main street into the warren of paths and alleys between the houses. The boy hurtled along the snowy pavements, through seemingly impossible gaps in walls, along alleyways in which the snow covered heaps of sodden rubbish, past pubs glowing with warm golden light. From one such, Thomas caught a thread of music – piano and a woman sadly singing: '. . . *and we'll never meet again, my love* . . .' Then it was gone, snatched into the distance as he ran on, struggling to keep up with the boy.

Despite the cold he was soon soaked with sweat and out of breath. Twice he fell over, sprawling in the snow, his senses deluded by the darkness. But the boy didn't relent. He was always just ahead, almost out of sight, looking back over his shoulder and beckoning Thomas to be quick.

'Come on! Come on! You have to hurry!'

Up a steep hill, almost losing his footing on hard pockets of grey, frozen slush – and then at the top a fence of iron railings and a wide view down, over the city cemetery where earlier in the day he had accompanied the other mourners to the funeral. Thomas grasped the rails and stood for a moment, breathing hard, seeing the white bowl of the cemetery, glowing in the moonlight. Long, blue shadows extended from the irregular columns of headstones and the forest of statues and spires. Down at the bottom of the hill, the dark line of cypress trees and the white marble chapel.

The boy chivvied him again. 'Quick now. Look lively!' He squeezed his tiny body through the fence, where one of the railings was slightly bent out of shape. Thomas tried to follow but he was larger than his guide and found himself wedged between the poles. The boy grabbed his arm and tried to tug him forcibly through the fence. Thomas yelped – felt his bones crushed and bruised – but he tumbled through, into the snow. The boy didn't wait for him – already he was running through the cemetery, leaping obstructions in his path. Thomas followed more cautiously, treading the boy's footprints in the otherwise perfect snow. Even so, he stumbled often, catching his toes on the snow-buried lintels around burial plots, and once, winding himself, tripped over a marble vase full of snow-crusted flowers.

Then, at last, the boy ducked into the shade of a yew tree – and seemingly vanished. Thomas slowed to a walk, brushing snow from his coat. Although his body was sweating his hands were cold as ice. The shadow, a skirt around the yew tree, swallowed him up. There was the boy – tugging at the sleeve of a humped shape. As Thomas's eyes adjusted to the greater darkness, the shape resolved itself. It was Lee, with his back to him, crouching low and peering out into the graveyard. Lee stuck his hand in his pocket and handed the boy some coins. Then he stood up, massive, stooped beneath the lower branches of the tree, and held out his fur-mittened hand to Thomas.

'It's good to meet you again, Thomas,' he said. 'I am sorry it's under such unhappy circumstances.' His voice was deep, his American accent musical. 'Constantine was a good man. The best of them.' Lee was wearing a long fur coat and a pair of tall boots, though his head was bare, his hair hanging blackly down his back.

'What are you doing here?' Thomas said. 'What's going on?'

Lee beckoned. 'Come and see.'

Thomas stepped forward and squatted beside the American.

'Look,' Lee said, extending his arm. 'Over there – see, where Constantine was buried.'

Thomas peered from the shadow into the moonlit basin of the cemetery. There, amid the graves, a solitary figure walked – a skinny man, all in black, with long, thin legs and a tight coat, a tall stove-pipe hat on his head, emphasising his height and narrowness. Tucked under his arm was a long, dark box. When he reached the new grave – already hard to distinguish because of the fallen snow – the man halted, opened his box and drew out a violin.

Thomas drew a breath. He looked up at Lee, about to speak, but Lee held out his hand to silence him. Thomas looked back to the man. Even from this distance, he could see the liquid glint of the moonlight on the body of the man's violin, as he raised it to his shoulder, flourished a bow and began to play.

The sound in the cold night air was clear and perfect. Like tangible strands, the notes undulated through the air. Thomas could see them – almost – like richly-coloured ribbons rising and falling in the darkness, threading through, creating patterns and pictures. And what colour would these ribbons of sound be? Bronze, honey and the softest antique gold. Pale primrose, conker brown, milk, amber, burnished copper. The music was smooth and sad, inveigling its way into Thomas's brain and stirring a host of memories – times of beauty or loss. And briefly the fragment of sentimental song he had heard earlier, coming from the pub, echoed in his head, as though it had been biding its time in the back of his mind until the trigger of the violin music lured it out again: '. . . *and we'll never meet again, my love . . .'*

He closed his eyes, soaking up the delicious sound, the tune he had last heard beside his grandmother's grave. Yes, oh yes it was the same. He had tried to recall it many times since then, but the tune had entirely eluded him. Now, so long after, he knew it at once. The music floated over the cemetery, taking him away from the winter scene to the day in the village churchyard when petals, not snowflakes, had fallen on the party of mourners. The scene rose up in his mind's eye, even the softness of the spring air, the scent of the blossom, the image of his mother and father walking ahead of him.

'Who is he?' Thomas whispered. 'Why is he playing over the grave?'

Lee shook his head. 'Tell me, Thomas, is this the man you saw before?'

'No. No it isn't. But he's playing the same music.'

Lee nodded heavily. 'I thought so.' Even in the dim moonlight Thomas could see some curious emotion playing over the American's square, masculine face, the dark eyes with strong, arched eyebrows. He peered at him, trying to read his thoughts.

'You know it, don't you?' Thomas said. 'The music? You've heard it before. And Blake knew it too. That's why he attacked the man – it wasn't that he knew the violin player, it was the music.'

Lee glanced at Thomas and for a moment Thomas feared the American would do as Blake had done – set off in pursuit of the violinist, leap on him, attack him. He didn't much fancy the violinist's chances if Lee got hold of him.

''S okay,' Lee said, clasping Thomas's arm in his mittened hand. 'I'm not going after him. We need a more subtle approach, I think. I don't know this guy's name but I think we can safely assume he is another member of the Guild of Funerary Violinists.'

'Hegel,' Thomas said. 'I'm supposed to be seeing Rupert Hegel – to meet the guild. That was what you all agreed at the meeting.' Constantine's death had pushed this to the back of his mind.

The violinist drew one long, final, undulating note from the instrument, tucked the violin under his arm, and bowed sharply over the grave. Then he put the violin back in its case and stalked out of the cemetery, his shoulders hunched against the cold, his thin legs throwing long, absurd shadows on the moonlit snow.

Lee and Thomas crept out from the shelter of the yew. Lee straightened up, brushing snow from the tails of his long winter coat.

'Come on, Thomas,' he said. 'Let's get you warmed up.' Then he was striding down the slope to the cemetery's main entrance leaving, like Wenceslas, a footprint trail to follow.

London's night streets were noisy and hectic after the tranquillity of the graveyard. Even at this late hour, carriages and hansom cabs thronged the streets, turning the snow to a mire of muck and slush. The wheels of one such veered perilously close to the pavement and threw a stream of watery grey slurry over Lee's coat. Lee, in a fury, raised his fist and boomed abuse at the driver. But the carriage was already passing out of earshot. The driver simply raised his whip – whether in apology or contempt it was impossible to tell.

Lee guided Thomas through streets and alleyways, away from the busy main roads. It occurred to Thomas that he was unwise to trust the American, who might, after all, be leading him into some kind of trap. Constantine had told him Lee could be trusted – but what had Constantine known? How far could his former guardian's judgement be trusted? Thomas fell further behind, entangled in thoughts and suspicions. They were close to the Thames now, in a poorer part of the city, walking through a maze of teetering pubs, small shops and boarding houses. Lee realised his companion was falling behind and stopped to wait for him, where the narrow street opened out to give a view of the river.

'You're shivering,' Lee said. 'We'll go inside and get some drinks, sit by the fire. We need to talk, Thomas.' The Thames at night was black as jet, and superficially as still. Several tattered sailing ships were moored to the quay on the far side, and all around them, a jam of smaller craft. Many of these were carriers of coal or timber. Some were elderly houseboats, rotting on the water, though bright light spilled from portholes and windows. Peering down the steep, muddy bank to the water, Thomas could see the fringe of chemical scum from the city factories, sodden rubbish and the slick, shiny hide of a dead rat. The river's breath, a mist rising from the water, carried the perfume of rot and sewage.

'I'm staying in a guesthouse over there.' Lee broke into Thomas's thoughts, with a wave of his hand. 'You're wondering why I'd stay in a place like this, when I could afford something a little more classy?'

Thomas didn't answer but he looked up at Lee and nodded. Lee laughed.

'Come on,' he said. 'There's a little place over there I like to eat at. I guess you could do with something to eat. I'm as hungry as hell.'

Despite the questions crawling in his brain, Thomas couldn't help but warm to Lee. It was his instinct to trust him – the American seemed straightforward and, despite his bluff manner, Thomas suspected he had a keen intelligence. He followed him to a public house on the river front. The front wall of the building leaned over the pathway. The painted sign portrayed a five-pointed star over a faded seascape. Lee had to stoop to pass through the slanting doorway. Inside, the room was hot and busy, full of smoke from the fireplace and the regiment of candles burning on the tables. A stew of smells – stale beer, overcooked food, heated unwashed human bodies, dogs, and the all-pervasive river.

Bent over beneath the low ceiling, Lee picked his way across the room to a battered armchair by the fireside and indicated a seat beside him for Thomas. A girl, about the same age as Thomas, came over and asked them what they wanted to eat. Lee ordered steak pie for the pair of them, beer for himself and tea for Thomas, who was peering round at the other drinkers and diners. They were an odd assortment – mostly people of a poorer sort than the customers who frequented Constantine's chemist's, but respectable-looking for the most part. Three French sailors were sitting at the closest table. Beyond them were an English man and wife tucking into plates of sausages and mash, and then two rather better-dressed young men who had obviously been drinking all night, because their voices dominated the room and they laughed very loudly.

Lee didn't say anything until their plates of pie had been placed in front of them. He loaded his fork with a substantial mound of beef and pastry, shovelled it into his mouth, chewed noisily and washed it down with a swig of beer.

'Aren't you going to eat?' he said, gesturing at Thomas's plate with his fork. 'It's good stuff, Thomas, and you look like you need some feeding up.'

'What do you think's going on?' Thomas said, picking at his own meal. 'Who killed Mr Constantine? Am I in danger, Mr Lee? Will they come after me?'

Lee shrugged his massive shoulders, still chewing.

'I can't lie to you, Thomas. You are a part of this, whether you like it or not. I'm sorry you were drawn in; I know this is really nothing you asked for. Yes. Yes you are in danger – but I shall do my best to protect you, for what it's worth. Constantine asked me to look out for you, and so I shall.'

Thomas put his fork down and swallowed hard. Feelings of grief stole over him again, taking away his strength, as he thought about the death of his friend and protector.

'I miss him,' he said, his eyes filling with unwanted tears. 'I miss him so much.'

Lee didn't speak, but he stretched out his arm and patted Thomas on the shoulder.

'I know you do,' he said. 'Don't be ashamed of how you feel, Thomas. I won't think any the less of you for your tears.'

Thomas picked at his food, struggling to eat. The heat of the room soon thawed his shivering body and the hot, sugary tea warmed him from the inside. When Lee had cleared his plate and polished off Thomas's leftovers, he leaned back in his chair, looked up at the ceiling and sighed deeply.

'So – what happens next?' Lee said. 'Who do we trust? Who is killing our friends, and what are they hoping to gain from it?'

Thomas shook his head. 'You are better placed to answer those questions than I am.'

Lee tipped back his head and laughed, his dark hair spilling over his shoulders. He stretched out his legs so his feet emerged from under the table.

'You're right, Thomas. The trouble is, I don't trust any of the others. Not Hegel, nor the old witch Lawrence nor Louisa Hudson – even though she looks like my dear old grandmother. Come to think of it, why should I count you out of my suspect list, Thomas?' His smile suggested he was teasing, but Lee had a shrewd glint in his eye. 'You've been suspiciously close to all three of my companions at the time of their murders – your grandmother, Nehemiah Blake and now my friend Albert Constantine. Maybe *you* are the connection.'

'I didn't kill them – it's nothing to do with me!' Thomas blurted.

Lee frowned, still staring at the boy, and then continued: 'I reckon you know more than any of us, Thomas, even if you don't realise how much.'

Thomas shook his head. 'I don't even know what the boxes are – what they do or where they come from,' he said. 'Why don't you tell me that, Mr Lee? Why didn't Mr Constantine tell me? Why do you all keep me in the dark? How can I understand why you're killing each other if I don't know that?' He was growing angry now, his voice rising. Lee was fishing, wasn't he? Trying to tease information from him without giving it back in return. Why did he trust this man? How could he be sure it wasn't Lee who had set up the murder of Albert Constantine?

Lee pressed his hands together, lost in thought for a moment or two.

'We'll go to my room,' he said at last. 'When we are alone, I will tell you what you want to know. Then you must go to Hegel as we agreed. We cannot waste any more time, Thomas. I have no idea who is next on the list, but I don't want anyone else to die.'

Two

The house had the name Nineveh chiselled in the stone lintel over the door. It overlooked a neat square with four park benches beneath ornamental trees. Doubtless in summer these provided shade while the sitter admired the carefully tended flower display, or chatted to friends, or watched over playing children. Now, in the thaw, the trees dripped cold, grey water and the park was a bog.

Thomas climbed three steps to the front door of the house. Before he had a chance to knock, the door opened. A smart, grey man in a dark suit – a servant – beckoned Thomas to enter.

'I'm Thomas Reiter. I've come to see Mr Hegel,' he began, as the servant led him along the black-and-white tiled hallway. His voice echoed loudly in the quiet house and the servant raised his fingers to his lips.

'Not so loud, Mr Reiter,' he admonished, ushering him into a drawing room. He closed the door very carefully.

'Herr Hegel is often unwell,' the man said. 'He suffers acutely.'

Thomas frowned. 'I'm sorry, I didn't know he was ill,' he said. 'What is the matter with him?'

'Neurasthenia,' the servant said in a low voice. 'His nerves. Herr Hegel has a very sensitive disposition. He is disturbed by any strong sensory stimulation – whether it is sound, a peculiar odour or some physical sensation. The merest touch – something you and I would not even notice – can cause him enormous pain if he is suffering one of his neurasthenic episodes, and these episodes are frequent.'

Thomas considered. 'Can I not see him? Mr Hegel arranged our meeting. He wanted us to go to the Guild of Funerary Violinists – this morning.'

The servant nodded, looking to the floor. 'Yes indeed. I know how important this meeting is, Mr Reiter. But I want you to understand and make allowances for my master's fragile state of health.'

Thomas cast his mind back to his first meeting with the German, how fastidiously he had picked at the meal and how little he had eaten.

The servant gave a modest smile. 'Come along,' he said. 'Herr Hegel is finishing his breakfast. You can talk to him while he eats and then I will help him dress and prepare.'

The carpet on the stairs was thick, muffling the sound of their footsteps. Curious paintings covered the landing walls – jewelled maidens, centaurs, sphinxes, fawns, in garish colours, in imagined landscapes both beautiful and grotesque. Too stimulating for one of Hegel's delicate constitution, surely? Doors led off to left and right. The servant stopped outside a room at the front of the house and knocked very lightly on the door. Once again he raised his finger to his lips – then he opened the door and indicated to Thomas to step inside.

A huge four-poster bed dominated the room, heaped with blankets and pillows. The air was hot and stifling, a huge fire burning in the hearth. Heavy crimson velvet curtains hung down the walls, presumably to muffle sound and conserve heat, so the room was a little like an exotic Arabian tent – or at least, what Thomas imagined an exotic Arabian tent might be like; all it needed was dancing girls in veils, and heaps of gold, and for Hegel to be dressed in a gown and turban, brandishing a scimitar. No such apparition materialised. Instead Thomas heard a weak cough from the mound of bedclothes and caught a whiff of infused lemon and peppermint, the perfume of the sickbed.

A pale hand flapped from the bedclothes.

'Thomas, come closer.' A feeble voice, the refined German accent. Thomas moved to the bedside, where Hegel lay propped on half a dozen white pillows, with a tray of what remained of his breakfast – two soft-boiled eggs and several thin slices of white bread, the crusts removed. For all of that, Thomas couldn't help thinking Hegel looked remarkably healthy. His face was bright, his eyes alert and shining. His physique – what he could see of it, throat, arms, chest – was that of a man who rode and ran and swam. Thomas wondered, of course, if Hegel was also a murderer. The duelling scars on the man's cheek caught his eye. So he kept his wits about him – observed all, stored up information in his mind. The German's keen blue eyes made a similarly keen assessment of Thomas.

'I am sorry for your loss,' Hegel said. 'Herr Constantine was a shrewd man, and a very kind one. He was a friend to me and understood me very well, I think.'

Thomas didn't reply at once. He noted, inwardly, how strange it was they all claimed to be each other's dear friends. Then he simply stared at Hegel, trying to see beneath the surface of the man, to assess if his sentiments were feigned or genuine. Then he said, with a bow of his head: 'Thank you. I appreciate your sympathy.'

They stared at each other for a moment, Thomas and Hegel, an unspoken conversation passing between them, each of them suspecting the other, each trying to uncover what the other was truly thinking. It was like a duel in its own right – mental fencing. Lunge, feint, riposte.

Thomas seized the initiative. 'You agreed we should call on the Guild of the Funerary Violinists this morning,' he said. 'I hope you are still well enough, Mr Hegel.'

'Yes, yes,' Hegel said with another wave of his hand. 'I am still recuperating from the latest attack. A curse – my nerves. But don't worry, Thomas. I shall not let you down.' Then, addressing the servant: 'Take the boy downstairs and tell the cook to give him something warm to drink – then come back to me right away and help me to shave and dress.'

The servant escorted Thomas from the overheated room, past the pictures of sphinxes and palaces, and down the stairs to the kitchen. The cook, a slender Indian man dressed in white, gave him a cool glass of milk and a slice of fruitcake. Thomas thanked him politely and ate in silence. The cake was very good, lightly spiced, full of nuts and fat sultanas. The cook smiled to see him eat so enthusiastically. Did the sensitive Hegel always dine on soft-boiled eggs, thin soups and invalid gruels? he wondered. The paintings suggested other, more exotic appetites, and – scanning the kitchen shelves, the jars containing a rainbow of herbs and spices – Thomas wondered again at the contradictions Hegel presented.

It took some time for the German to ready himself for their outing. When he'd finished his cake, Thomas allowed himself to think about the events of the night before – the trip to the cemetery with Lee, their talk in the old pub by the Thames and then, in the American's little locked room above the bar, the moment he had drawn out from a locked tin chest beneath his bed – of course – a smooth wooden box.

*

Lee's box was made of the darkest wood – a viscous black, like jet, like the surface of the water in the Thames outside. And like the river, Thomas sensed currents moving beneath the surface of the solid wood. A complex pattern of gold was etched into the top of the box, a miniature maze of intricate paths, coils and shapes. How Thomas had itched to trace this pattern with his finger, to explore and resolve it.

Lee held the box lovingly between his hands.

'Tell me what you know, Thomas,' he said. 'I shall try and fill in the gaps as best I can.'

Thomas looked around the tiny, dingy room. A small bed (Lee's feet would hang off the end, surely), a dingy chair by the fireplace, a jug and bowl for washing. If Lee was as wealthy as the others, why had he chosen such a low place to stay? As he was learning, appearances could not be trusted; so many layers of disguise to uncover.

'Mr Constantine told me about the Guild of Medical Herbalists, about your discovery of the archive. Maud told me more – she called you a band of witches.' This he said with a glance at Lee, but the American gave no visible response. 'She told me there were seven boxes. And I have seen for myself the two . . . gardens. Broceliande, the Garden of Dreams, and Arcadia, the Poison Garden. They are connected, aren't they? The boxes and the gardens that don't exist in the real world.'

Lee nodded heavily. 'Arcadia is a strange place, yes. A necropolis – a city of the dead.'

'So how does it work?' Thomas was impatient now. 'Mr Constantine told me about the thought forms – took one out of me, out of my head. I want to know, Mr Lee – how do these things work? *Are* you a witch?'

Lee raised his hand. 'Steady on,' he said. 'I'll tell you what you want to know, but it is hard to explain and hard to understand. I don't think you have ever opened your box, Thomas? There is a maze on the lid, like this one, right? Your grandmother should have shown you the way to solve the puzzle and no doubt she would have done so, if she had had the time – if death had not surprised her.

'The puzzle on the lid is the lock, you see. If you don't know how to solve it, you won't be able to open the box.'

'What's inside the box?'

'Why, the garden, of course. The garden!' Lee said. 'I think you discovered that for yourself. Have a little more faith in your own judgement.'

'How can a box hold a garden?' But as he asked the question, a scene rose up vividly in his mind, looking out the window of his grandmother's house and seeing the garden's odd perspective – its curve, as though it were contained within a ball of glass – a snow globe like the one Mrs Constantine kept on the mantelpiece in her parlour. He thought for a moment, and Lee simply watched him, prepared to let him work it out from what he already knew.

'That's why Blake came to the house,' he concluded. 'That last night at my grandmother's, to show me. The box was open and I walked in it, and so did Blake and the man who killed him. And the revenant – my grandmother's ghost – that was in the box too.'

Lee nodded. 'You're right,' he said. 'The gardens can be, well, unfolded, for want of a better word. At home, in our safe places, we keep the boxes and therefore the gardens open, so we can use them. There are gates between the gardens too – I suspect Blake wanted to pay his respects, and passed from his garden into hers.'

'How do I open it again?' Thomas demanded. 'I want to see it for myself! Do you know how to solve the puzzle? How do I do it? What's in your box?'

Lee held up his hand. 'Patience, young man.' He sighed, his fingers still unthinkingly playing over the surface of the ebony lid. 'Back home,' he said, 'out in the desert, I have a ranch. A thousand acres of dust and rock and cactus, and my house in the middle of it, miles from anywhere. I bet that doesn't sound like heaven to you, but it is a beautiful place, Thomas. Better than this damp, grey, miserable country. I built the ranch myself, out of red earth, and I called it Acoma, which is the name of a city that's hundreds of years old. Some of the Pueblo Indians reckon it's the oldest continuously inhabited city in America – a settlement built on the top of a huge sandstone mesa, hundreds of feet in the air. My mother was a Pueblo Indian, Thomas. She lived in Acoma. So I created the garden in my box out of the love I have for this place – my true home.'

'If you open the box now, will everyone see it?' Thomas said eagerly. 'Will it cover a slice of London?'

Lee laughed. 'No, Thomas. There are doors and gateways into each garden, which I can leave open, or lock, as I please. Imagine the gardens are pieces of a great circle, and each has a gateway into its two neighbours. We know the doorways into each other's gardens. I don't know how this stranger found his way into your grandmother's garden though.

'And while I have been happy to talk about the gardens unfolding, in another sense they are always contained within the box. When we step into them, we become tiny. Each garden is a world within the ordinary world.'

'So, if we step into the garden, we disappear from the ordinary world? The experience isn't – a dream. How does that work? How do you shrink?'

Lee smiled and shook his head. 'These are difficult questions, Thomas, and ones I cannot offer you a simple answer to. We don't entirely understand it ourselves. Do you shrink when you dream? The dream takes place within the walls of your skull – a bone box. Do you feel smaller in the dream?'

'That's different. You don't disappear when you dream. Your physical body is still there – still the same size.'

'Well, that's true. Still, the comparison holds out, I think. The dreamer believes he is somewhere else. Think about this – how many angels can dance on the head of a pin? If I raise my hand I can blot out the moon, so is the moon smaller than my hand? How big are we anyway? Perhaps the whole world is an apple in the hand of one of those angels dancing on the pin's head.'

Thomas listened to Lee's words but the American's philosophising interested him less than the gold and ebony box in Lee's hands.

'Enough talking, huh? You want to see?' Lee nodded. He took a deep breath, sat up straight and pushed his hair behind his ears. Then, with his forefinger, he began to trace a winding path through the golden maze on the lid of the ebony box. His face was tense with concentration as the tip of his finger proceeded and backtracked and looped through the complex pattern. How did he remember it? Thomas held his breath. The fire seemed to still in the hearth. The voices of the men in the bar beneath the room were far away now, the energy in the room, of the present moment, focused in the movement of the American's hands on the box in his lap.

A loose windowpane rattled. Suddenly the fire blazed up, filling the room with yellow light. The floorboards creaked, as though invisible people were walking in the room. Thomas felt the air stir, a cold draught ruffling his hair, making goosebumps on his skin. The golden maze on the box lid began to glow, beams of hot yellow light shooting up between Lee's hands, spelling out the word Acoma, the name of the ancient Indian city. Thomas felt the chair shift beneath him and, with a loud crack, the china jug on the table split in two, spilling a great gush of water over the floor. Light shone from the box and illuminated Lee's face. He drew his hand away, with a smile, as the lid rose up and swung open.

Thomas breathed the perfume of dust and dry air.

'Come see,' Lee said, rising to his feet. They looked through the window. The London scene had disappeared – instead, stars glittered over a plain of sand and rocks. A huge, low moon – silver pocked with grey – painted long shadows behind each stone, cactus, clump of dry, night-blue grass. Thomas grinned. The prospect delighted him. And it was as he had remembered – the slight horizon curve, a sense the view was out of kilter in a way he could not precisely define . . . as though he could reach out and hold it in his hand. A scene in a snow globe, yes, that was it.

The expanse of desert was bounded, like his grandmother's garden, by a high wall. Strange dark shapes rose out of the ground far away, which resolved themselves under his attention to be ruined temples, broken villages, platforms and stairways and pyramids of stone.

'Shall we go?' Lee said. 'This way, Thomas.' He opened the window, lifted a leg over the sill, swung round and dropped to the ground. He moved with surprising grace for such a big man.

'Jump down,' he called up. 'You'll be fine. It's not as far as it looks.'

Thomas climbed out of the window, crouched on the windowsill, closed his eyes and cast himself down. Lee was right – the distance wasn't as great as it should have been and in any case Lee half caught him as he hit the ground. When he turned back, the window was a tall wrought iron gate in the wall that extended around the desert garden.

'Let me show you the place,' Lee said. The moon hung like a slow-burning lantern over the garden, impossibly low, as though they could reach out and touch it. Thomas looked up at a huge red rock, the size of a castle, carved with peaks and runnels by the wind and sand. High up, near the turreted peak, the clustered forms of small, flat-roofed buildings huddled together.

'The Indian city.' Thomas wrinkled his brow. 'How does that work?' he said, his voice a little short. 'This isn't a real place – so there aren't really Indians living there? Where do these witch boxes come from? How do they work? How did you create this place?'

Lee laughed. 'Ah, so much to learn, Thomas. I created it from my memories, my desires, from my imagination. It is hard to explain, but when you master your grandmother's box I can show you. You will change it to suit yourself. Then it will truly become yours.'

They seemed to walk for miles. The castle of rock fell behind them and they reached the first of the old stone temples, the dry bones of ancient buildings, the hide stripped away by time. Lee sat on a step and rested his elbows on his knees. Thomas took his place beside him.

'Mr Lee, if my grandmother's garden was the Garden of Dreams, and Mrs Lawrence's is the Poison Garden, what is yours? What sort of garden is Acoma?'

'It is the Garden of Journeys, Thomas.'

'What does that mean?'

'It means that the plants I cultivate and create here in the desert, these strange cacti, these stringy little shrubs, and the many roots you cannot see which lie waiting under the ground for the spring rain to make them flower, possess powers related to journeys. And I don't mean your regular kind of journey – but

140

voyages up here.' Lee tapped the side of his head. Then he bent down and picked up a tiny cactus shaped like a sheep's hoof.

'This one, if it is dried and eaten, would take you on a journey back through your own memories and further, into the memories of your parents and grandparents, back through generations. Well, so the old documents tell me. I haven't got it quite right yet, but I'm working on it.'

Thomas remembered sticking a finger in some of his grandmother's jam and licking it, with her warning him it would give him bad dreams. Now he realised the fruit must have come from her Garden of Dreams, that perhaps he hadn't eaten enough because he had suffered no effects he could recall.

'You know Rupert Hegel plays the violin,' Lee said. 'Well, he wrote that piece of music you heard in the graveyard where Constantine was buried. And you tell me that was the same tune the funeral violinist played over your grandmother's grave, right?'

Thomas nodded quickly and said: 'He wrote it? Does that mean Hegel is the one? You think it's him?'

Lee raised his hand. 'Steady on. Not necessarily, but it surely looks a little incriminating. I just want to tell you, Thomas, when you go to see him, when he takes you to the Guild of Funerary Violinists, you must keep your wits about you. You be careful, okay?'

Thomas bit his lower lip. 'How do you know he wrote it?'

'We spent a lot of time together on an expedition many years ago. Hegel played the violin a good deal. I remember that piece very well. He was very proud of it, and it is beautiful.'

'But to play it over the graves – that must mean something. Does it have some particular significance?'

Lee's face crumpled into a frown. He looked away from Thomas, as though something had just occurred to him. When he turned back there was, for the first time, an unexpected evasiveness about him.

'Not that I can think of,' he said, rising to his feet. 'We have to get back now. And in the morning, you go to Hegel's house.'

'Are you ready to go?' Hegel stood in the kitchen doorway, immaculately turned out in a grey suit and white cravat, a black coat collared with fur over his arm. His face was smooth from shaving and Cologne scented his skin. When they reached the front door, the servant helped Hegel put his coat on, handed him a red silk scarf, a pair of black leather gloves and a fur hat.

They tramped through the melting snow to the road, where Hegel hailed a hansom cab and told the driver to take them to Cavendish Square. The wind was achingly cold, and even inside the cab Thomas shivered. The wheels hissed through the slush. Thomas told Hegel about his late-night trip to the cemetery – and described the violinist playing over Constantine's grave. He didn't tell him Lee had recognised the piece of music, that he knew Hegel himself had composed it.

Hegel held the silver head of a walking stick in both hands as he peered into Thomas's face.

'You understand what we are doing?' Hegel said.

'Going to the Guild of Funerary Violinists,' Thomas answered, boldly returning the German's stare.

'Yes. And there we hope to find the name of the man or woman who commissioned the violinists to play over the graves of your grandmother – and Albert Constantine.'

'You said – at the meeting – you had some connection with the guild.'

'I am a violinist, Thomas, and these men are most talented. They have an archive of ancient music, some of which I have studied.'

Thomas continued to stare at Hegel, trying to work out if he knew it was his music the funeral violinist had played. If he had made the commission, then obviously he would know. If he hadn't – well, he would have no idea.

The journey took about twenty minutes. They drew up outside a tall, three-storey town house. Hegel paid the driver and walked up to the front door, kicking through the grey snow with his long, leather boots. Thomas scurried after him, suddenly very nervous. His heart seemed to plummet inside his chest.

It was a perfectly ordinary town house, except that the brass plaque by the door carried the name of the guild and a picture of a death's head. The plaque was tarnished however, the paint on the window frames peeling. As he looked more closely Thomas observed the whole building had a faint air of neglect. Hegel raised his walking stick and rapped it smartly on the door.

They waited several minutes. Thomas wrapped his arms around himself in a bid to keep warm. Hegel's breath puffed in a warm cloud in front of his face. Then, at last, the door swung open and a short, stout man with mutton-chop whiskers stood in the doorway. Thomas's mouth dropped open. He knew this man. His thoughts seemed to clamber over each other in sudden disarray. He was about to utter some shocked exclamation, except that Hegel, perhaps sensing some indiscretion, clapped his hand on the boy's shoulder and drew him to his side.

Thomas gathered his wits and closed his mouth. He was cross with himself now for so nearly giving himself away. The man at the doorway scowled at them both, looked them up and down, and scratched his greasy forehead.

'Hegel, isn't it? This your son?' His voice was gruff.

'I am Rupert Hegel, yes. No, this isn't my son.' The German's lip curled slightly, though whether it was the possibility of Thomas being his son or the guild man's rude manner that was so distasteful to him Thomas couldn't decide.

'You'd better come in, then,' the man said, turning his back on them and tramping up the corridor, expecting them to follow. Thomas glanced up at Hegel and they stepped into the cold house.

Thomas knew the man, oh yes. He was a little greyer and distinctly more stout than he had been four years ago at his grandmother's grave, when Blake had jumped on him and pinned him to the ground. The seams on his black suit were strained, the fabric worn smooth on the collar and elbows. He looked as though he hadn't shaved in several days and smelled distinctly unclean. Perhaps that was the source of Hegel's distaste.

Inside, the signs of dilapidation were more evident. The walls in the hallway were grey, punctuated by cleaner white squares where pictures had once hung. The tiles on the floor were cracked and soiled. The whole place smelled of dust and damp and over-boiled cabbage. Evidently funeral violin playing was not paying well. The guild had seen better days.

'In here,' the man said, dabbing his nose on his jacket sleeve. He pushed open a door and led them into a large drawing room, where two men sat at a round table playing cards. One Thomas recognised from the night with Lee in the graveyard, the long, skinny man who played over Constantine's grave. The other was an elderly man with lank, grey locks, also dressed in funereal black, with a seamed, grimy face. He cast one quick glance at the visitors and then focused again on the fan of cards in his hand. He wore a pair of fingerless gloves and indeed it was cold in the room, despite the efforts of a lacklustre fire in a grate full of ash. Whenever the wind blew, smoke from the damp wood puffed into the room so the atmosphere was gritty and thick. Rupert drew a handkerchief from his pocket and waved it in front of his face.

'It's Hegel,' said the man who had opened the door. 'Wants to talk to you.' The old man with the mittens looked up again, with a scowl, as though irritated to have the game interrupted.

Tatty oddments of furniture filled the room – mismatched and dingy, perhaps picked up randomly from junk shops. Again, pale squares on the wallpaper indicated missing pictures. In one corner, damage caused by a long-ago fire hadn't been repaired. Floorboards were burned away, revealing a hole down to the basement through which a chilly draught blew. Above the hole, the walls were charred and blackened.

Hegel tutted, impatient for attention. The old man sighed deeply, cast his useless hand of cards face up on the table. Even the creased, discoloured cards had seen better days. The old man rose to his feet.

'Simon Goldsworthy? Vice-president of the Guild of Funerary Violinists?' Hegel demanded, banging his stick on the floor.

The old man looked at him sideways, with the hint of a smirk. He took a clay pipe from his pocket and began to stuff it with tobacco from a pouch in another pocket.

'Mr Hegel,' he said slowly. 'I'm sorry we aren't better set up to receive you. We don't have many visitors these days.'

'No matter. I won't be long. My question is simple.' Hegel lifted his stick and indicated the half-dozen violins hanging from pegs on the back wall. The instruments were clean and glossy, free of the patina of dust and soot covering everything else in the room. The scrolls at the end of each neck were carved with the guild's traditional death's head.

'Who commissioned you to play at the funeral of Augusta Williams, some four years ago, and again, at the funeral of Albert Constantine just yesterday?'

145

The skinny man, who was drawing the pack of cards together, looked a little shifty. Presumably he hadn't realised he'd had an audience in the cemetery. Thomas stared at him – his anger at Constantine's murder rising up like a storm inside of him, thickening in his throat. He clenched and unclenched his fists and pressed his teeth together. Hegel, perhaps sensing the change in Thomas, lightly placed his gloved hand on the boy's shoulder.

Goldsworthy smiled. 'Is that it? Well, I'm sorry you've had a wasted trip, Mr Hegel. Our patrons are guaranteed privacy. It is a sacred trust. There is no way I could possibly tell you any such names.' He stuck the pipe in his mouth, gripped it between brown-stained teeth and then lit it using a taper from the fire. The smells of soot and dust were quickly overlaid with the perfume of cherry tobacco. Hegel wrinkled his nose and sighed. He drew out a wallet from his coat pocket.

'Very well, Mr Goldsworthy. How much do you want?'

Goldsworthy grinned, still puffing on his pipe. 'You dishonour me, sir. Do you think I'm open to bribes? This is a proud guild with a long and distinguished tradition.'

Hegel glanced around the room in a way that suggested the state of the place did not inspire his faith. He drew out a five-pound note. Both the skinny man and the violinist with the mutton chop whiskers looked up from their cards and stared at the large paper note.

Goldsworthy continued to grin and puff but his eyes were fixed on the money.

'If you can't reveal the name of your patrons, could you tell what music it was you played over the graves?' Thomas blurted.

Hegel shot Thomas a look of annoyance because Goldsworthy snatched the money from Hegel's hand and stuffed it inside his waistcoat pocket.

'I see no reason why not!' His voice was bright. He looked very pleased with himself. 'Gentlemen? Who will do the honours?' This to the card-players. For a moment or two neither of them stirred. Then, with a sigh, the man with the whiskers rose to his feet and took down a violin from the wall. He held it under his chin, plucked at the strings to check the tuning and picked up a bow from the table.

Thomas stared at Hegel, eager to gauge his reaction as the violinist lifted the bow, placed it against the strings and slowly began to play . . .

Three

As the delicious, brooding, melancholy notes floated from the violin, Hegel's pale, scarred face seemed to tighten. He pressed his lips together and his hand squeezed the head of his walking stick. He looked . . . stunned. There was no doubt about it. When Hegel flapped his handkerchief again, Thomas saw his hand was shaking. The German was trying so hard to contain himself, but his emotions were getting the better of him.

The music continued – its beautiful, sorrowful grace seeming to melt away the gloomy surroundings. Sitting at the table, the skinny man closed his eyes and sighed with pleasure.

Then the tune was over and the spell broken. The whiskered man stopped playing, stuck the instrument back on its peg, threw down the bow on the table and returned to the playing cards.

Hegel struggled to restrain himself, his body tense with fury, his nostrils flared. Then the walking stick dropped from his hand and he launched himself at Goldsworthy, grabbing him by the grimy collar and half knocking him from his feet. He thrust him against the wall, with some angry exclamation in German. The two other men jumped up, ready to step to their boss's defence.

Hegel spoke in German again, a fine sweat breaking out on his face. He raised his clenched fist towards Goldsworthy's face, struggling to restrain himself, and the other men stepped closer.

'Let him alone!' shouted the skinny man. 'Let him go, Hegel.'

The moment stretched – Goldsworthy gasping against the wall, Hegel trying to overcome his urge to hit him. Slowly, slowly, Hegel lowered his fist and loosened his grip. Goldsworthy began to breathe more easily, though Hegel still held him.

Hegel said: 'Who gave you that music?'

Goldsworthy wriggled. 'Let me go. We'll talk more. Be reasonable!'

Hegel glanced round at the other two men, who were closing in on him now, evidently planning to pull him away from Goldsworthy. He gave his head a terse shake, tutted and, with a visible effort of will, let the violinist go. He stepped back, as Goldsworthy scowled and brushed himself down.

Thomas was intrigued. Hegel looked genuinely stunned by the revelation that his own music had been played over his fellow guild members' graves. He had momentarily lost self-control – his fury had taken over. Did this mean Hegel could be trusted? That he *hadn't* organised the killings? It was possible, of course, that someone other than the murderer had arranged the musical tribute for the passed-on.

Hegel took a deep breath and regained his self-possession.

'Where did you get the music?' he asked again. 'It is very important I know.'

Goldsworthy shrugged and turned to a large wooden cabinet next to the door. He tried to look nonchalant but he kept half an eye on Hegel all the same, wary of another attack. The cabinet contained a haphazard pile of sheet music, printed and handwritten, some in folders, some gathered together and tied with ribbon, some stray pieces floating about loose, variously crumpled, folded, scrunched up. Without any thought, Goldsworthy simply pulled the pile off the shelf and out of the cabinet so it fell on the floor with a soft thump and the various piles, sheets and books spilled out in a papery puddle.

'It's here somewhere,' Goldsworthy said, pushing at the mound with his toe. 'Why don't you help me look?'

A tremor from Hegel – so clearly disturbed by the dirty, damaged room, by the violinists' casual manner, and the disrespectful way Goldsworthy had pushed the precious collection of music on the floor. Stepping carefully, Hegel crossed the room and crouched down to peer at the sprawl of paper.

Thomas looked to the stout violin player. Did he remember Thomas from their encounter in the churchyard four years ago? Probably not. The funeral violinist had had other things on his mind then – principally how to defend himself from Nehemiah Blake. While Hegel was looking through the music, Thomas gestured to the burnt floorboards, and said to the violinist: 'What happened to you? To this place?'

The man shrugged. 'A long time ago,' he said, picking up the eternal pack of cards. 'Twenty years now. The guild has all but died away. So few people calling for funerary violinists any more. We've sold nearly everything. Which is why this commission was so important to us.' He shot a glance at Goldsworthy and Hegel, turning over pages on the floor. 'Our client paid us very well. Should have known it would be trouble.'

'This is what you want,' Goldsworthy said. He jumped to his feet and flourished a piece of yellowed manuscript paper. He waved it above his head. Hegel tried to take it from him but Goldsworthy held on to it for a moment, relishing the German's impatience and his own moment of power.

'Let me see it,' Hegel demanded. 'Give it to me.'

Goldsworthy made a show of checking it over – then passed it to Hegel. Thomas stepped up beside him to see for himself. The paper was badly damaged, with grimy seams where it had been folded and refolded. Two of the corners had been torn off and the page possessed a curious, exotic scent – detectable even above the overwhelming odour of damp, soot and cherry tobacco in the room. Something piquant and spicy – a little like the herbs his grandmother had grown in her garden, where he played as a boy. The music was handwritten in a light, precise style. Hegel scanned the paper. His nostrils flared again.

'It's a lovely little piece,' Goldsworthy said. 'Not your traditional funeral music of course – no, it's far too light to be part of a funerary suite. The work of an amateur I would guess. An accomplished amateur, but an amateur all the same. I imagine it must have had some particular significance for the late Mr Constantine, God bless his soul. Perhaps from some long-lost sweetheart?'

Hegel bridled at this assessment of his work. Presumably he considered himself – wealthy, over-educated, refined and well-dressed – to be the superior of this scruffy, impoverished funeral violin player.

'A long-lost sweetheart?' He almost spat the words. 'You are not thinking. And was this sweetheart also Augusta Williams' sweetheart?'

Goldsworthy smiled. 'You know the provenance of the music, sir?'

'I am familiar with it, yes,' Hegel said.

'How?' Thomas piped up, though he knew the answer. There was something about Hegel that provoked in Thomas an urge to be cheeky, to wind him up. Would Hegel admit he had written it himself? Probably not, since Goldsworthy had accurately

151

dismissed it as the work of an amateur. Hegel would consider himself not an amateur but an artist.

Hegel shook his head. 'I know it, yes. I know the man who wrote it. What I cannot understand is how you possess it. Who gave it to you? Who paid you to play over these graves?' His voice was rising again, with its implication of threat. Goldsworthy scowled. The men sitting at the table were slipping cards onto the table but Thomas sensed they were alert and paying attention.

'Please,' Thomas said. 'It is very serious, Mr Goldsworthy sir. This isn't just about sweethearts. Augusta Williams was my grandmother, and she was murdered.'

'Thomas!' Hegel interrupted. 'Be quiet! You don't know what you're saying!' He looked furious but, undeterred, Thomas ignored him.

'You know yourself how dangerous guild rivalries can be,' he persisted, 'and I am afraid the Guild of Medical Herbalists itself is under threat. We need your help. Was there not once, long ago, a friendship between your guild and ours?'

Goldsworthy furrowed his brow. 'The Medical Herbalists, you say? There is mention of it in our own histories. I didn't know it still existed. That is who you are? Why didn't you say?'

Thomas's heart beat so furiously in his chest he felt the other people in the room would surely be able to hear it – and thus to deduce he had lied. A friendship between the guilds? This he had entirely made up, in the moment. Perhaps not so much a lie as an invention. A dubious distinction, of course, and Hegel would know he was bluffing. The German was standing stock-still, apparently stunned by Thomas's new approach.

Goldsworthy looked them over again, as though seeing them for the first time. 'The Medical Herbalists, eh?' He sucked his lower lip, ruminating on this new information. 'There were many guilds once. Ah but we are fading now, all of us.' Then he said: 'Sit down, Mr Hegel. And you, Thomas.' He drew two chairs forward and took another seat for himself.

'This puts another slant on the matter,' he mused, clasping his hands together. 'There are loyalties to our clients, yes, but also ancient loyalties among guilds. Rivalries, yes – sometimes murderous rivalries. But comradeship too. But guild brothers – should we not help each other from time to time?'

Hegel quivered. Perhaps he was reluctant to own brotherhood with the down-at-heel violinists in their decaying, smoky home. So Thomas stepped in. He was thinking fast.

'Yes!' he said. 'Yes, we should. The Medical Herbalists are small in number, but wealthy still. One of our members is Mrs Lawrence. You may have heard of her? There may be opportunities for us to help you.'

At this prospect, a distinct spark lit up in the eyes of all three violinists. The game was momentarily forgotten. They looked one to another.

'Mrs Lawrence? Charlie Lawrence's widow?' he said. It seemed the funerary violinists were well aware of this London *grande dame*'s reputation.

Thomas nodded. 'She would be very grateful. She would owe you a favour.'

Goldsworthy leaned forward confidentially.

'You will understand, Master Thomas, that commissions are not always straightforward and so much is the case this time,' he said. 'I cannot tell you the name of the client for the simple reason I do not know who he – or she – might be. The instructions and payment were entirely anonymous.'

Hegel made some indignant sound, but Thomas ignored him. He gestured for Goldsworthy to continue. 'So tell me –

how did the commission come to you? The instructions, the money?'

Goldsworthy glanced at the skinny violinist, who nodded and pulled open a drawer under the table. He took out a handful of papers, rummaged among them and picked out three envelopes. These he handed to Goldsworthy, who took out the letters and unfolded them on his knee.

'This was the first,' he said, handing one to Thomas. 'You see, it is dated some five years ago now. My first thought – it was a nasty joke. Or worse, the work of a madman.'

Thomas looked at the letter. Black ink, confident, sloping handwriting. Was the author a young man, perhaps? The style suggested masculinity, and an impetuous nature. He began to read:

'To the honourable Guild of Funerary Violinists –

My client extends his greetings to this notable guild, now sadly occluded. He wishes you to enjoy his patronage for an indefinite period. During this time, you will be called upon to play a specified piece of music at the graves of our dear-departed. The names of these honoured persons will be revealed to you one at a time at the appropriate moment – for whosoever knows the time of their departure?

You will not play at the funeral, but after it, when the mourners have departed. You may not hear from us for many months – perhaps for years. But you will remain at our service as long we continue to pay into an account the sum of £50 a year and when you receive word, we expect you to fulfil your obligation.

This commission is a private one and my client a powerful individual so do not betray our confidence.'

No name at the bottom – only the address of a bank in Mason Street.

'So you had to be sure this wasn't a trick,' Thomas said. He passed the letter to Hegel. 'You went to the bank.'

'Yes. I told them my name and I found out the sum of £50 had been deposited for the guild. You see how straitened our circumstances are – this money was a lifeline and we took it. We heard nothing until the following spring when another similar letter arrived with the name of your grandmother, the date of her funeral, directions and the piece of music Mr Hegel has already examined. Despite the mystery surrounding our benefactor it seemed honest enough.

'It wasn't until my colleague was so fiercely assaulted that we understood the contract might be more than it first appeared.'

'And the second commission?' Thomas said.

Goldsworthy picked up the last letter. 'Albert Constantine. I knew him by reputation. And now I see he was a member of your guild – a herbalist turned chemist. Of course! It all falls into place now.

'We were cautious this time – went after dark.'

The skinny violinist piped up. 'But I was watched, I tell you. I could feel them – eyes on me. An audience for my playing – and not just the cold ones in the ground. I think we should abandon the contract, money or not.'

Thomas said to Hegel: 'Do you recognise the writing? Does this help us at all?'

Hegel folded the letter. 'What will you do, when the next instruction arrives? It may be my funeral. It may be my grave you dance on.'

Goldsworthy stared at him. 'We'll wait and see, Mr Hegel. We'll wait and see.'

Thomas followed Hegel through the cold, slushy streets. Hegel walked briskly, lost in thought, seemingly forgetting the boy beside him. His mind was focused inwards, away from the noisy traders and endless horse-drawn traffic, to the knot of the problem – the guild's mysterious patron. Whenever Thomas volunteered a thought or raised a question, Hegel raised his hand in annoyed dismissal. He didn't want to talk.

'I am thinking!' he exclaimed. 'Leave me in peace.'

So Thomas mulled over the situation on his own account as the spray of filthy, melted snow from the road gradually soaked his boots. It was bitterly cold, miserably damp. The low grey sky threatened rain to come.

They returned to the overheated embrace of Hegel's house. Hegel looked very pale. The scars were a livid scarlet against the almond-white of his face. The servant took his master's coat, pulled off his boots and escorted them to the drawing room where a fire burned in a marble hearth. Above the mantelpiece, a nearly naked maiden, as white as milk, danced before a shadowed throne. Thomas, still shivering, peered at the picture while Hegel dropped his long, bony feet into a basin of hot water. The servant disappeared and returned again with cups of hot chocolate. As Thomas raised the cup to his lips he realised his teeth were chattering. The drink burned his lips.

The servant moved a chair closer to the fire and indicated he should sit down. Gradually they warmed up, Hegel and Thomas. Hegel was still lost in thought. The flames reflected on his glasses as he stared into the fire. Thomas began to doze, lulled by heat and weariness. Later the servant bustled in again and set up lunch for two on a small table in the corner of the room. They dined on a thin, flavourless chicken soup, and then a dish of lamb in spicy sauce, roast potatoes and beans. Still Hegel wouldn't speak. In the end Thomas gave up trying to engage him in conversation. Instead he focused on his meal, enjoyed the excellent stodgy treacle pudding that followed, and then curled up in his warm chair by the fire. Outside, daylight began to fade. The servant cleared the table and drew the long curtains. Firelight danced on the white body of the maiden in the painting.

'May I go home?' Thomas said at last. 'Mrs Constantine will be expecting me. I have work to do at the chemist's shop.'

A flicker of irritation crossed Hegel's face. He shook his head.

'She will manage without you,' he said. '*Gott im Himmel!* You are not a floor-sweeping shop boy any more, Thomas. You will soon be a member of the guild.'

Thomas scowled. 'It is not the floor-sweeping I'm worrying about,' he jumped in. 'I don't want Mrs Constantine to be concerned about me.'

Hegel shook his head. 'A note will be sent. You must stay here tonight, Thomas Reiter.'

'Why? What are we going to do?'

'We have to meet. I shall send a message now, to the other members.'

Hegel left the room. He was a while, leaving Thomas to his own devices. There was little in the drawing room to entertain him so he gazed at the fire and turned over, yet again, the events of the past few days: Constantine's death, his visit to the cemetery with Lee, and the encounter with the funeral violinists. He had been very suspicious of Hegel – but the German's shock when he discovered he was the author of the music played over the graves seemed genuine enough. Who did that leave? Mrs Lawrence,

Louisa Hudson and Mr Lee. He thought about them all, his impressions of them, the things they had said and done. Miss Hudson he knew the least – indeed he had hardly exchanged a word with her. He felt he could trust Lee – but was he right in this? There was no way of knowing. He pushed the possibilities around his mind like chess pieces on a board. Best trust no-one.

Then he thought about the wooden box, stowed in the chest beneath his bed. A magic puzzle box. A box of tricks. Did it truly contain his grandmother's garden? The evidence of his own senses told him this was the case – hadn't he seen for himself how the boxes worked? Mrs Lawrence's necropolis where he had played tea parties with Maud; the desert garden Lee had revealed the night before; the orchards, herb beds and bluebell wood of his grandmother's box . . . Did the revenant haunt it still?

Hegel woke him. Thomas had fallen asleep again, in the chair, dreams swallowing his procession of thoughts.

'It's time to go,' Hegel said quietly.

Thomas assumed Hegel had organised a meeting somewhere in London – perhaps Miss Hudson had already travelled up from her country house? The German, however, headed upstairs and opened a door off the landing, beckoning Thomas to follow him into a well-furnished library. An ochre globe stood on a large leather-topped desk. Books lined the walls on ranks of glass-fronted shelves. A host of botanical drawings were pinned to a board above the fireplace. Swiftly Thomas scanned these details – before his eyes locked on a pale wooden box, standing on a low table in the middle of the room.

A sound, like a sigh, passed through the room. The box didn't move – but Thomas could sense movement within it. It was as though with each passing day, with every new visit to the secret gardens, he became more attuned to the boxes – to the power they

158

contained. He thought of his own box, miles away across the city, and yearned to take it in his hands, to run his fingers over the patterns inlaid in the top. He wanted to open it and climb inside the folded acres of his grandmother's garden, to that magical, intoxicating place now so vivid in his memory.

He stepped closer to the low table, conscious of Hegel's eyes upon him. Then he knelt on the rug and stretched out his hand so his fingers very gently skimmed the lid of the box, barely touching it at all. Still the box reacted. A hum, more felt than heard, emanated from the honey-coloured wood. A word glowed among the coils carved into the surface. It was the name Hegel had carved over the door of his house.

Thomas looked back over his shoulder. 'Who made the boxes?' he said.

'We each had them made for us, following one pattern,' Hegel said. 'That is why they are all different – though essentially they are the same.'

'Your garden is called Nineveh? What is its other name?'

'The Perfume Garden.' Hegel gave a half-smile. 'Nineveh was an ancient Assyrian city,' he said. 'It was built two thousand years before Christ was born. It was the city dedicated to the worship of Ishtar – goddess of love and war.' He shrugged. 'It was my fancy, merely, to name my secret kingdom so.'

Thomas touched the box again, and watched the letters glow, spelling out the name of the ancient city.

'The Perfume Garden,' Thomas mused. 'So you cultivate herbs and fruits to make perfumes?'

Hegel laughed. 'Yes. And many of my perfumes have very special qualities. Some make people stop loving each other, others drive you mad with longing, or make you hate with a passion.'

'Are any of your perfumes poisonous?'

Hegel assented. 'Yes. Yes indeed.'

'Such plants could make you very powerful.'

Hegel inclined his head. 'My work in this field is in its infancy, but one day, yes, you are right.'

'Where are we meeting the others? Are they coming here?'

Hegel shook his head. 'No, Thomas. We shall meet another way on this occasion. We shall travel through Nineveh and meet at the confluence of these seven secret places.'

'Lee told me something about doors,' Thomas interrupted. 'He said you could choose to leave doorways open so friends could come and go, those that knew the way.'

Hegel pursed his lips. 'Listen to me, Thomas. There are those doors, yes. But there is another, more secret, door that only the owner of the land will know. It is this we must pass through to reach the place where the lands meet – where they are one. Although Miss Hudson is a hundred miles away, she will be able to meet with us. Mrs Lawrence will not have to step into the cold night.'

Thomas pondered. 'Is that how Lee travelled to Miss Hudson's house for the dinner, from America? Did he pass through his garden – his land – and then through this secret way into her garden, and into the house?'

'Yes, yes. That is how he did it. How long would it take him otherwise, on a ship across the Atlantic sea? Many weeks, certainly.'

'But that means he carried his box with him – as he walked through the garden. How can that happen? I know it is true because I carried my box through my garden.'

Hegel laughed. 'Ah, you are a philosopher, Thomas. You can carry a box through the garden, because then it is just a box. It is the contents that make up the garden.'

Thomas stepped back. 'Shall you open the lid now? Shall we go?' he said. Excitement was rising. He was eager to gaze at the wonders of Nineveh – for surely eccentric Hegel, with his strange nervous ailments and mysterious, ornamented paintings, would create a land worth seeing?

Hegel stepped forward and took the box in his hands. He pressed his palm onto the lid, closed his eyes and drew a deep breath. The solid wood appeared to ripple and – as he took his hand away – the lid opened in a smooth arc. A dark golden light poured from the box, congealing into vegetable tendrils that curled over Hegel's hand and down to the ground, snaking across the floor, over the walls of books. The light flared once, so bright the room was entirely extinguished for a moment – and then went out. The room was as before, and the box inert, though the lid was open still.

'Which way do we go?' Thomas asked.

'Ah, through the door of course.' Hegel gestured with his hand. For the first time, Thomas noticed Hegel had changed his clothes. Instead of a suit he was wearing a long soft silk jacket, without buttons. Underneath it his chest was bare. Around his throat, a necklace of hammered golden plates; a dark blue cloth was tied around his waist. Thomas could sense Hegel's excitement, the physical quiver of anticipation as he drew the study door open.

'Come, Thomas,' he said. 'Follow me.'

They stepped into the warm, perfumed air of an Assyrian night. Unfamiliar coils of stars burned in the clear sky – close and brilliant, like jewels that could be plucked at an arm's length. They were standing in a walled garden, full of shadows and the sound of falling water from a fountain Thomas could not yet see. Hegel pulled the door closed behind them, and it merged into a wall overhung with climbing briars upon which monstrous roses

161

blossomed – dark red in the moonlight, breathing a thick, syrupy perfume. Fallen petals lay on the stone-paved ground like drops of blood.

Thomas stepped forward. It wasn't so dark, now his eyes had adjusted. A huge crystalline moon hung in the sky, casting a hard white light, striping the garden with shadows. From far away, he heard the blast of an archaic horn, a long, melancholy note. More petals dropped from the roses, as though disturbed by the sound.

'Do you like it?' Hegel spread his arms, proudly, to encompass the garden.

'Yes,' Thomas said. 'Yes, I do.'

He was accustomed, now, to the disorientating geography of these places – the sense of huge distance and close containment at one and the same time. The walls reeled away to a dim horizon, with a peculiar curving perspective. Symmetrical paths outlined a mosaic of garden plots. In the centre stood the fountain where a white statue of a woman held aloft a lotus flower, from which water ceaselessly tumbled, silver in the moonlight. Slowly they walked through the garden. Each bed of earth was well tended and carried a harvest of herbs and flowers like no others Thomas had seen before. Blue-green spikes, feathery herbs, red and yellow flowers shaped like wine glasses, twisted fruits, frail dry pods from which seeds drifted like smoke. And a palette of odours as they passed one bed and another: smoke, honey, spice, rotten flesh, burning wood, here and there intermingling into a brew that seemed to penetrate his brain and set his thoughts alight.

He looked again – with new eyes – at the forest of herbs, fruits and flowers in Hegel's garden. What powers did each possess? What preparation, what dose? Ah, how much Constantine could have taught him. He felt the sharp stab of grief, to have lost him, to have appreciated so little the true extent of his knowledge.

'Tell me something about these plants,' Thomas asked. 'What do they do?'

Hegel smiled. Abruptly he changed direction, taking a side path to the left and heading with purpose to a garden plot in the shadow of the wall. There he crouched and plucked a skinny and anaemic-looking stalk, adorned with half a dozen white-blotched leaves. From the bottom of the broken stalk a thick, creamy liquid oozed.

'What is it?' Thomas asked.

Hegel frowned. He wiped the drop of liquid with the tip of his finger. 'You are acquainted with this one. It isn't an impressive looking plant, but looks are often deceptive. If you pulverise a handful of stalks, extract this substance . . .' he rubbed it between his fingers '. . . stew and reduce it, swallow the correct dose – why, then it gives you the power to create thought forms.'

'Thought forms!' Thomas said. 'I've seen them! I had one inside my head. Mr Constantine took it out.' The recollection made him shudder and he stepped back, fear making him angry.

'Maud said you were all witches!' he said. 'She was right. Thought forms – making magic. Let me out of here, Hegel. I don't want to go any further. Take me home.'

Unperturbed, Hegel looked over his shoulder.

'Magic? No, I wouldn't call it magic. It is science, Thomas. The science of plants. Magic is the word we apply when we don't understand how something works. So many of these plants enhance and amplify the abilities of the mind and body you see. Just as bread and meat nourish the strength of the body, these special foods nourish the mysterious brain.'

He gave a swift, manic smile and licked the juice from his fingers.

'Come now,' he said. 'You are not going home and we must not be late.' He turned on his heel and strode through the garden. Thomas hesitated. Should he run away? Try and find his way out? Worry vied with the desire to find out what was happening, to know more. He looked back the way they had come, and then at Hegel walking away from him, deeper into the garden. He looked again – and then followed Hegel.

'What's it called?' he demanded. 'The plant, for thought forms, what is it called?'

'Its common name is nightbane,' Hegel said, with a flourish of his arm. 'Don't forget it, Thomas! You have a lot to learn.'

The garden didn't end where it should have, of course. The far wall, not so far away when viewed from the first door, seemed to recede as they began to drop down a hitherto unseen hill. The vista of the garden expanded. Further down, the gardens merged into a cityscape of reddish flat-roofed houses, columned temples, open market places, a warren of lanes and alleyways. Lights glowed in the windows of the houses. Torches burned in the streets. Flowers and herbs tumbled from terracotta pots.

'Is that Ishtar?' Thomas pointed to a statue he could see through the doorway of a temple. A musky incense blew towards them. The light inside was the colour of bronze, perhaps a temple fire reflecting from the tall, polished body of the slender goddess. Her face was fierce and beautiful.

Hegel didn't answer but he headed into the temple, bounding up the steps and into the body of the fragrant, dimly-lit building. A woman in a white dress tended a fire in a flat copper basin. Dark kohl lined her eyes. She had straight black hair wound in an elaborate plait. She paid no attention to the visitors, instead focused on the task in hand, scattering resins on the fire. Thomas yearned to accost her – to see if she would speak, if she was insubstantial as Hegel had claimed – but the German would not allow it, ushering him instead into an antechamber behind the statue.

'Turn your back to me, Thomas,' he said. 'Cover your eyes. This is my own secret, the doorway to the connecting place. It is my right to be the only person to know it. Turn away.'

Thomas did as he was instructed. When he closed his eyes he lost all sense of the garden, the city of Nineveh. He wondered, dizzyingly, if he was in fact still standing in the study at Hegel's house, under the enchantment of the box. But the box had taken him, or shrunk him – a homunculus – and swallowed him into its depths.

'Come now,' Hegel ordered. 'I have opened the door.'

Thomas looked around. A space had opened on the wall beyond which the statue was standing. This space was a black void – offering no tantalising glimpse into another strange and exotic garden. Thomas was taken aback – momentarily afraid. A shocking sense of his own vulnerability assailed him. He was alone here. Hegel – who may have already killed – could do what he liked to him. No-one would know. No-one could help. The opening in the wall – its emptiness – filled him with fear. He backed away, eyes wide.

Hegel made some sudden irritated exclamation in German.

'I will go first!' he said. 'But you must follow me. Do you understand? Follow me!' Without hesitation he stepped into the black space – and disappeared.

XANADU

The Garden of Time

So twice five miles of fertile ground
With walls and towers were girdled round:
And here were gardens bright with sinuous rills,
Where blossomed many an incense-bearing tree;
And here were forests ancient as the hills,
Enfolding sunny spots of greenery.

Coleridge

One

Thomas stepped through the doorway into the darkness. Now – without any sense of an interval, or of distance travelled – he was standing in a cold stone corridor. In front of him, Hegel waited impatiently.

'Where are we?' Thomas said. He glanced up and down the corridor.

'Come along.' Hegel set off at a brisk pace. Thomas followed him along the stone path. There were no lights but Thomas found he could see perfectly well. After a time they reached a Roman arch and the path opened into a square with three other similarly arched exits. Without a thought Hegel took the arch to the right and they walked again along another corridor. So it went on. Very soon Thomas lost track of the turnings they had taken. The paths of stone looked one and the same – each conjunction also. Trotting to keep up with Hegel, Thomas felt the clutch of fear again. Was Hegel intent on losing him here? Or causing him harm? How would anyone ever find him?

But what could he do? If Thomas drew back now, if he lost sight of Hegel, he would neither find his way in or out of the maze. Best keep up as well as he could.

'Wait for me,' he called, the note of fear in his voice perhaps sounding like irritation. He didn't want Hegel to know he was afraid.

Hegel twirled around. 'Keep up,' he barked. And Thomas wondered, beneath the briskness and the Teutonic scowl, was Hegel afraid too?

It was hard to know how long or far they walked. Possibly they walked in complex circles, crossing their own path, backtracking, retracing steps. Hegel turned left and right without a thought, as though he had taken this journey many times before. Like the paths in his grandmother's garden, Thomas saw that the stone corridors did not conform to normal expectations of perspective. Sometimes the walls leaned out or in – sometimes the path tunnelled steeply downhill, although his body detected no sense of this incline. Once it occurred to him that Hegel and he were growing smaller and smaller the further they proceeded, that the maze was closing in – and they were shrinking along with it.

'Here it is.' Hegel stopped suddenly and Thomas almost ran into him. They were standing in another stone square. This time, the facing archway contained a wooden door. Hegel reached out – but before he touched the door he wiped his face with his hand and drew a deep, strained breath. He pressed his teeth together, so the muscles in his cheek were momentarily tense.

'Stay close to me, Thomas,' he said. 'Watch, listen. Pay attention. And be careful.'

Hegel turned the metal handle and pushed the door open. Thomas followed him into a huge, circular room – a great dome. Curved black walls raced away to left and right and gathered seamlessly together in the ceiling above. It was as though they were standing beneath a huge, inverted bowl made of polished onyx.

'This is the centre,' Thomas whispered. 'The place connecting all the gardens.' He didn't know why he kept his voice so quiet –

perhaps it was the atmosphere of the place, the vaulting space, the sense of infinity contained, that kindled his sense of reverence, reminding him of London's magnificent cathedrals.

'Yes.' Hegel also whispered. He put out his hand to keep Thomas by his side.

'What is it?' Then he saw for himself. Emerging from the darkness, a tall, thin woman and a girl dressed in white. Curious how the darkness seemed to unwrap from them.

'Maud!' Thomas cried out, all caution thrown to the winds. He ran up to her, astonishingly grateful and glad to see her quirky little face in this palace of the strange. She put her hand over her mouth and giggled.

'Hello, Thomas,' she said. 'Isn't this a marvellous place? I saw a ghost when we came in, on the other side. At least, I think it was a ghost. And then a silver palace floating in the air. There is so much to see!'

The widow Lawrence harrumphed. 'Maud, be quiet,' she said.

Thomas looked around him. So much to see? The dome contained only a folding darkness – shifting, formless, almost palpable. As though Thomas could reach out and hold it in his hand. This made him think of the thought forms, the black shapes stealing through his grandmother's house and into his brain . . . was there a connection?

'Are the others here yet?' Hegel stood upright and correct. Mrs Lawrence, in her habitual armour of jet jewellery, could have been an embodiment of the dome itself – a miniature goddess of this reverse cauldron of simmering, glittering dark.

'I'm here.' Lee emerged from the left and, beside him, plump Mrs Hudson. And so they were assembled, all that remained of the Guild of Medical Herbalists. The four survivors – and their two apprentices.

'Shall we sit?' Mrs Lawrence said. Without waiting for an answer, she pushed the dark aside like a curtain – to reveal a long table with six high-backed wooden chairs. A brace of candles burned in a complex silver stand on the table. A tea set, porcelain whimsically decorated with forget-me-nots, stood waiting on a tray.

'How civilised,' Lee commented, with a wry smile, as he took his place.

Mrs Lawrence sat at the head of the table. 'I'll be mother,' she said.

There were scones too, still warm from a non-existent oven, and dishes of jam and cream. Maud's eyes, wide as saucers, lighted on the refreshments and without waiting for permission she began to fill her plate. Thomas sat down beside her.

'Aren't you afraid they might be poisoned?' he whispered.

Maud laughed. 'Don't worry, Thomas. This meal is the safest you will ever eat. It won't satisfy you either. Don't you see? It doesn't truly exist. It is a phantom we've created between us, from the substance of the dome.'

Hegel and Miss Hudson took the other seats. Miss Hudson folded her arms under her bosom and smiled at Maud as she spooned bright strawberry jam onto a scone. Lee, uncouth, placed his giant elbows on the table while Mrs Lawrence picked up the pot and poured steaming tea into six cups.

For a moment, Thomas was so enchanted by the scene he forgot the truth of their situation. His busy mind quickly wove in the missing details to fill out the picture. Walls, a hint of paintings, a carpet, a fireplace – they painted themselves around the table setting to create a full-fashioned room, as though the dome itself was plucking out memories from his mind so it might embroider the scene more completely.

Did the others see the same room? Perhaps this curious place of potential drew on all their memories to create this scene, where they might dine on moist scones and sip sweetly-scented Earl Grey tea.

'So – where do we begin?' Mrs Lawrence had taken on the mantle of authority. Her voice was brisk and businesslike.

Thomas tried to imagine the meeting as it might have been, in the past. His sour grandmother Augusta, avuncular Albert Constantine and eccentric Nehemiah Blake – now all dead – along with the giant American, fastidious Hegel, homely Miss Hudson and the grand Widow Lawrence. They were such a curious collection it was hard to imagine them together. Now, of course, they would never be together again and Thomas reminded himself, looking at the four survivors, that one of those here, sipping tea and eating scones, had killed, or arranged the killing, of the other three. He looked at their faces, one by one. How can you tell? How do you ever know another's thoughts if they do not care to share them?

Lee cleared his throat. 'I went to the cemetery, in the night, after Albert's burial,' he said. 'I took young Thomas along too. The funeral violinist appeared and played a piece of music I recognised. You would all know it too.' This with a look at Hegel.

Hegel picked up the story. 'I went to the Guild of Funerary Violinists, yes. I have a connection there, from long ago. At least, enough for them to grant me an interview. I play the violin myself, as you all know.' Thomas could see Hegel was nervous. Perspiration glittered on his high forehead. The scar flushed red. He balled his fists and stretched his fingers, working out the tension.

'The guild is much diminished now,' he said. 'Only a handful left, and they are impoverished. And yes, I know the music they played over the graves. How could I not? It is a piece of music I wrote myself.'

173

Miss Hudson's eyes widened. Mrs Lawrence pursed her lips. Thomas observed Lee watching them both very closely.

'It is the piece I wrote when we were travelling together – for our companion – for my beloved friend – Wilhelm Karsch.'

Hegel was sweating profusely now. He drew out a handkerchief from a fold in his tunic and wiped his face. The others remained perfectly still. They were focused, all of them, on Hegel – academic, musician, neurasthenic – as his usually impervious self-control faltered and broke into pieces. Even the illusion of a room faded momentarily, the table and chairs and tea and scones melting away, as Hegel pressed the heels of his hands to his eyes and began to sob.

Time stretched. Hegel, a spiral of grief and loss, seemed to draw the potent darkness in a whirl around himself. The cloak of it brushed against Maud, Thomas and the others, infecting them with Hegel's pain.

But Lee broke the spell. He stood up and reached out to Hegel. He put his arm around Hegel's shoulder in a rough, manly embrace.

'Hey, Rupert, hey,' he said. 'Don't get so upset. It's over and done with. It was a long time ago.'

Hegel looked at Lee with a sense of disbelief.

'A long time? Have you no heart, or any sense of the depth of my feelings?' he said. Nonetheless, Lee's tactic did the trick. Hegel was snapped from his moment of emotional abandon. His pride rallied. He didn't want this comfort and he pushed Lee away with an expression of contempt.

Thomas glanced at Maud. She was staring, open-mouthed, at Hegel and Lee. Then she looked back at Thomas and the question hung between them. Who was Wilhelm Karsch, so beloved by Hegel?

Mrs Lawrence said in a brisk voice: 'Wilhelm Karsch was the

eighth member, in the early days of the guild's revival. He was German, like Hegel. They were friends and companions.'

'Well, then,' Thomas burst in, impetuous. Suddenly the answer was obvious. 'Surely he is the one – the killer. Why did you not mention him before? Or tell us about him? It's obvious, isn't it?'

They stared at him, all of them. Lee shook his head. Hegel shot him a glance of such pure, venomous hatred that Thomas quailed.

From the other side of the table Mrs Lawrence tutted. 'Oh no, Thomas,' she said. 'You don't understand at all. It cannot possibly be Herr Karsch. He died many years ago. There was an accident, you see, when we were travelling together. Wilhelm Karsch is dead.'

Maud and Thomas glanced at one another. Maud piped up: 'What sort of accident? How did he die?'

'A climbing accident,' Miss Hudson said. 'Please – leave the subject. It is a very painful one for all of us.'

Lee stepped in, eager to move the discussion forward. 'Rupert, tell us what you found out from the funerary violinists,' he said. 'Who instructed them? How did they obtain your music?'

Hegel took three quick, short breaths and stood up very straight. 'They do not know themselves,' he said. 'Anonymous instructions, a yearly fee deposited in a bank. This has been a long campaign, and has taken a great deal of planning.'

He went on to tell them the story of their visit to the funerary violinists – though Thomas noted his own role was entirely written out. Hegel, of course, gave himself all credit for wheedling the truth from Goldsworthy and his friends.

The non-existent fire crackled in the fireplace as they mulled over Hegel's report. How would they unearth the truth? They each suspected the other of course. Thomas looked from one face to another. Who did he think it was, trying to take the boxes, desirous of amassing their powers for him- or herself?

Thomas watched as Mrs Lawrence took Maud's smooth, white hand in her thin, onyx-ringed fingers. She cleared her throat and announced imperiously: 'There is one matter of the utmost urgency, which we have not yet touched upon. We must initiate the children into the guild. I entirely appreciate they are very young – much younger than we would have chosen – but we are so diminished now, and the boxes are very vulnerable.'

Lee frowned and shook his head. 'They are way too young,' he said. 'We don't know what might happen.'

Maud licked her fingers, looking indeed like a little child. But Thomas knew it was an act, this little-girl mask. Her mind was acute – although they were almost the same age in terms of years he sensed the depth and intelligence she kept hidden away behind all the doll-playing. Watching her now, he observed how she absorbed every nuance of the conversation.

'We have no choice,' Mrs Lawrence said sharply. 'We are three down. I have Blake's box for Maud – he left it in my safe keeping. Thomas has Augusta's box, and we must be certain to secure Mr Constantine's also.'

She looked to Hegel and Miss Hudson. Would they back her up, against Lee? Miss Hudson said: 'I didn't know you had Blake's box. How did it come to you?'

Mrs Lawrence gave an icy smile. 'When Blake disappeared I took it and kept it safe,' she said.

'But you didn't tell us?' Lee asked.

'Did it not occur to any of you that we needed to secure it?'

Hegel sighed. 'I agree with Lee, that Maud and Thomas are too young. Children merely. But we have no choice. We do not know who opposes us, but they have resources and determination. We have to make the best decision based on what we have.'

Lee took a deep breath. 'Then we are decided,' he said. 'Though

I have to tell you, I'm not happy with this decision. We don't know what might happen – to Maud and Thomas – or to the boxes. We might be letting ourselves in for a whole load of different trouble.'

Maud looked pleased, however. She dabbed her fingertip in the last blob of jam on the edge of her plate and licked it clean, a steely glint in her eyes and a private smile on her face. Looking from Maud to Lee and Hegel, a flicker of unease passed through Thomas. No doubt there was something uncanny about her, little black-and-white Maud. She had called them all witches – but she looked most like a witch herself. A girl witch. A witchling.

'The children must come with me,' Miss Hudson said. 'We have no time to waste. Rupert – take Thomas home. Let him collect Augusta's box and see if you can take Albert's into your protection. Maud, also – fetch Nehemiah's box from your guardian's house and we shall meet here again so I can take you and Thomas through Xanadu to Huntington Hall. Then I can proceed with the initiation.'

Lee rose to his feet. 'I wish to be there too,' he said heavily. 'May I come with you now? I want to help you with this – to help them.'

Mrs Lawrence and Hegel looked at one another. They were all insecure, unable to trust one another. Was Lee declaring some kind of alliance, or loyalty? Would some private confidence be passed between them? Hegel frowned.

'You would be most welcome,' Miss Hudson said, rising to her feet. The others, likewise, stood up and the table, tea service, fireplace and scones all vanished into the roiling darkness that made up the interior of the dome. What about the insubstantial scones in Maud's stomach? Thomas wondered.

London's streets were cold, ankle-deep in slush and filth. A wind blew, its edge sharp enough to hurt nose and ears and cheeks. Above the city, the sky had blown clear, and through the dark mesh of the city's perpetual shroud of coal-smoke, the stars glittered like broken pieces of ice.

Thomas and Hegel hurried along the pavement towards Constantine & Blacklow's. The window was dark, the shop closed up for the night. For Thomas, after his voyages, it was the material city that seemed eerie and unreal. The muffled faces looming from the darkness, the glimpses into candlelit rooms where phantasmal people talked or worked or dined, the dark, clopping forms of the horses on the streets – characters populating a dream perhaps. Hard to know what is real, when you come to the crux of it.

Hegel knocked on the door and peered through the glass with a hand cupped by the side of his face. Within a minute or two, James the elder apprentice came sloping through the shop and unlocked the door. His hair was standing askew, his face crumpled with sleep. He peered out, not recognising Hegel.

'The shop's shut,' he said. 'If it's an emergency you'll have to try somewhere else.'

Thomas stepped forward. 'James, it's me. We need to come in.'

James opened his eyes properly. 'Thomas – where've you been? Mrs Constantine has been at her wits' end – cos you didn't come back. That and everything else that has happened. She thought something had happened to you, too.' He stepped back, letting the two new arrivals into the relative warmth of the shop.

'Didn't she get the note from Mr Hegel?' Thomas looked at his companion, confused.

'No,' said James crossly. 'Who's your friend?' He glanced at Hegel with some suspicion.

'This is Rupert Hegel. He was a friend of Mr Constantine's.'

'Then why wasn't he at the funeral?'

Hegel sighed with exasperation. 'We have no time for this. Thomas – collect what you need and take me to Constantine's study.'

James frowned. He stood up straight, rising to his newly-adopted role – man of the house. 'I don't think I like this. I'll wake the mistress – I can't let strangers roam around the house in the middle of the night. Where d'you find him, Thomas? How do you know who he is?'

But Thomas sidestepped his fellow apprentice and skipped into the next room, to the locked trunk under his bed. He took out his grandmother's box, the red bird's-eye maple with its inlaid lid, the patterns of gold and mother-of-pearl, and hurried back to Hegel.

'This way,' he said, leading the way upstairs to the study while James still protested behind them.

They were too late, so much was immediately obvious.

The study had been turned upside down. It still possessed the air of recent occupation – the intruder had climbed a ladder and broken through the window but the room still seemed to hold a little warmth. Papers and books lay over the floor, as though an enormously energetic storm had whirled up the contents of the room. Some stray pages still hung, momentarily suspended in the air, or teetering from the edges of shelves and desk. Papers flipped in the draught from the broken window. Had no-one heard anything? Then again, the burglar hadn't stepped out of the study and neither Mrs Constantine nor her daughters had bedrooms on this floor. Presumably they had slept through the entire event.

'Do we know for sure that Mr Constantine kept his box in here?' Thomas whispered. James stepped up behind them, peered through the doorway and gasped at the spectacle of destruction.

'No,' Hegel said, his face a cold mask. 'But whoever came here seemed to know this would be the place. I think we are too late. If the intruder hadn't found what he was looking for he would have searched the rest of the house.'

He strode into the room, over the river of papers, the broken equipment, the jars of herbs and chemicals strewn on the floor. The large desk near the fireplace had four large drawers – usually locked. These had all been forced open – most expertly, because the wood was only a little damaged.

'But we don't know for sure, do we?' Thomas said. 'They might have heard us coming and made off. Maybe the box is hidden somewhere else. Maybe it's still safe.'

'Perhaps,' Hegel said. His lips were pressed into a thin line. His face was tense and thoughtful. Plainly he didn't believe Thomas's optimistic interpretation.

'We have to go, without delay,' he said. Then, turning to James: 'You can tell your mistress Thomas is with her husband's friends. Be kind to her. She will be most upset when she sees what has happened. Tell her to call the police.'

They stood in a circle, in the dome that joined the seven gardens, like the hub at the centre of a cartwheel – Maud and Thomas, Hegel, Mrs Lawrence and Louisa Hudson – as Hegel recounted the details of the burglary and his fear that the box had fallen into the hands of their unknown, unseen enemy.

'We must shut all the gateways – seal up the secret places,' Mrs Lawrence said. 'There is no time to lose.'

She and Hegel disappeared into the darkness. Miss Hudson smiled at Maud and Thomas. 'Come and see the gardens of Xanadu,' she said. 'The Garden of Time.'

She led them, a curiously comforting and motherly figure, through the wall of the dome. Bright sunlight washed over Thomas's face, heated, scented with summer. The shock of it stopped him in his tracks. He heard Maud gasp.

'It's a forest,' she said. Thomas opened his eyes again, breathing delicious warm air into his lungs. They were standing in a clearing – a circle of vast beech trees. Smooth, grey trunks reached up, like a cathedral's stone pillars. Enticing paths led away at the cardinal points.

'This is Xanadu, your garden?' Maud marvelled. 'You all chose such marvellous and exotic names.'

'Ah but your aunt named her garden Arcadia,' Miss Hudson said playfully. 'She has a necropolis where she grows the most perfect poisons. Do you think, perhaps, it is her joke? A counterpoint?'

'Or perhaps she just likes the name,' Thomas offered.

'Perhaps she does,' Miss Hudson responded. 'Come along now. We have no time to lose.'

They moved through the glorious forest, along paths lined with wild flowers, where the purple towers of foxgloves nodded and honeysuckle clambered along the branches. As the path progressed they stepped from the summer sun into an autumn season, October's copper leaves lying dense on the floor, where fallen branches ached beneath the weight of huge, brightly-coloured fungi – strange growths like melted wax, or splayed fingers, or huge whorled ears. Miss Hudson saw how Maud's attention focused on this fungal harvest.

'My speciality,' she said. 'I have cultivated them for years, Maud. They are the most remarkable things, fungi.'

'Why is it the Garden of Time?' Maud asked. 'What powers do your fungi possess?'

Both Maud and Thomas were keen to look more closely but Miss Hudson hurried them on, obviously afraid despite her sympathetic demeanour.

'When people find themselves in the utmost danger – in the moments before a potentially fatal accident, let us say – they often find time seems to slow down,' she said. 'Clearly, the mind alters –

181

at least, its perception of time. I have grown a fungus here which, when consumed, creates this alteration in the mind so a man with only an hour can read and digest an entire novel. That is just one of my discoveries. There are many more I hope I can share with you, when this crisis is over.'

And so the forest of Xanadu altered, a map of months – splashes of January cold, glades of spring flowers, melancholy autumn groves. The year was arranged in a patchwork overlaying the forest. Here all things could germinate, flourish, bud, flower and harvest according to need.

Once or twice, out of the corner of his eye, Thomas sensed movement among the trees. He wondered if spectral deer roamed the forest but when he mentioned this, under his breath, to Maud she shook her head and said: 'Yes I have seen them too. But they're not deer, Thomas. Can't you see?'

She stopped and raised her arm – pointing to a wisp of palest blue, rising like smoke from the moist soil between the trees. The wisp opened like a fan – solidified – details etching in over three or four seconds, to create the impossibly tall and narrow form of a girl – though her body was featureless. She had long, slanting eyes and tendrils of green hair that moved as though suspended in water. The girl held up her hands and spread her long, severally jointed fingers in some curious greeting before melting away again, into the air from which she had come.

Thomas felt his mouth drop open, the beat of his heart against his ribs.

'What was that?' he said, with a shiver of unease.

'Why, a fairy,' Maud answered. 'What else, in a forest?' She grinned, fey herself, and twirled in a delighted circle.

'No time for playing,' Miss Hudson called. 'Come along. Don't lose me. We are nearly there now.'

They ran to catch up, as Miss Hudson switched from path to path. She stopped seemingly at random – but as he looked more carefully, Thomas saw the long line of wall stretching through the trees in front of them. The wall seemed not to be made of stone, but of bark. Whorled, mottled bark with veins of lichen – a living thing. Miss Hudson smiled to see them wonder at it. As she stretched out her hand a narrow wooden gateway appeared in the wall. This she unlocked and opened, before ushering them through into a small, damp parlour.

The room was an unpleasant antechamber to the forest of Xanadu. Cold, pokey and furnished with several faded armchairs, the dismal surroundings seemed to swallow the recollection of the glorious garden as soon as they stepped into it. Thomas saw Maud's face fall, the corners of her narrow mouth curl down in distaste. On this side, the wooden gate was a cupboard door which Miss Hudson spent some time locking and bolting.

'We have to be careful,' she said. 'You heard what Herr Hegel thinks. There must be no doors left open or unlocked until we know Albert's box is in safe hands.' She led them from the gloomy parlour, through long shadowed corridors to the kitchen, where at least a fire was burning.

'Don't you have any servants?' Maud asked, glancing at the kitchen's disarray.

Miss Hudson laughed. It was odd how girlish she sounded.

'I do have servants when I need them, but I don't want anyone living in. I like to be private – to have the place to myself. If I need extra help, then I hire it. The rest of the time, I can behave as I like without raising any questions.' She grinned wickedly, and unbidden images arose in Thomas's imagination – cosy Miss Hudson dressed in trailing black and casting brightly-coloured fungi into a cauldron.

She had no cauldron now, however. Instead she picked up a large black kettle, filled it with water and placed it on the range. She had no fresh scones to offer, instead placing a substantial brown loaf on the table, along with a slab of pale cheese, a jar of conker-brown pickle and a pat of butter. The plates she doled out were none too clean but Thomas was too hungry to quibble. He placed his box on the table beside him and began to eat. In any case the tea, when she poured it, was strong and hot and satisfying.

'Well,' Miss Hudson said, drawing up a chair for herself. 'We shall find Mr Lee and then I think you shall look in your boxes.' She smiled, as though proposing a pleasant picnic in the park. Remembering Lee's concern, however, Thomas felt a quiver of fear. What would happen to them? He glanced across the table to Maud. She, also, had placed her box on the table. It was less elaborate than the others he had seen – strongly built from oak, with a strong, waving grain. It might have been a document box for a farmer.

'Before we begin, I would like you to tell me what you know about the boxes, and the guild. There is a great deal for you to learn very quickly.' Her voice was very serious, but Louisa Hudson's eyes still possessed a twinkle as she looked from Thomas to Maud. 'We have never tried this before – passing a box from its maker to a successor. When we resurrected the guild, we began anew – created the places ourselves. So there is some uncertainty as to how it will work when you take one for yourself.'

Thomas swallowed hard. A lump of bread had caught in his throat. When he picked up his teacup he realised his hand was shaking. The cup rattled in its saucer. Miss Hudson observed – but continued to speak.

'Of course we know it must work. After all, in times past the guild passed on its garden through the generations – over hundreds of years. So do not worry overly. It can be done most successfully; it is only that we haven't done so ourselves. So,' she said, sitting up straight and clasping her hands together on the table, 'tell me what you know.'

Thomas swallowed again, trying to clear the impediment in his throat. Maud jumped in.

'My guardian has told me a lot,' she said. 'You are the Guild of Witches. You have divided up a magic garden where you grow the plants and herbs for all your magic.'

Miss Hudson laughed. 'We prefer the title the Guild of Medical Herbalists. That is our oldest and most accurate name, Maud. Now, Thomas – what did dear Albert tell you?'

Thomas took a deep breath and cast his mind back to his last visit at Huntington, and more specifically to the conversation at the inn on their way back to London – how the disparate researchers came together and unearthed an archive so that they might bring back to life a lost tradition and a wealth of knowledge that had lain hidden and forgotten.

'Why did you want to resurrect the guild?' Thomas said. 'What was your purpose?'

'We all had different reasons,' Miss Hudson said. 'Perhaps that is where our weakness lies. Albert Constantine wanted to find new medicines, to heal and cultivate health – but Mrs Lawrence seeks only to develop poisons, as part of her quest for wealth and power. We had in common a thirst for knowledge – but the ends to which we might put this knowledge have clearly torn us apart.'

'That much I know and understand, to a degree,' he said. 'But what the boxes are, how they work, where they came from – that I don't know.' He placed his hand on top of his grandmother's wooden box, sensing the energy within it – the movement like flowing water beneath the solid, patterned surface.

'You have visited a few, I think.' She gave him an intense, acute look, as though to see inside his head and unravel his perception of the condensed, curving worlds contained within the several boxes.

'Yes,' he nodded, counting on his fingers. 'Five, I think. Arcadia, Xanadu, Acoma, Nineveh – and my grandmother's garden, Broceliande. All different – and all the same.'

Miss Hudson said: 'Broceliande, yes. The ancient mythological woodland that lay across northern France. The enchanted forest where Merlin was caught in a tree.'

Thomas nodded. He had enjoyed the Arthurian legends as a child, and his sister Christabel had read them to him. He liked the name.

'And you have both experienced the black space at the centre of the seven gardens,' Miss Hudson continued. 'That, perhaps, has shown you the material from which the gardens are made.'

Maud and Thomas looked at each other. Miss Hudson tutted.

'I am sorry,' she said. 'I know it is hard to understand. We are ourselves only just beginning to learn about it. So much was lost. Perhaps the best I can do is to tell you what happened – how they came to be created.'

'And Wilhelm Karsch,' Maud piped up. She had a sly glint in her eye. 'The one who died. Tell me about him too.'

Thomas stared at her. He wanted to know more about Karsch too. For even if he were dead, there had to be some connection with the killings. Why else would the funeral violinists be paid to play a piece dedicated to him over the graves of the dead witches?

Two

Miss Hudson led them along a dark corridor. She carried a brass lamp in her hand. The shadows of tables and stands with vases fled before and behind them. Within its radius of yellow light, paintings briefly loomed – inoffensive landscapes, horses with glossy bodies. They climbed a flight of stairs. Miss Hudson was talking to Maud but Thomas, trailing behind, couldn't hear what she said. Her long, dark dress swung from side to side as they ascended. The treads of the stairs creaked underfoot.

'Here we are,' Miss Hudson said, stopping beside a door. She took out a long key from her pocket and slotted it into the lock. 'The guild library. It doesn't belong to me, or to any of the members, but to the guild present and future. I am the librarian only.'

With a dramatic flourish she opened the door and gestured them to step inside. It was dark, of course. Miss Hudson's lamp made little impression on a room of such size. Dimly Thomas saw huge shuttered windows, towering bookshelves. Miss Hudson bustled from desk to desk, lighting a host of somnolent table lamps so that piece by piece the room began to take shape around them.

'I am sorry it is so cold in here. If I had known, I would have arranged for a fire,' she said. Neither Maud nor Thomas was bothered about the cold just then. The lamps provided a lake of warm light, illuminating the size of the library – surely two or three rooms knocked into one? Bookshelves covered the walls and stood in free-standing ranks to left and right of the room. Glass fronted display cabinets held collections of yellow paper covered in unfathomable writing. The two young people didn't speak at first – instead they looked and marvelled. They wandered from bookcase to bookcase. Thomas plucked out a book at random and turned over pages (written in some kind of archaic German?) and observed botanical drawings of barbarous plants the like of which he had never seen – plants like warriors armed with blades and spears, helmed flowers. He couldn't understand the text but the accompanying diagrams (a symbolic rose, joined hands) suggested the application of this deadly-seeming flower might, strangely, concern love. The book, the picture, disturbed him. He slid the book back into place. Its brothers and sisters seemed to pull it from his hand – to suck it back in place with an audible sigh. Thomas saw that his hand, still suspended in the air, was trembling. The nerves along his spine tingled from the base to the join at the back of his neck, where the intricate tower of bone joined his skull. And his skull began to hum.

The books on the shelf in front of him seemed to call for his attention. He wanted to touch them – but dared not. So he stepped away and continued along the corridor between the shelves to a glass-topped display cabinet. Maud emerged, like a ghost, from the shadows on the other side. She too stood beside the table-cabinet and they looked down into its depths, like children enchanted by a rock pool. A piece of parchment lay unrolled on a bed of green velvet. It was pinned in place at each corner with lumps of rough quartz that glittered in the light.

Painted on the parchment, in thick black ink, was a diagram linking twenty or more different flowering plants. Some, like enchanter's nightshade, Thomas already recognised. Others were new to him – perhaps related species. The diagram itself was organic in style, so many fancy curlicues and tendrils. The flowers seemed to move as he continued to stare. Maud stretched out a finger and poked the glass – as though it were indeed a pool of water and she wanted to disturb a crab or anemone she had spied in the depths. The hum in Thomas's skull grew louder – a physical vibration that began to make his head ache. Beneath Maud's finger, under the glass, the design on the parchment rippled and the nightshade-cousin depicted in ink raised its petalled head. Maud gave a delighted laugh. She looked up at Thomas with mischief in her eyes and poked her finger on the surface of the cabinet a second time – another nightshade-cousin stirred and shifted its carefully drawn roots, like a lady adjusting her skirts. Thomas felt a stab of pain at the back of his skull.

'Don't,' he said. 'Can't you feel it? Can't you hear the horrible noise?'

'What noise? There isn't any noise, stupid,' she said.

Miss Hudson loomed beside Thomas and with a gesture brushed Maud's hand from the cabinet. 'Leave it be,' she said.

'I can make the pictures move,' Maud said, pettishly, sticking out her bottom lip.

'Can you indeed?' Miss Hudson said. 'How can they move? They are drawn on paper. You think you are the cause of this movement – but look at it another way. Perhaps the diagram itself – or the perfumes infusing the paper, potent even through a cabinet of glass – have caused the incorrect functioning of your organs of perception?'

189

Maud frowned. Thomas said: 'So the nature of the diagram – or the potion in the paper – are making us see what isn't there? It isn't really moving – it's a hallucination.'

Miss Hudson smiled. 'It is something you should consider, isn't it? Best not to jump to conclusions, I find.'

Thomas rubbed the back of his head, where the pain was at its worst. When he stopped looking at the parchment he found the discomfort faded – though the sense of the hum in his skull didn't entirely disappear.

They followed Miss Hudson through the library. From time to time she stopped to show them something – rarely making anything more than a brief comment as she did so. There were long flat drawers which she slid open to reveal piles of papers covered in botanical drawings, or lengths of papyrus riddled with Egyptian hieroglyphs, or scrolls in Arabic scripts, or Russian or ancient Chinese, as well as languages and alphabets she said they could not identify at all – coming perhaps from lost places, or countries that had existed only in the imagination. Finally, at the far end of the library, they passed beneath an archway of books into an alcove furnished comfortably with armchairs. Here the fire was already set, so all Miss Hudson had to do was light a taper from her lamp and apply it to the neat assembly of kindling and logs. Within a few minutes the fire was throwing out heat and warming the little enclave in the corner of the library.

Maud was sitting with her legs curled under her. Thomas took the chair on the other side of the fire. Miss Hudson took the chair in the middle. She sat up straight, her hands folded in her lap, the warm red firelight playing over her face.

'Well,' she said. 'This is the first time I have had to share this particular story. We have necessarily kept it to ourselves, the seven guild members. And of course we are now four so the story is dying with us. A story only exists in a mind – and if all those story-possessing minds are extinguished, the story is too. So I need to share it, don't I? To pass it on so its life continues, even if the creators and players of the story do not exist any more.

'As long as people have existed on Earth they have used plants to eat, for medicine and magic. They learned what tastes good, what nourishes the body. They have observed how plants can affect the body – how they might cleanse and heal wounds, reduce pain, speed the heart, cure illness. In the same way there are plants which increase the body's strength for a time, or its flexibility, endurance, ability to withstand pain. And again, they observed how certain plants, fruits, seeds and roots affect the mind – creating dreams and illusions, confusing the senses or heightening powers of observation; there is one special fungus which, when dried and eaten, can empower the eater to observe a man's body language so closely and exclusively he can tell you what he is thinking.

'Is this magic, do you think? Or is it science – the cunning application of knowledge to create an effect? Maud calls us witches, and certainly many others have done so over the centuries. If a woman can effect a miracle cure, if a man possesses the strength of an ox for the length of a battle, if another can evidently read minds, or conjure up demonic hallucinations, the unknowing could certainly be forgiven for calling this magic. Albert would certainly say it was science, though, wouldn't he?' This with a smile at Thomas. He nodded.

'He told me you found the lost archive in a basement in London,' Thomas said.

'A large portion of what you see came from that archive, yes. But over the last twenty years we have continued to build up the collection, to accumulate the books and papers you see now in this library. It's been a mighty labour, and it has cost us dearly in time and resources. It is precious, this store of knowledge. And the two of you can choose to become members of the Guild and custodians of the library. There is so much to learn. We, the first members of the restored guild, have only just begun the journey. We've dabbled at the edges, turned over a few stones.'

'But what about the gardens? What about the boxes? What happened to Karsch?' Thomas was impatient to know more. Albert Constantine had told him this much. 'You can't tell me the boxes and the gardens aren't magic – how can you explain those?'

Miss Hudson nodded. 'Ah, Thomas. Albert told me you were a hothead. Can you not listen patiently? What I'm trying to illustrate is that we often describe something as magic when we don't entirely understand how and why it works. If you don't know about stars and planets, why then the sun's rising and declining every day might seem to be the work of the gods, might seem to be magic.'

Thomas compressed his face into a frown and balled his fists. This conversation was starting to annoy him. Why couldn't she just tell him what he wanted to know? Miss Hudson looked at him, and then at Maud. Her face was shrewd and calculating.

'Very well,' she said. 'Wilhelm Karsch. He was German, like Hegel. They were friends. He was tall, blond and very handsome. An aristocrat – and an athlete, swordsman, scholar, musician, dancer, horseman and soldier. A veritable Renaissance man. It was Karsch who gave Hegel those scars upon his face in a university duel, and still Hegel loved him. Karsch was instrumental in the discovery of the lost archive. He, more than any of us, believed we could resurrect the guild.' Miss Hudson stretched out her hand and took down a slim white book from a shelf beside her. She flipped open the cover and presented it to Maud.

'There he is,' she said. 'Wilhelm Karsch. He wrote a number of books on a variety of topics.' She sounded proud, Thomas thought. Like a respectful mother boasting of the accomplishments of a successful son. Maud passed the book to Thomas. The title was written in German but judging by the drawings inside it was some kind of treatise on botany. On the frontispiece Karsch stared out from a black-and-white photograph. He was indeed handsome – also imperious. Thomas gazed at the face for a few moments, committing it to memory.

'How long ago was this taken?' Thomas said.

'About twenty years ago.'

'So he would be in his fifties now, if he were still alive?'

'Yes, that is true.' Miss Hudson nodded. 'I should add, Thomas, that we are all older than we look. While none of us has yet created an elixir of youth, we have all worked most industriously on creating concoctions to prolong our lives and boost our health. Think how successful Albert was with his beauty creams and remedies for ladies – there are many commercial uses for the knowledge we possess and Albert did very well from them.'

They were getting sidetracked again. Thomas didn't want to know any more about Mr Constantine's chemist business so he pulled her back to the story. Despite her declared intention to tell them, he sensed she was evading something. 'The gardens,' he said. 'How did they happen? How were they created?'

Maud had been very quiet, letting Thomas do the talking. He glanced over at her. She had a cool, calculating glint in her eye though – she was just as hungry for this elusive piece of information.

'We found the archive, and we built it up,' Miss Hudson began. 'Over the years we all established gardens – ordinary gardens – to grow the plants we were learning about. We also travelled, either

193

singly or together, to places all around the world looking for those more exotic specimens which we would bring back to cultivate in hothouses. They were fascinating times and we had many adventures together, adventures which bound us as a guild and as friends too. Of course there were rivalries and arguments and some fallings-out as you will find among any group of people but altogether we were bound to a single cause, a quest for knowledge, and through this knowledge, the quest for power and wealth. For centuries the early scientists have searched for an elixir of life, a potion promising eternal youth, and we hoped that this too might be uncovered in our researches.'

But as the years went by, she explained, they began to realise there was a great void at the heart of their cargo of knowledge and growing expertise. A manuscript written in the fifteenth century called for the use of a plant known to grow only on the banks of the River Nile in ancient Egypt. Other recipes required the cultivation of lichens that thrived only in the northern tundra, or mushrooms specific to one dry desert on the other side of the world. Other books listed hundreds of species, with detailed botanical drawings, which they did not recognise at all and could find no record of in any part of the world. At first some of the members suspected these collections were entirely fantastical – drawn up as a game or whim. Surely they were wasting time trying to find the origins of plants that had never existed in the known world? But these plants, it seemed, were also the most powerful. They had to find them – or forever be amateur dabblers. Miss Hudson told them how the story unfolded.

Karsch took the initiative. He devoted months and years and a personal fortune uncovering this most hidden secret of the Guild of Medical Herbalists. He was convinced they had overlooked something of great importance – the key to unlock the treasury of the guild's lost heritage. His first discovery – in a jewelled, illuminated book created in a medieval monastery by a monk who was undoubtedly also a member of the guild – was a beautiful picture of a circular garden.

Ringed by a high wall, containing orchards where maidens plucked apples from trees still curiously also in blossom, the garden was crossed by a merry stream and contained diverse and fantastical plants as well as several mythological animals – a unicorn, a dragon, a centaur.

The garden piqued Karsch's attention. The others didn't at first believe in its significance and dismissed it as a religious allegory, a depiction of Eden perhaps. A garden of earthly delights. But Karsch wouldn't let the idea go. Something about the picture and the book itself suggested to him that the garden existed – and that it was a place where all manner of plants might be generated, as well as such creatures as unicorns and dragons. The puzzle obsessed him. He wrote and researched. He travelled far and wide, writing long letters to his fellow guild members. Perhaps there was a link with the biblical Garden of Eden, he speculated. Eden was the first garden, the beginning place, created by God to be a home for Adam and Eve. Was there some link between the idea of Eden and the creation itself? Did the Garden of Eden possess a power to generate – an energy of potential from which flowers, trees, herbs and fungi might be created and grown? Was there also a link between Eden and the Celtic myth of the Cauldron of Plenty – the huge bowl from which any manner of good things might be summoned?

Karsch continued to explore his ideas while the other members dismissed his obsession and cultivated their gardens, and collected books and papers relating to the guild. At last Karsch made the discovery he had been longing for. He summoned them all to dinner at Huntington Hall and, here in the library, he brandished a large piece of paper, soft and yellow with age, marked with unidentifiable stains.

Karsch made them wait, of course. They dined and talked for hours, eager to find out what Karsch had discovered but loath to ask him directly. His manner was maddeningly triumphant – and perhaps he had a right to be so since they had poured cold water over his dreams for so many years. In the end, after midnight, when the bottles were empty and the plates cleared away, Karsch raised the paper in his hand once more.

'You doubted me, I know,' he said. 'You joked about me behind my back.'

'*Nein*,' Hegel piped up. Then in German he pleaded his innocence, his faith in his friend.

But Karsch brushed away his protestations and continued: 'Here I have a letter written by the last president of the Guild of Medical Herbalists before it was broken up and forgotten a hundred years ago, in the so-called Age of Reason. The guild has always had enemies – those who accused its members of witchcraft, who persecuted, tortured and executed them. By the last century, the guild members were dwindling and the last president feared for the safety of their most powerful and profound secret – the garden – Eden shall we call it?'

They stared at him, the doubting seven. Then Lee said: 'Where did you get the letter from? Where is it, Herr Karsch? Where is this garden? Does your letter say?'

Karsch gave a slow, cold smile. 'The letter, Mr Lee, was folded inside the cover of a book I bought at a great country house in Russia. The owners were selling up an entire estate to cover gambling debts. I called by, to examine the contents of the library because an earlier correspondence revealed the grandfather of the feckless, house-selling gambler had once been a member of our lost guild. His botanical collection hadn't been touched for years. Dozens of books lay covered in dust or thrown into boxes ready for removal. A little old lady dressed in black with a shawl over her head showed me where to go and for an entire day I had the library to myself. Can you imagine it? Beyond the open doors a forest of silver birch trees whispered in the summer breeze, while I sat at a table turning up books, manuscripts and drawings for our great collection. *Ach*, it was worth the journey even before I found the letter. I didn't stumble upon that until the end of the day. Darkness didn't fall till very late. The old lady came in again to light the candles and present me with something to eat. I was very tired by then. I had sorted all I wanted to buy and was readying myself to leave. But the old lady, seeing what had caught my interest, drew my attention to a locked drawer in the desk. She drew out a bundle of keys and unfastened the drawer. We chatted together and she indicated to a drawer and pointed to the books I had gathered. I could see it contained handwritten papers and thanked her most courteously. Then when she had gone again I sorted through this second resource – one I had so nearly overlooked.

'Our Russian colleague had studied most diligently. There were his own researches into the properties of the flora in the forests surrounding his home, and investigations into their uses. There was a modest notebook in which he had a collection of field drawings, notes and observations. And it was here, tucked inside the cover, that I found the letter I now hold in my hand.'

They were attentive now, all of them. The seven stared, eager to find out what the letter might say. Karsch looked from one face to another. The four men – Blake, Hegel, Constantine, Lee. The three women – Hudson, Lawrence, Williams. Their eyes were bright and hungry. They all wanted to know.

'At the time this letter was written, the guild was almost entirely diminished and its knowledge was fading from the light,' Karsch said. 'Only two men knew about Eden, and where to find it. It was at this time that the last president, an English botanist, wrote to our Russian and said he would hide it.'

'How can you hide a garden?' Albert Constantine demanded. 'In any case, even if you *could* lock it away, it would be overgrown after a hundred years. It wouldn't be a garden any more – it would be a wilderness!'

Karsch gritted his teeth and his face flamed red. 'You ignorant man!' he retorted. 'Haven't you listened all these years to what I have been telling you? Don't you understand at all? This isn't a garden like the stodgy plot behind your house, Herr Constantine. It is a tool, an energy. It is a place of potential and generation!'

'And how will this manifest itself? What will it look like?' Mrs Lawrence, who could even then match Karsch for imperiousness, would not stand for any nonsense. Karsch lowered his voice to a more respectful level.

'In all honesty, I do not know, madam,' he said. 'I shall know it when I see it. And see it I shall. The English botanist had a house in Devon, not far from the sea. He was very old at the time of writing – close to death, I think, and with no successor. This is why he wrote to his Russian friend. He doesn't refer to the garden specifically in this letter, but talks of the guild's most precious treasure and he says he will keep it forever safe and close.'

The room was silent for a moment. Lee's voice first: 'What does that mean, safe and close?'

'I would think it obvious,' Thomas's grandmother said, acid as vinegar. 'When did he die? And where is he buried?'

Next to her Nehemiah Blake grinned. 'Clever,' he said, inclining his head to Augusta. 'Very clever.'

Within the week the eight were travelling to Devon. They took a train and then a coach to a small, impoverished fishing village overlooking the Channel, where they took rooms at the inn. It was quite an event, to have so many visitors in such a quiet place – and with their international contingent they attracted considerable attention. The village lay wedged in a cleft of the cliff, opening down to the sea. On the day of their arrival, Louisa Hudson and the American Lee strolled down the single street past the facing lines of low, dark fishermen's cottages to the shore. It was June, the weather breezy, fitfully hot and cold as wreaths of cloud passed in front of the sun. Stripes of brilliant blue and dour grey moved across the fretful sea.

'Do you think he is right?' Miss Hudson said, shading her eyes. They were standing on a strip of pebbles by the tiny harbour. Seaweed lay across the stones. The air carried a faint aroma of dead fish.

'I don't know,' Lee admitted. Standing on the stone pier, three stunted fishermen were staring at the long-haired giant, pointing at him, talking to one another. Lee ignored them.

'He is a remarkably intelligent man, and his research has been painstaking,' Lee said. 'We know already that the world contains more marvels than most of us could ever imagine – and if he's right, what new wonders will we discover? What plants, what powers?'

'So you think it is worth our while – this journey? The committing of a crime – this desecration.'

Lee sighed heavily. 'Perhaps,' he said. 'If you think about it, this man wanted to keep his Eden safe. He wanted to protect it because the guild had lost its way. But we are the guild reborn – surely it is ours, then, by right of inheritance. Wouldn't he want us to claim it?'

'You are right.' Miss Hudson inclined her head. 'Still, I cannot help but feel a profound unease at the action we are contemplating.'

Lee didn't answer. He stared out at the sea. The wind lifted long streamers of his hair and blew it around his face. What was he thinking? These years of research, of laying down the foundation for a new Guild of Medical Herbalists, had been compelling, fascinating, marvellous. Now though, she felt a nagging anxiety – a tightness in her chest at her heart – when she contemplated their next step. She had long fought against the notion that the medical herbalists were witches – but wasn't the act they were contemplating akin to the traditional practices of witchcraft?

They dined together that night, in an upper room at the inn, away from all the curious ears and eyes. The food was basic – boiled fish, potatoes, cabbage. Hegel refused to eat anything but bread. The midsummer sun shone through the small windows late into the evening, filling the room with a soft, syrup-coloured light. The eight guests made plans.

There was no need for them all to go, of course. Thomas's grandmother, who had organised the booking, had told the innkeeper they were botanists, come to sketch the summer sea flora, and to this end they came armed with paper, pencils, paints. The hours of darkness were short – from about ten until four or five in the morning – so the protagonists in this particular grisly drama would have to act fast. There was, already, a palpable air of suspicion among the group. Nothing was said – no overt accusations – but Miss Hudson sensed it all the same. They were all wondering if they could trust each other, if Wilhelm Karsch might trick them or betray them in some way. He was keyed up and tense. His narrow, aristocratic face was bright with a passion he was trying to hide. But there was no disguising it, the energy in his body, the lust for possession of the mysterious creating garden he had such faith in. And who could blame him? He, all along, had believed in it. He had worked, travelled, studied and researched for years when all the others had been sceptical. Didn't he deserve this hoped-for hour of triumph?

Karsch, of course, would lead the expedition. He wanted Lee for his physical strength and Blake for his cunning and talent for dealing with the uncanny. The others would remain at the inn and cover for the absence of these three. Hegel was disappointed – he wanted to be Wilhelm's right-hand man – but Karsch insisted that the fewer in the team the better, and the less chance there was of discovery.

So when darkness fell, the three men slipped away from the inn and headed across the fields. The five remained in their private room, the three ladies talking and playing cards, Constantine reading a book. Hegel took up his violin. The sound of his curious, mournful tunes drifted through the floor and walls, and were heard by the other more regular patrons who were drinking at the bar or sitting by the fire.

Miss Hudson didn't witness the events of the next few hours but Lee, afterwards, recounted to her what happened. She said she had no reason to disbelieve him.

It had been a bright, cool night. Grey dew on the grass, a furnace of stars. The great house loomed blackly against the dark-blue velvet of the night sky but it was not to the house the three men were heading. Instead they turned to the parish church, built on a hump above the fishing village. It was a squat Saxon building with a square tower. The churchyard fell away in a dark-green skirt all around it, hemmed by a low stone wall. They passed through an iron kissing gate at the rear of the church and stepped into an unkempt field of graves. Low, mossy, tumbled by time and the slow slippage of the land into the sea, the crop of headstones was obscured by long grass, dandelions and an overgrown rambling rose.

'Do you know where the grave is?' Lee whispered. He carried a shovel over his shoulder.

'Yes,' Karsch nodded. 'I came this afternoon, to find it.' He raised his hand and pointed. 'It's over there, near the wall, with the white marble cross.'

Lee glanced over at Blake who, whimsical as always, was hopping between the old headstones and peering through the darkness at the weathered names. Karsch frowned.

'Blake!' he called in a low voice. 'Please, this way. We have to be quick. We cannot waste any time.'

Three

Lee took a deep breath. The breeze carried the scent of the sea. He fancied he could hear it too, the endless rasp of the waves gnawing at the edge of the land. He was sweating now, hacking into the hard earth. The two other men stood and watched as he jammed the shovel into the ground, wrenched out a clod of earth, tossed it to the side of the grave plot. On and on, arduously digging down and down towards the coffin. He was a strong man but the soil was dry and dense. The ground held out against him, only grudgingly, forced, piece by piece, did it surrender.

From time to time Karsch urged him on. Blake, however, didn't say a word. Once, like a scene from a ghost story, a veil of cloud covered the face of the low half-moon, immersing them in a deeper darkness. With a similar sense of the appropriate, a bleached barn owl hooted from the church tower and floated like a phantom over the heads of the men and away into the night.

Lee rested a moment, wiping the sweat from his face.

'You must hurry,' Karsch ordered. 'You cannot stop.'

Lee pulled a face. Karsch didn't intimidate him. Instead he found him irritating, with his old-world airs and graces, his assumption of superiority. He waited a moment more, willing the ache in his muscles to subside. The skin on the palm of his hand was burning, warning of a blister to come. The cloud passed. Lee began to work again.

Perhaps an hour passed – it was hard to tell. The digging grew harder the deeper the hole became. Lee found it difficult to manoeuvre in the limited space. He had to reach higher to throw out the excavated soil. Then, at last, the shovel thumped into a hard wooden surface.

'I've found it,' he called out, standing up straight, feeling the twinge in his back. 'Now what d'you want me to do?'

Karsch fluttered some words in German. He stared down into the mouth of the grave.

'Can we lift the coffin out?' he demanded, then more German which Lee couldn't understand.

'No,' Lee responded. 'How can we lift it out without digging all around it? How will we find any purchase on the box?'

Karsch was agitated now. 'Then we shall have to break into the lid where it lies,' he said.

'We?' Lee was tired and short-tempered now. 'We? You mean *I* will. Or are you planning to hop down here and smash the lid yourself?'

'You! Of course you. Be careful, though. Very careful. You mustn't damage anything.'

'Well, I can't promise that.' Lee backed to the foot of the coffin. The wood creaked beneath his feet. Perhaps the lid, already decayed by years under the soil, would simply collapse beneath his considerable weight. What if he jumped on it? Of course Karsch would fuss and squawk. So he lifted the shovel high, and dropped it near the head of the coffin. The blade sliced down and jammed like a knife into the wood. Lee wriggled it from side to side, splintering the lid, slowly making a narrow hole. The wood squeaked and screeched in the night-time quiet.

'Here.' Blake lowered a lantern into the grave. The shutters were closed but once the light was safely below the level of the ground he opened them to cast a yellow light onto the defiled surface of the coffin. Lee had now created a long gap though which he could see pale bone.

'Thank you,' he nodded to Blake. 'That makes my job a whole lot easier.' He continued to work more carefully, enlarging the hole in the lid with the shovel and then his hands. Slowly the skull-face of the interred body was revealed. It stared at them, passive, from its deep eye sockets. The old guy'd had good teeth, Lee mused. He stood up straight, leaned against the soil wall. Moonlight shone on the skull. After so many decades underground, how strange for the body to be illuminated again. Lee felt a quiver then, a foretaste of his own mortality. One day his own dead body would be hidden in the ground, never to be touched by the light again. It was only a brief interval, wasn't it, this sojourn in the light? So much darkness before and after.

'Get out now,' Karsch ordered. Lee stared up at him. Who did he think he was, to order him about like that?

'Get out now,' Karsch repeated. His eyes were shining, his expression hectic.

'I've done all the work, but you want to be first to get your hands on the reward, huh?'

'All the work?' Suddenly Karsch was furious. 'All the work? All you've done is dig a hole. I am the one who undertook the work – for years!'

Lee shrugged. For now he owned the grave, because he was in it. For all his bluster, Karsch was no match for him physically. He couldn't take possession by force. Lee didn't say this, but he implied it by his presence, and with a cold stare into Karsch's face. Then he heaved himself out of the grave.

'Be my guest,' he said. Out of the ground, he stretched his arms and wiped the grave dirt from his hands. Karsch hopped lightly down to the coffin and squatted over the opening in the lid. He slipped his fingers inside.

'Be careful,' Blake piped up. Lee caught the warning note in his voice.

'What is it?'

'Be careful, Karsch,' Blake repeated. He was shaking and backing away from the edge of the grave. But Karsch ignored him. He was probing the contents of the coffin, nudging the bones aside, looking for the artefact this last president of the Guild of Medical Herbalists had promised to keep safe in perpetuity. He made an excited exclamation. Presumably he had found something. He broke off more of the wood and groped around inside the coffin.

'Karsch!' Blake barked. In the moonlight his face was whiter than the skull.

'What are you afraid of?' Lee asked. He knew Blake had a sixth sense, that his intuitions, however random, should be trusted. Lee was also torn. He longed to see what Karsch had discovered but he knew that if Blake was agitated he also had every good reason to be afraid.

Deaf to the warning, Karsch put both hands into the coffin and drew out a flat, black box. The night stood poised all around them – as though the attention of the world itself was focused for that moment on the grave, the four men (one long dead) and the box emerging from its long sleep in the ground. No owl now, no skein of cloud. The stars froze. Lee felt his heart suspended between one beat and the next.

The sound of a delicate breakage, the collapse perhaps of thin glass. A long, slow hiss from the coffin.

Without a thought, Lee threw himself away from the grave. Blake was already some way off, still stepping backwards towards the body of the church. Lee landed with a heavy thud, bruising his hip and ribs. He was overcome with panic now, dragging himself away from the grave with his hands, clawing at the grass in a paroxysm of dread. Behind him Karsch gave out one long, thin, terrified cry. The sound imprinted itself on Lee's brain, a kind of aural scar he would never afterwards be rid of.

He covered his ears with his hands, squeezed his eyes shut, tensed his body to close out the night.

Still, he could smell it faintly. The lemon taint of poison. The perfume of death. Even this far from the coffin the last dying threads of it touched him and teased him. So he lay there, clenched against it, waiting for the horror to disperse. Where was Blake? Surely far enough away to be safe. In any case, he had to admit, nothing mattered just then but self preservation. He pressed his face into the ground.

Time passed. Hard to know how long. Did he lose consciousness? Was the thread of poison strong enough to have stolen him for a time? He woke to find Blake patting his shoulder. There was no light yet but the general stirring in the atmosphere suggested sunrise could not be far away. A solitary bird sent out a few tentative notes.

'Lee, wake up,' Blake whispered. 'Karsch is dead. Come and see.'

Lee's head thrummed with pain – as though he'd been beaten over the head with the shovel still lying at the graveside. He struggled to his feet, every muscle stiff and protesting. His hands were numb, his fingers barely capable of flexing.

'I breathed some of the poison, I think,' he said. Even his lips were thick and clumsy.

Blake peered up into his face and nodded. 'Yes, I should think so. You don't look wholesome. But you were lucky nonetheless.'

'Are you sure it's safe now?'

'Yes. The poison has dispersed.'

'He set a trap, didn't he, the dead guy? So no-one would take the box unless they were clever enough to know. And Karsch wasn't as clever as he thought.'

'Yes.' Blake stared to the east. 'Perhaps there was a sign in the letter that Karsch overlooked. A warning he didn't see.'

The two men gazed down into the grave. Karsch was curled on top of the coffin. His body had contracted into a foetal ball, the muscles pulled tight, his eyes open, his face caught in a spasm of pain and terror. His lips were stretched wide open, in a horrible and eternal grin. Blake jumped down into the grave and placed his fingers on Karsch's neck.

'Cold and dead,' he said. 'I think his heart stopped.'

Lee tried to quell a rising sense of panic. 'What are we going to do?' he said.

'We are not responsible for his death,' Blake said. 'Though I am sorry for it. I didn't like Karsch, it is true, but I regret any loss of life.'

'Karsch brought this on himself,' Lee said. Still he felt no easier about it. They should have been more careful – should have anticipated this trick. 'But what shall we do? We can't leave him here.'

'There is only one thing we can do,' Blake said. 'We fill in the grave again.'

Lee frowned. 'You mean, leave Karsch where he lies? Cover him up? Bury him with the other guy?'

'That is exactly what I mean.'

Lee's mouth felt cold. He swallowed.

'Do you have any better suggestion? Notify the police, the coroner? Do you think he, or his sisters, would thank us for revealing he was robbing a grave? Should we carry the body away and hide it somewhere else? Where better to hide it than in a grave.'

Slowly Lee nodded. Far away on the horizon the first streaks of daylight had emerged. Another bird piped up. Down in the village the fishermen would soon be rising.

He picked up the shovel.

Blake, still in the grave, picked up the box. Lee narrowed his eyes.

'You're taking it?'

'Why not? Karsch wanted the guild to be resurrected. If he is right, then we have the means right here. It will be his lasting memorial – his greatest achievement. How will it serve him to bury it again?' Blake dropped the flat, featureless black box on the graveside. It was about twelve inches square, scattered with soil. Lee stared at it with a sense of misgiving. Then looked down at the body. Blake had closed Karsch's eyes, laid him out as best he could – so now Lee began to fill in the grave again.

He worked quickly and without thought, like an automaton. Slowly the exercise restored the vigour and flexibility to his poisoned muscles. In the east the sun ascended and soon he began to sweat in the early summer heat. He tried not to look into the grave as he laboured, not wanting to see the dirt falling on Karsch's face, covering his body. He switched his mind off, focusing on the task at hand. Blake was sitting on the grass meanwhile, holding the box in his lap. Blake was right – there was no sense in burying the box, nothing for Karsch to gain by keeping it beyond death – but still he felt a sense of foreboding, an instinct that this was not

209

right, not moral. The whole horrible situation filled him with painful unease.

At last the job was done. He and Blake trampled the grave flat, tried to disguise the disturbance. They didn't do a good job, however. Anyone looking would notice the ground had been broken. They would have to rely on the villagers' neglect and indifference. Judging by the state of the churchyard that should not be a problem.

None of the others had gone to bed that night. They were sitting up, in silence, in the room where they had eaten supper the previous night. Their faces were wan and tired.

Hegel jumped to his feet when Blake and Lee walked into the room.

'Where is Wilhelm?' he demanded.

Blake placed the box on the table, next to the pack of cards.

'Where is he? Where is Wilhelm?' Hegel's eyes were wide. Clearly he sensed something terrible had happened. Blake and Lee looked at one another.

'He's dead,' Lee said. Hegel froze, his eyes intent, his mouth open. The others looked at Blake, who nodded confirmation. Then they stood, all of them, in various poses of shock – a curious tableau of expressions and attitudes.

'What happened?' Albert Constantine said. He took out his handkerchief and mopped his face. The others, too, began to move.

Lee and Blake sat down. Lee brushed his hair from his face and pushed it back over his shoulders. He told them everything.

Maud and Thomas listened intently. Miss Hudson had been talking for a long time, and she had carried them with her. The scenes rose up in Thomas's mind – the journey, the inn, the churchyard. He could see them, the players in the unravelling drama.

'What happened next?' he said.

'That following day was the longest in my life,' Miss Hudson said. 'We didn't know what to do. It was agreed we should try to act normally, so we set off on a walk along the coast, ostensibly to collect plants, to draw. Hegel was utterly devastated – heartbroken. There was no consoling him. He insisted we carry out some kind of funeral service – a valediction. A ceremony of mourning and farewell at the side of the grave. We argued this was foolish and would draw attention to us and the disturbed grave, but Hegel insisted and perhaps deep down we all believed it was a duty.

'So that night we set off, in the dark, to the churchyard and Hegel said prayers in German over the grave. Then he took out his violin and played a piece of music – his own special composition. It was beautiful and haunting – it moved us all, I think.'

Maud clicked her tongue. 'The music he played at Karsch's grave. It was the same piece, wasn't it? The melody the funeral violinists have been paid to play over the graves of Albert Constantine and Thomas's grandmother.'

Miss Hudson nodded. 'Yes, it was. But what does that mean? So few of us even know about the death and our graveside vigil. Who is doing this?'

'What about the box?' Thomas said. 'When did you open it? What was inside?'

Miss Hudson rose to her feet. 'Come with me,' she said. 'I'll show you.' She took them back into the library proper and opened a cabinet on the south wall. Inside, on a shelf, was a shallow black box. It was just as Thomas had imagined from Miss Hudson's

211

account. She lifted it out and placed it on a table. The candles on the table flickered, their light reflecting in the dim glossy pool of the lid.

Maud tilted her head to one side. 'There's nothing inside it now, is there?' she said. Miss Hudson didn't answer – instead she lifted the lid to reveal the empty space inside.

'We didn't open it for a long while,' she said. 'We were all so shocked by Wilhelm's death and afraid what consequences it might bring for us if the desecration of the grave were discovered. Hegel moved to London and kept the box safe. I think he believed he had claim to it, by right of inheritance, since he had loved Wilhelm so dearly.

'Months went by. We avoided each other – tried to continue with our lives – until at last, the following spring, Hegel sent us each an invitation to his new home.'

They had assembled, the seven remaining members of the revived guild, at Hegel's house. It was early March, chilly and rain-splashed. The first daffodils were buffeted in the garden square. Miss Hudson had travelled up from Huntington Hall. Lee had not returned to America after Karsch's death – probably because the mystery of the box remained to be unravelled – and he journeyed from the North Country to attend the elegant dinner Hegel had prepared for them.

Hegel had become more eccentric. He had scarcely left the house since the expedition to Devon – indeed he had become a virtual recluse, finding escape in whimsical obsessions. He had three white cats with jewelled collars. His house was furnished with exotic paintings. One of the upper rooms he had turned into a perfumery, using his herbal learning to create fabulous scents. His taste in clothing had become outlandish too. On the night of the dinner he wore a black silk robe, like an Arabian prince. They were concerned, the other guild members, about his state of mind. Hegel had turned his back on the real world, it seemed. Now he was obsessed with dreams and fantasies. Grief had tainted his common sense. That and the luxury of a private income, of course.

Along the centre of the table tall Venetian glass vases held the stems of copper and flesh-coloured orchids, or pure white lilies with waxen petals. They dined on quails' eggs, roast peacock, venison in a redcurrant sauce, on meringues stuffed with cream and hothouse grapes, apricots steeped in Madeira wine, sugar sweets flavoured with aniseed and rosewater. They drank champagne, and a succession of antique wines and liquors. The meal lasted for several hours. At the end of it, they were all intoxicated by the rich food, its manifold perfumes and flavours. Their senses were heightened and disorientated at once. None of them knew what Hegel intended to do but once the table had been cleared he disappeared for a moment – and returned with Karsch's wooden box.

He placed it on the middle of the table – then returned to his chair. The guests didn't speak for a few minutes. They stared at the box, and each other. Hegel was very much master of the situation. He made no comment; instead he waited for the others to offer a suggestion or remark. In the end it was Albert Constantine who spoke up.

'Have you opened it yet?'

Hegel shook his head. 'No. I wouldn't do that without you all being here. It doesn't just belong to me. It belongs to the guild – and we are the guild together.'

'What do you think is inside it?' This was Augusta, Thomas's grandmother. 'Isn't it a risk, lifting the lid? What if there is another poison waiting?'

Hegel inclined his head. 'That is a risk, of course,' he said. 'Now we have to decide if we want to take that risk. I have not been entirely idle these past months. I have undertaken some useful work – including the study of Karsch's notes on the secret garden. I engaged the services of a man possessing certain useful skills, and paid him to travel to Prussia with the purpose of breaking into Karsch's house and taking the documents, books and notes we needed. Of course I realise this is not entirely ethical behaviour but I think Karsch would have approved of my actions. His work belongs to the guild and will become a part of its library.'

'So what's inside?' Lee placed his strong hands, palms down, on the table. He stared at Hegel.

'A garden,' Hegel said. 'A garden with the power to grow and create all kinds of plants. A reservoir of generative force.'

A murmur of voices. How could a box contain a garden?

But Lee was impatient. He banged the table. 'Then what are we waiting for? Open it up.'

'Don't be hasty,' Mrs Lawrence jumped in. 'Remember what happened to Wilhelm.'

Lee looked at Blake. 'What d'you think, Nehemiah? You have an understanding of these things. Should we open it?'

Blake scratched his forehead. Then he shrugged. 'I don't know,' he said. 'It seems foolish to have it and not to open it.'

They all looked at one another again. A kind of unspoken agreement had been reached. Hegel nodded and drew the box towards him with both hands.

There was no lock on the box – no bolt, latch or lock to undo. The box was finely made – the lid fitted perfectly and gave the faintest hiss when it lifted off, smooth as silk. They were all tense, waiting for a whiff of poison, for a second booby trap. Hegel stared into the box. Then they all stood up in a rush, overcome by a wave of excitement, eager to see what lay inside. And what was it?

A low hemisphere of dark glass.

It rested on a bed of green velvet. About the size of a dinner plate, absorbing the light, its surface was perfectly smooth – like a summer pond in the shade.

'That's not a garden,' Lee said. But Constantine shushed him. Hegel slowly reached into the box and placed his hands on each side of the hemisphere. He lifted it from the box and placed it, so carefully, on the table. Lee crouched down to stare through the side of the glass. He moved his face towards it. Moments passed – he gazed as though he were mesmerised. A great sigh passed through his body. The substance of his physical self began to fade before their eyes . . . how could this be? He became insubstantial, like a ghost, thinning and contracting. Then, impossibly, he disappeared for a moment, a beam of light sucked into the dark heart of the glass.

Then, almost in the blink of an eye, he was back by the table. His eyes were wide.

'What is it? What happened? You disappeared!' Miss Hudson said. She put her hand on the big man's shoulder.

'It is a garden,' he whispered, still intent on the glass. 'There is a garden inside it. He was right! I can see it. And it is the most beautiful place you can imagine.'

He rose to his feet to make room for Miss Hudson. She took his place and bent down so her eyes were level with the glass hemisphere. At first she could see nothing – the glass was opaque and unyielding. Then, as she continued to look, a part of her internal landscape began to open. There was some curious alchemy between the glass and her mind's eye – as though the organs of perception within her imagination were latching on to the signals the glass was sending out. Her own creative powers worked together with a kind of metaphorical fertile soil within the glass. She peered inside and a vista opened up – a garden, much like the one depicted in the medieval manuscript Karsch had found, the wall and orchards, the stream running through the centre, the ghostly maidens plucking apples and plums. The closer she looked, the more detail emerged. It was as though she too were slowly being sucked inside. Soon she could see silver fish in the stream, the individual petals of the apple blossom and the border of embroidered daisies on a maiden's skirt. The horizon curved. The walls leaned out. And Lee had left his creative footprint here already. A spiny cactus grew in a bed of golden lilies. Presumably she too was scattering the seeds of her imagination in the generative soil of this magic garden.

'Louisa. Louisa!' A voice called her. How quickly the garden had swallowed her up. Now she was back in the room and Lee had his hand on her shoulder.

Disorientated, she glanced at the hungry faces of the fellow guests. They wanted to know what she had seen.

'Yes, yes it is true,' she said. 'It is the most astonishing thing I have ever beheld. And look!' She opened her hand – to reveal half a dozen pink silk petals, plucked from a tree in the garden.

Their voices rose, in discussion and argument. They were all eager to gaze into the glass themselves, disputing how best to preserve the garden, what should be done with it, how it might be used. One by one they fell under its enchantment, and emerged delighted and astonished. The discussion went on into the night and far into the small hours. Who should be its custodian? Who should shape it? Cultivate it? In the end Mrs Lawrence suggested they find a way to divide up the glass hemisphere and its garden cargo so that each guild member should make it as they wished and pursue their own creative interests.

Of course this started another argument. Could the glass be divided? What effect might this have? Would its powers be weakened? Hegel said he would continue to mine Karsch's research and asked them all to leave. He would keep their glass Eden, he said, until they were all agreed about its fate. Already the others were reluctant to leave it but dawn was almost upon them and they were tired to the point of exhaustion. Hansom cabs were called. The guests slowly departed for their homes or hotels.

'We know what happened,' Thomas said. 'You did divide the garden. At least, to a degree. They are still part of one whole, though, aren't they? In some way they are joined up.'

Miss Hudson agreed. 'Imagine a pie in seven pieces, though still contained within one dish. That is how our Eden works. And there is the central space, to which we can all travel.'

'So you all went off and had your boxes made,' Maud said. 'But how did you carve up the glass?'

'Carve? What a brutal word. Yes, there were many similarly violent suggestions put forward – that it should be cut, smashed, melted, broken. In the end, though, the process was so much more simple and obvious. Although it looks like glass the substance is not actually glass as we know it. Its nature, its origin, those we haven't worked out. One of the stories in Wilhelm Karsch's collection suggests the glass fell from the sky – a meteorite, perhaps. Is that the connection with the mythological Garden of Eden? Did this uncanny cauldron of plenty, so long ago, seed the Earth with its countless plants? There is so much we do not know – that future members of the guild may learn in the years to come.

'It was Blake who understood that, in essence, all we needed to do was to wish it to be divided. The glass, for we continue to call it such, responds to the will and imagination of its beholder. Why then, all we needed to do was to want and to imagine in one concerted effort – the seven of us. This we did, entering into communion with the glass together and using the power of will to separate the garden into pieces. When we emerged, there they lay. Seven globes of glass, smoky at the edge, darkly opaque at the centre, each of a size to sit in the palm of a hand. We locked them in our boxes, named them, cultivated them each as we wished. We used them over the years to invent, shape and grow flowers, trees, herbs, fruits, fungi with all manner of properties as we have already discussed. To heal, poison, possess, intoxicate. To boost the powers of mind or body. Witches or herbalists? Magic or science? That too we have touched upon already.' Miss Hudson smiled.

'It has been an adventure unlike anything I could have imagined. All these years later, and three of us are dead. What's happening? I'd hoped we could teach you slowly over several years but now it seems vital you stake a claim on these gardens left behind by Blake and your grandmother. We don't know who has Constantine's box and I am very afraid there will be more deaths if we can't discover and defeat our enemy.'

Miss Hudson put the empty box away in its cabinet. Maud put Blake's box on the empty table. Thomas followed suit with his grandmother's bequest. When Maud ran her hand across the lid of her box the word Albion emerged in a glowing ivory script.

'I haven't seen Mr Constantine's garden,' Thomas said. 'He told me it was called Tadmor, the Garden of Healing.'

'It is a fruitful cottage garden brimming with herbs, fruits and flowers,' Miss Hudson said. 'They are all very fanciful, the names we chose. But why not? It seemed appropriate. As for your grandmother's garden – see for yourself.'

Thomas had caressed the smooth wood of this precious casket so many times and never had the name emerged before. Would it now? Was he more receptive to the powers it contained? He took a deep breath and stared at the box in his hands. He felt the buzz of energy, the ripple of contained potential, as though the contents of the box were straining to be free. The inlaid patterns shone in the dim light of the library.

'What does it say?' Maud asked. Patiently, Miss Hudson waited.

The letters lifted from the pattern. Obvious after all – they had always been there, in disguise, waiting for him to notice.

'It is Broceliande,' he said. 'Her magic wood, her orchard and bluebells.' He laughed.

ALBION

The Garden of Love

This royal throne of kings, this sceptred isle,
This earth of majesty, this seat of Mars,
This other Eden, demi-paradise . . .

Shakespeare

One

Winter sunshine poured through the kitchen window. The servant girl, come in from the village, opened the door on the mighty black range to reveal the ferocious gold fire, the mouth fed with buckets of coal. A bare ash branch tap-tapped on glass, agitated by the wind. Thomas and Maud were eating toast and butter at the long table. Miss Hudson poured them all cups of strong, scalding tea.

'Did you sleep well?' she asked. Maud nodded, her mouth full of toast. Thomas said: 'Surprisingly, yes. After last night – all you told us – I wasn't expecting to rest easily. But I fell asleep in an instant.' He wasn't sure how late it had been when Miss Hudson had guided them each to a bedroom. He had placed his garden-box on a table, quickly undressed and then washed his hands and face in the icy water from the ewer on a stand in the corner. He had hopped into the high old bed, beneath a mound of old but scrupulously clean blankets, blown out his candle – and then what? He'd been too tired even to think over the revelations of the evening.

'I slept well too,' Maud said, still chewing. 'I was woken up by a crow on a tree outside my window. It was very loud.'

The image rose, unbidden, in Thomas's imagination: Maud

with her glossy black hair and long white petticoat, standing at her bedroom window and glowering at the noisy, sable rook beyond the glass. A smile flickered across his face.

Miss Hudson laughed. 'Huntington is a popular place for rooks,' she said. 'They roost in the old woods behind the house and fly around in circles over the trees making a terrible racket. Not that I mind it so much myself but I know other people don't like them.'

Thomas slid the blade of his knife through the butter and spread it on his wedge of hot toast. His mind strayed back to the night before, the gloomy library, the book with inked-in tendrils that moved (or appeared to move) on the page, the stories Miss Hudson had told them about the guild and the recovery of the secret garden. Today – the promised next step. They would enter and claim their gardens, seal up the gateways, protect them from possible invasion by their unknown opponent. Unless, of course, they were already too late. Thomas felt a peculiar twist in his belly to think of it. He was excited yes, but anxious as well. They were stepping into an unknown. What might happen? What if the enemy (an enemy who killed) was already waiting for them? Thomas stared at Maud, wondering if she too was apprehensive about the morning's appointment. She was hard to read beneath the illusory whimsical-little-girl exterior. Even now, she was humming a little tune to herself, sucking crumbs from her fingers.

Miss Hudson left the young people to their breakfast to make preparations, she said. As they were finishing their meal and growing bored with the waiting, Lee appeared in the doorway.

'Good morning,' he said, tugging his long jacket around him. 'This place is so cold. The damp gets into my bones. I don't know how you stand it.'

Maud looked at him quizzically. 'It's not as cold as all that,' she said. 'Perhaps you should take more exercise, Mr Lee. That would warm you up.'

The servant girl frowned at Maud and gestured to the American to sit on the chair beside the range.

'Here, sir. Take no notice of young miss. Sit in the warm, and I'll make you some tea.'

'Coffee, please, if you have some.' Lee, ever the gallant gentleman, gave a little, grateful bow. The servant girl blushed and hurried to the cupboard. He sat down, filling the wooden chair, and looked into their faces, Maud and Thomas.

'Louisa has told you about the gardens and how we came by them,' Lee said. 'I can't say I'm happy about the next step in this process, but you know that already. It occurred to me that any one of us adults could simply claim the extra gardens and add them to our own, thereby saving you from any danger. But Louisa thinks there is safety in numbers. And since we are already reduced to four, she may be right.' His voice was low, deep and serious. He held their attention.

'I shall take you to the library, and all being well, you shall make these special places yours.'

In the daytime, the tall wooden shutters folded back, the library was a very different place. With so much sunshine pouring in through the high windows, there was a sense of height and space that the darkness had obscured. And colours, too. The glint of crimson and emerald green on the heavy book covers, the ubiquitous glint of gold etched into the leather bindings, the jewelled glow of the illuminated pages and manuscripts. Maud and Thomas wandered in a renewed bubble of delight.

Lee and Miss Hudson spoke together quietly. Then they summoned the two young people, bade them sit down on ornate wooden chairs to either side of a low table. Thomas and Maud each placed their boxes – Broceliande and Albion – on their laps.

'One at a time?' Maud said. 'Or together?'

'Together I think, Maud,' Miss Hudson said. She stood behind the girl, and placed her soft little hand on Maud's shoulder.

'What do we do?' Thomas asked. 'You haven't told us that yet.' His apprehension was getting the better of him now, and the words came out a little more belligerent in tone than he had intended. He reined himself in: 'I mean, will you explain to us, please.'

Lee nodded, his face receptive and sympathetic. 'Of course, Thomas. Of course. When we took the gardens and created them for ourselves, they had lain pretty much dormant for decades. Although the ancient template remained in place, the archetypal garden you saw in the medieval picture, the impressions left by so many subsequent guild members, had faded away. Not disappeared, mind you. I don't think any information, any creation, actually disappears from the store of knowledge in the garden – but they might not always be manifest. They are potential plants – idea seeds, if you like. Part of our work has been discovering and recreating some of these.'

'So, the gardens are like a miraculous glasshouse – where you can grow long-lost plants, and generate new ones. Plants that may have all sorts of powers,' Thomas said. 'You can take them out of the garden, carry them out into the real world, just as you could with an ordinary glasshouse. But what about the revenant of my grandmother, the fairy we saw in Miss Hudson's garden, the ghostly people in yours and Herr Hegel's? They aren't plants, are they?'

'They are not,' Lee agreed. 'Like the structures, the landscapes, they are different to the plants. The gardens generate real, substantial, viable plants – the other things you see could be considered painted scenery. Illusions, dreams. The material within the globes is so hungry to create that it takes them from our thoughts and builds them. Some of this we have chosen – playfully, perhaps artistically – others arise from the darker side of ourselves, and by dark I do not mean necessarily evil, I mean from those parts of the heart and soul we might not even be aware of – the fount of our dreams, maybe.'

'But what about the revenant – the girl who was my grandmother?'

Lee shrugged, though his face was very serious. 'I am not entirely certain – remember I'm no authority – the things I tell you are my best guess so far, right? I think the ghost was the last dying echo of your grandmother, still clinging to the garden, maybe preserved there in some form. Perhaps there are other ghosts in all the gardens, like the idea seeds I spoke about. Maybe all our ancestral herbalists are inside the garden still, as revenants, and we haven't yet discovered them.'

Miss Hudson pursed her lips uneasily. 'We haven't time to speculate and philosophise too much. Tell the children what they need to do,' she urged. Maud and Thomas exchanged a glance. Maud was wringing her hands together, surreptitiously in her lap. Thomas wanted to reassure her – but what could he say? He was just as afraid.

'You will each open your box, and inside you will see a globe of black glass,' Lee said. 'You are thinking that when the other boxes have been opened – like mine, Thomas – that you have simply stepped into them – that you haven't seen the glass at all. Well, that is because we are masters of those gardens and that is what we have allowed. These gardens, once controlled by your grandmother, Thomas, and by Nehemiah Blake, Maud, have no master. They have been closed down and locked up. So you will behold the globe, you will move inside – and then you shall see what happens. You will find your own way. Most important of all, you must find the gateways into the other gardens and make sure they are locked.' Lee sat back. Thomas swallowed. He felt none the wiser. What manner of instruction was that?

'I'm ready,' Maud said, without a moment's hesitation. Thomas wasn't fooled. Her skin was waxy. Perspiration glistened on her forehead.

Lee looked at Thomas. He nodded. 'I've never succeeded in opening the box before,' he said. 'How do I do it now?'

'You will do it,' Lee nodded. 'The key, the password, is your own receptiveness – your understanding and wish. You didn't know before – you weren't ready. Now – I hope you are ready.'

Thomas drew a deep, tense breath. He and Maud exchanged one last look – and then he placed his hand on the top of the box.

Almost in that instant, the name emerged from the patterns inlaid on the lid. The wood was warm and soft, like syrup beneath his fingers. He tried to empty his mind, not to think. Instead, remembering how Lee had opened his box, he waited for its mysterious contents to reach out to him. Slowly, slowly, his fingertips teased out the patterns, the binding holding the box closed. A knot to untie, a long unravelling. How many times had he tried this before – and failed? He had been too demanding – he had never tried clearing his mind, and waiting, asking for the path through the maze into the heart of the box.

His fingers glided over the lid, round and back, looping and turning. As the moments passed, the box grew heavy on his lap as though loaded with stones. Sensations of hot and cold passed through his hands. Then his fingers stopped. He opened his eyes to see a blaze of light through the letters spelling out its name. He drew his hand away and the lid lifted open on its own, in a smooth, graceful arc. It folded back – revealing inside a globe of dark glass. Thomas stared. He had never seen it before, but how familiar it seemed. Across the table Maud was opening her own box. Lee and Miss Hudson were watching over them, but it was as though they didn't exist. The entire world receded from Thomas as he stared at the glass. The globe was a little larger than the size of his fist, transparent at its outer curve, densely black in the centre. The surface was so smooth it looked not less like glass than like water. A huge, dark-hearted dewdrop.

He stared into the globe, was lured to it irresistibly. It was like jumping into a shadowed pool, feeling the weight of its liquid substance drawing him down and down, into the depths. The glass closed over his head, the light slipped away, and all sense of his material surroundings. Everything collapsed.

He stood in a garden, before a tunnel of thorny stems. The sky a brilliant blue, punctuated with fluffy, scudding clouds. Hot sunshine, the earth and grass scent of his grandmother's garden. The shock was so great he laughed out loud. He squatted down and picked up a handful of dirt, feeling the grit drain through his fingers. He plucked a leaf, scrunched it in his hand, and lifted it to his face to smell the perfume of bitter sap. Then he laughed again. The place was so utterly, blissfully familiar. His fear melted away – a feeling of warmth and lightness expanded inside him. Some five years of life and memory seemed to fade away, leaving him back in this place of childhood. His grandmother's death, Blake, London, the Constantines, the guild – how real were they? Nothing existed but now, in the garden. This familiar, beautiful place. If he turned back to the sundial he might visit his siblings, his mother. He wrapped his arms around himself, a little boy again, living in the eternal present, the here.

Except that he was afraid to turn back. If he could stand here forever, poised between return and stepping forward, into the thorny tunnel, he might maintain forever the illusion he was only a step away from childhood and irresponsibility, that he could run home to his mother, that he had no problems to deal with. But you can't go back, can you? However much you want to, the past is gone and familiar places change. *You* change. To go back is to be disappointed. He wrestled for a few moments with this dilemma. He couldn't go back but he wanted to hold on, for a little while at least, to the idea that he had that choice. The feeling of returning to this long-lost childhood place, the ache of nostalgia, was so sweet and delightful he couldn't quite let it go.

The garden called. A whisper, a hiss, through the passage of thorns. Something uncurled in Thomas's mind, a little brain weevil. An idea, a reminder, of his purpose in coming here. He had to move on. He took a deep breath, and another, let go his longing for the vanished past and stepped through the tunnel into his grandmother's garden.

Except, of course, it wasn't quite as he had remembered it. The original garden archetype was emerging, as Lee had suggested it might, the garden of earthly delight illustrated in the medieval manuscript had begun to assert itself again. His grandmother's creation – the map of cultivated ground, the rhododendron bushes, the pathways, the orchard and bluebell wood – was itself becoming a little ghostly. He wandered down a long hill to the orchard, a stump of stone in its centre. The black goat mooched up to him and bleated. Thomas remembered to close the gate behind him so the goat wouldn't escape.

But once in the orchard, his sense of purpose melted again. The place was so perfectly lovely, so blissfully calm. He lay down in the grass on his back and watched the apple trees and their cargo of blossom fade in and out of existence. Soon he would find the narrow iron gateway into the bluebell wood, but first he would rest awhile. His eyes grew heavy, his body seemed to melt into the ground. How relaxed he was, no tension, no worry. It was easy to lie and dissolve, to linger on the delicious cusp between waking and sleeping when dreams begin to invade the mind . . .

Curious dreams. The teasing out of memories – of his childhood in the village, his brothers and sisters, his grandmother's face, her funeral in the graveyard with the petals blowing over the mourners. Except the mourners turned into a parliament of rooks, as wild and clamorous as the real birds circling the woods of Huntington. The priest was a rook, his white surplice hanging around his black, feathered neck. He held the prayer book in his giant claw and intoned: 'Man that is born of a woman hath but a short time to live, and is full of misery . . .'

The rook-mourners were not well-behaved, crying hoarsely to one another. The Blake rook emerged from a hedge, his top hat at a jaunty angle, a waistcoat fitted closely around his wings. He winked at Thomas as he strode past on his scaled rook feet.

'Let me out!' A hammering from the coffin in the grave. 'Let me out!'

A girl's voice, querulous rather than panicked. Shouldn't it be the body of the old lady in the long wooden box?

'Let me out!'

Thomas felt a leap of agitation. They couldn't bury a little girl in the grave! The funeral service had to be stopped. None of the mourners seemed to notice the girl's cries so Thomas tried to call out and tell them. But his voice wouldn't work. He couldn't make himself heard. The rook-mourners began throwing handfuls of earth into the open grave. These balls of soil thumped onto the lid of the coffin and sprawled over its surface. Very soon the grave began to fill, though the girl's voice grew louder.

'Let me out! Let me out!'

Thomas was afraid now. He tried to stop them burying the coffin but the rooks seemed not to notice him at all – they were all too intent on their own rookish business at the graveside. Except for Blake, who winked at him again and hopped away towards the churchyard wall and a narrow gateway that led into a bluebell wood. He seemed to suggest Thomas should follow him. So Thomas tried to break away . . . but the dream faded. Briefly he was back in the orchard, in the garden of Broceliande. The sun shone upon his face. The ground cradled him like a hand. He drifted again, to the antechamber of sleep.

The chemist's shop – Constantine & Blacklow painted over the plate-glass window. Standing behind the counter were a young man and a girl with chestnut brown hair. They looked familiar to Thomas, this twosome. They were hard at work – the man was grinding a powder, the girl pouring a treacly substance into a dark blue medicine bottle. Thomas stepped into the shop.

'How can I help you, sir?' asked the young man.

'I'm looking for Mr Constantine. Is he at home?' Thomas said. The girl smiled. They were, of course, Nehemiah Blake and his grandmother Augusta.

'I'm afraid not,' said Blake, shaking his head. 'He is dead and buried. You will find him in the city cemetery, in a smart new grave. There is nothing of our dear friend Albert here, you know. But Augusta and I – well, we shall help you as much as we can.'

Thomas frowned. 'Am I dreaming?'

'No, no,' Augusta said briskly. 'The garden is exploring you, that is all. Making a little harvest, gleaning seeds from your thoughts and memories. Nehemiah and I are both a part of the garden, of course – and we have a connection with you.'

'But what about the other man – the one who killed Blake and died in the garden. That means he's here too.' Fear took a hold of him, like cold water rising. An image rose vividly, the young man with flaxen hair striking Thomas across the head, and again, wrestling with Blake, then lying with a knife embedded in his chest.

'Don't worry, Thomas,' Blake said, still pounding his powder. 'We shall keep an eye on you.' They faded away, and Thomas found himself standing in an empty London street. Hard to tell if it was day or night, the sky was a dull monotone, a grey stripe between the towering houses to left and right. Thomas began to walk, wondering where the usual crowds might be, the traffic and the traders. The buildings looked deserted, no lights or movement. He walked a long way, straight along the road, till he reached the gates of the city cemetery where not so long ago Albert Constantine had been buried at the end of a lavish funeral. Thomas strode along the avenue of yew trees and found the freshly-turned earth of his friend and teacher's grave. There was Constantine, sitting on the grass beside his own marble headstone. Thomas smiled to see him.

'How are you, Thomas?' Constantine enquired.

'You must have visited my grandmother's Garden of Dreams, I think, to have left some trace of yourself here,' Thomas said. 'Are you a dream, or a revenant, or something spun from my memories?'

'Ah, Thomas – perhaps a combination of all three?'

'How do you find it, being dead?' Thomas asked.

'I have no idea,' Constantine answered. 'I wasn't dead when I visited this garden, and you, naturally, have no memories of how

I feel now I *am* dead so we are – neither of us – any the wiser on that score.'

Thomas turned this over in his mind. 'So what am I supposed to do here?'

'You are doing it,' Constantine said. 'And the garden is doing it with you. Look around – what can you see?'

Thomas raised his eyes from the grave. The cemetery was dissolving into a colourful circus in which places and people from his fourteen years of life were parading. There he was, a baby, in a flash of sunlight with a stripe of birth's red blood on his face; there was his father, holding out his hands; his big sister Christabel dreaming over a book and nursing a baby sister in her lap; games in his grandmother's garden, dull Sundays in the cattle-stall pews in the church, traipsing in the mud to school, lying by the fire in the dark winter days . . .

Thomas woke with a start. He had fallen over the brink into sleep proper. His quasi-dreams faded. He was still in the orchard but the stupor had fallen off him. He felt fresh and alert.

Thomas climbed to his feet and looked around him. He was different. The garden itself was also different. To begin with, it looked very similar to the garden his grandmother had created – after all his memory of the place was very strong and he liked it. The orchard was just the same, including the goat, but the rhododendron maze had disappeared and in its place were stretches of elegant parkland, like the green spaces of London Thomas had enjoyed so much when he first moved to the city. Giant ornamental trees, flower gardens where he might begin his own botanical experiments, still lakes where swans glided among pearl-white water lilies. And what about the bluebell wood? He hurried to the narrow archway. Oh yes, there it lay, the pale gloom of the beech trees, the lakes of purple-blue. Would he encounter the revenant there? Blake and the blond man had died in the wood – would their bodies still lie among the bluebells? Horrible thought. First he had to walk the perimeter of the garden to be sure the doorways into the garden were shut and locked.

He sensed his new connection with the garden. It no longer disorientated him, or threw him off track with its curious perspectives and leaping scenes. He could identify the outer wall (and see through the scene-setting brick to the opaque glass beyond) and he followed it easily. First there was the pathway through the thorny tunnel, which he would close when he left the garden. Elsewhere there were two other gateways into the neighbouring gardens, Albion and Xanadu. The first was already closed and locked – a gate of iron rails looped with rusty chains and a vast padlock.

Finally, no avoiding it, he passed into the eerie half-light of the bluebell wood, the wood within the garden, in search of a third gate. It was just as he remembered. Moonlight and white moths. The curve of the beech trees above the endless lake of lilac-blue. Of all the places he had seen in these enchanted gardens, this was the most captivating, the most beautiful. A little sinister, yes, with the faintest skeins of mist floating above the flowers and the tremble in the air that hinted at so many unseen presences. Had this secret wood sprung from his grandmother's memory and imagination? Or had she discovered it and made it manifest again, the gift from an earlier garden visitor? Perhaps his guild ancestors had each loved and shaped and sustained it over the centuries, because of all the places in the garden of Broceliande it seemed the most ancient, imbued with time and the unseen presence of those who had come before. He wondered about the eternal bluebells. Were they different from their ordinary counterparts, the flowers he saw every spring in the woods around his home village? Were they grown like this because they possessed a particular potency, perhaps to create dreams and visions?

He was unnerved but not surprised to behold the revenant again, a movement of white glimpsed from the corner of his eye. He continued to walk. Would the ghost approach him? The wood curved over, the moths danced in piercing swords of silver moonlight. The air was crisp and cool, perfumed by the bluebells. What about Blake and the blond man, who had died here four years ago? Would they be preserved, just as they had fallen – or would the magic substance of the glass have absorbed them and taken them apart, using them to nourish the garden? He found it impossible, even now, to work out the place where the fight had taken place. The wood still managed to fold itself around him, to defy his instinct to map it.

The ghost was standing some way in front of him now – tempting him to acknowledge it. Thomas smiled and bowed, though his teeth were chattering.

'Grandmother,' he said. 'Hello again.' The ghost didn't reply, but moved away from him, leading the way along narrow pathways through the bluebells of the beech cathedral to the brick wall at the perimeter. Thick ivies and other climbing plants with glossy leaves dangled over it. Pushing these aside Thomas saw the narrow gothic archway just large enough for a man to walk through. And beyond it – he gasped to see it again after so long – a wide vista of rolling chalk hills, faraway white cliffs and a sweep of the eternal sea, grey-blue beneath the sky. Seagulls, with breasts of angelic white, soared and cried over the water. Waves crashed and recoiled on beaches of cream and smoke pebbles. It was Albion, the Garden of Love: Blake's garden kingdom.

Thomas turned, intoxicated by the view. How he wanted to visit this world – this garden passed by right of inheritance to

Maud. And she was in there now, wasn't she? Exploring it, making it her own – perhaps changing it? He ached to step from the closed world of Broceliande into this new kingdom, the place of space and distance and the sea. Except that it was an illusion, he reminded himself. The leaping sky, the expanse of sea were both contained within a ball of glass he could hold in his hand . . .

He had to close the gate and lock it.

Something niggled. The night of his grandmother's funeral – his adventure in the garden with Blake and the blond man. Clearly Blake had passed from Albion into Broceliande through this gateway – but how had the intruder gained access? Perhaps he had followed Thomas along the thorny path, through the entrance his grandmother had left open for him. Thomas sighed. He drew shut the wooden door, blocking the glorious view over Albion's vista of sea and hills. The door had a key which he turned in the lock and then deposited in his pocket. Then he turned away, regret mingled with relief. Surely he was safe now. The garden was secured.

A sound like a long sigh moved through the trees. The revenant had moved away from him. There she was, in a glade, the moon poking white fingers through her insubstantial body. Thomas felt a leap of fear – sensing an intruder in the garden, the place to which he was now so intimately embroidered. He backed against the wall. Someone was coming after him – hunting him down. Who was it? Why could he not see them? For a horrible moment he was afraid it was the blond man Blake had killed. In his mind rose the image of the long-dead body, climbing from the garden's nurturing soil, the knife poking from his chest, still fired by the will to hunt Thomas down and steal his inheritance. He pressed himself into the wall's veil of ivy, as though the dangling leaves would cover and hide him. He could see no-one – but the sense of the invader was strong still. The sense of threat. The revenant moved again. Did she want him to follow? Could he trust her? What else could he do? Soon this rising sense of terror would paralyse him completely.

Thomas broke away from the wall and ran through the bluebells, in desperate pursuit of the revenant. She was hard to follow, because she appeared and disappeared at random, not taking any straight path. Once he ran past the phantasmal forms of Blake and the blond man fighting with each other – but the temptation to stop and look was overwhelmed by his sense of panic, the sure knowledge that something terrible had happened. The thought flashed into his head – of Lee and Miss Hudson sitting in the library at Huntington waiting for their protégés to emerge from the gardens. Were they in danger? What about Maud? What was happening? He hurtled out of the bluebell wood and into the orchard where the standing stone stood among the blossoming trees.

A man was standing there. He was tall, slim, beautifully dressed. At first Thomas thought it was Rupert Hegel – something about his haughty bearing, the dark blond hair. His thoughts tumbled over each other, trying to make sense of what he was seeing. He recognised this man, oh yes. But it couldn't be – unless he was a revenant too, a ghostly presence in the glass shell. How could he be? This man never had an opportunity to step inside the gardens he had chased for so many years. He had died before he got the chance.

Thomas ground to a halt and stared. He was hot and breathing heavily. His heart banged against his ribs. The man regarded him without any obvious emotion and Thomas struggled to speak.

'How did you get in here?' he said at last, forcing out the words. 'What have you done to the others, to Lee and Miss Hudson?'

The man made no response.

'I know who you are,' Thomas blustered. 'I know your name. They said you were dead but I saw your picture. You're Wilhelm Karsch.'

At last the man responded. At the mention of his name he stood up straight and clicked his heels together, military style.

'You are in my garden,' Karsch said. 'I claim it – it is my right.'

Two

'How did you get in here?' Thomas said. His eyes were fixed on Karsch and he struggled to breathe, his heart seeming to swell in the cage of his ribs. Karsch didn't speak – instead he cupped his hands together, opening them to reveal what looked like a silver-grey egg. As Thomas watched, anaemic yellow root tendrils thrust themselves through the clay-like substance and curled over the edge of Karsch's hands.

'I closed the gate,' Thomas blurted, struggling to distract Wilhelm, to put words in the way of his fear.

Wilhelm shook his head. 'Too late,' he answered. 'You were too slow, Thomas.'

'How did you get in? Through the gate from Albion? Where's Maud?'

'Albion,' Wilhelm smiled. 'Such romantics, aren't they? And Maud – well, Thomas, I am claiming Maud's garden too. They're all mine, as I think you understand. They told you what happened.'

Thomas glanced into Karsch's hands. The seed, for so it must be, had entirely broken apart. Karsch moved his hands gently underneath this burgeoning vegetable growth as though it were a creature he was cradling and encouraging.

'They said you died,' Thomas said, his voice belligerent.

Wilhelm shrugged. 'And yet – here I am. Isn't that curious? So you see, they lied to you.'

'But you killed my grandmother,' Thomas said. 'And you killed Albert Constantine. Why did you do it?'

'A punishment,' Wilhelm said. 'Justice.' He moved his head, and the moonlight reflected on his glasses. Despite the calm demeanour, a skim of perspiration glittered on his skin.

'But I haven't wronged you,' Thomas continued. 'Why punish me? What have *I* done?' While his mouth worked on, his mind was busy on its own account. Where was Maud? How exactly – by what path – had Wilhelm come to Broceliande? Had he passed into Maud's garden through the library at Huntington? If so, had he overcome Miss Hudson and the formidable Lee? Or had one or other of them assisted him? Perhaps he had passed into Albion by a different route. There was a possibility he had an accomplice among the other members of the guild – Mrs Lawrence, Rupert Hegel – and perhaps they had granted him access to Albion and therefore Broceliande through their own garden. His mind whirred, weighing up the possibilities. Who should he trust? Clearly they had lied to him about the demise of Wilhelm Karsch, for here he was, standing in front of him. And where, where was Maud?

He could resist it no longer. The tendrils hung over Karsch's hands now, like long dry worms. Violet bands circled the pale roots. The questing tips reached the ground, like an animal's claws, which it used to pull itself entirely free of Karsch and over the ground towards Thomas.

'What is it?' Thomas began to panic, backing away from the plant-creature. It travelled swiftly, still growing, now thrusting out green spiky stalks, articulated like fingers.

'Call it off,' Thomas said, retreating through the bluebells. 'Whatever it is, stop it. Stop it!'

Karsch sighed. Plainly he would not waste any further time conversing with Thomas. He paid no heed to the boy's cries.

'I'm sorry,' Karsch said. 'I understand you are not to blame for what happened to me. But you are in my way now – you have taken the garden for yourself and I shall wrest it from you.' He kept his eyes fixed on the plant-creature, as though it were the strength of his will that kept it moving and growing. It pulled itself over the soil, still increasing in size, an accumulating wave of roots and spikes and leaves crawling and rolling faster and faster.

Thomas ran backwards, overwhelmed by dread, afraid to turn his back on his pursuer. His feet were awkward on the uneven ground; his legs felt clumsy and heavy. The plant-creature moved towards him, inexorable, impersonal, a blind force of nature over which Karsch had somehow gained control. Then Thomas fell, his feet failing to negotiate the root of a beech tree. He landed heavily on his hip and shoulder, a hot dart of pain shooting through his wrist as it was crushed under his body. He looked up – and in a moment the creature was upon him, all over him. Thomas shrieked. The cold roots slid over his skin, beneath his clothes, around his limbs. The sharp tips pressed into his flesh. Within a few seconds it had swarmed all over him. Roots twisted in spirals around his arms and legs. A fat stem circled his neck, almost cutting off his breath. Then it tightened, slowly and inexorably, every time he moved.

Karsch stepped closer. He stared down at Thomas, his eyes cold.

'If you keep very still, the roots may relax a little,' Karsch said. 'Fight it, struggle, and it will tighten again.' He looked away again, through the dim wood, and continued to speak. His tone was level, mildly curious – like a lecturer before a class of students.

'It is a most remarkable plant, is it not? I don't suppose your tutors described it to you. There are carnivorous plants, Thomas. The Venus fly-trap, for example – perhaps you have heard of that? Or pitcher plants, which capture insects in rolled-up leaves and slowly digest them. They evolve in environments where the soil is thin and short of nutrients, compelling the most vigorous species to develop an alternative method of feeding.'

Thomas struggled to control his movements. His wrist throbbed with pain. Even the rise and fall of his chest as he breathed caused the plant to tighten. He fought to suppress panic; taking slow, shallow breaths so the roots shouldn't throttle him altogether. It wasn't enough, though. A shortage of oxygen was leaving him faint. A red haze rose in front of his eyes. He felt his mind begin to drift. Still Karsch continued to speak.

'This variety, the most impressive carnivore in the plant kingdom, originates in South America. It was never so large nor so mobile, of course. In its natural state it is no larger than my hand and has to wait for its prey to crawl onto it – small snakes, beetles, mice – before the tendrils close over the victim. Then it releases digestive juices from the mauve bands you can see on the tendrils there. It has taken me some years to develop that modest Peruvian original into the voracious lion that has you in its maw, Thomas. Certainly it would not have been possible without the powers of this miraculous glass garden. But I hope you are impressed with the fruit of my labour. I am certainly very happy with it.

'Of course in the natural world any prey is usually throttled before it is digested, but a human? Well, humans have more self-control than many animals and insects. If you lie still enough, it may begin to digest you first.'

243

Thomas was beginning to pass out of consciousness. Karsch's voice seemed far away now. The hurt in his wrist was distant, a pain belonging to somebody else. The tendrils tightened again around his throat and chest. Even fear began to melt away as the small, bright room of his mind began to shrink and dim . . .

Then, far away, he saw Karsch waving his arm. He let out a low cry – fear, distress. Thomas strained his eyes to see. A ribbon of pale phantasmal material had manifested in front of Karsch's face. This transparent white streamer undulated around him. Karsch staggered back, into the bluebells, still waving his arm. Thomas could make no sense of what was happening, but the problem no longer seemed to concern him. Miles away, thorns pressed into his skin and began to sting. He closed his eyes.

'Thomas!' a girl's voice hissed in his ear. 'Wake up, Thomas. Why are you lying there? Why have you given up?' It was the voice of the revenant. Briefly lifting his eyelids he could see her, translucent, standing over him. Only her mouth seemed solid, her lips and teeth dyed with blood.

'This is your garden, Thomas. You are master here, not Wilhelm Karsch. The garden accepted you and now you are the creator in Broceliande. Karsch can only take it from you once you are dead.'

Thomas had awareness enough to know he would be dead very soon. And how could he fight it? He could barely breathe, the plant held him in iron bands. Its digestive poisons had already been injected into his skin . . . strange vegetable dreams were crowding in the shadows at the edge of his mind. Images of soil and death, of dark harvests and unnatural growth.

His grandmother urged him to fight. But what should he do? Karsch had moved away, still batting at the miasma of supernatural white gauze floating around his face. Perhaps drawn by its light, half a dozen moths were dancing about Karsch's head. They seemed to leave trails of dust behind them, pathways hanging in the air. Thomas closed his eyes. He was the creator in Broceliande. The garden had tuned itself to his mind, his memories and imagination. But he was young and untutored – he had no idea how to use the glass garden's creative powers and he was partially asphyxiated already, his mind beginning to blur. Help me, Grandmother, he thought to himself. I don't want to die. Tell me what to do.

When he opened his eyes again the revenant was floating above him. Her face was above his, staring down. Her ghostly hair drifted in slow Medusa coils, as though she were under water. He couldn't speak or move – could only ask the question in his mind and hope that she heard it. How could he fight Karsch? How to escape the plant that had him bound and poisoned like a midge in a web? By effort of will he resisted the lure of unconsciousness and fastened his attention on escape. What could he summon up to help him? An image flashed into his mind. He had to be quick.

Straining to open his lips, to find the breath to speak, he said: 'Grandmother, the black goat. Open the orchard gate and bring it here.'

Above him, the revenant smiled. She melted away – like snow fallen into water. Thomas felt the shadows close around his mind again. The plant's poisons, carried by his blood, were creeping into his brain. The garden dissolved from his awareness and he fainted away.

How long was he unconscious? Impossible to tell. Moments or minutes? The first thing he heard was a rip, as though a dense fabric had been torn across. Then a crunch, another rip, and a hearty munching. The pressure eased from Thomas's throat. He opened his eyes, gasping for breath. There it was – the black goat from the orchard but repeated six times. Six identical black goats all feeding voraciously on his plant captor, cheerfully tearing it apart, grinding it to pulp between their teeth as though it were the most delicious meal they had ever eaten. Under such an onslaught the plant grew slack. Its upright stems were plucked and consumed. The coils about Thomas's arms and legs fell away leaving long, red snake-like welts on his skin. Puncture marks, like blisters, rose at intervals along the welts.

'Where's Karsch? Does he think I'm dead? Where has he gone?' Thomas pushed away the remains of the plant and scrambled unsteadily to his feet. His wrist hurt. His skin itched and stung. He addressed the revenant.

She raised her white hand. 'He's still in the garden,' she said. 'He's making his way to the stone in the orchard so that he can claim the garden in the instant that you die. Of course, when that instant doesn't come, when it doesn't reach out for him, he will realise you are still alive and come after you again.'

Thomas's thoughts turned over. 'What about Maud? What did he do to her?' He was afraid Karsch had come through the garden of Albion. Perhaps he had loosed a murderous plant on her too, so that he might also claim Albion for himself.

'I have to find Maud,' he said. 'I'll unlock the gate into her garden and try and find her.' The image rose in his mind's eye, of Maud lying bound, throttled, poisoned. The revenant opened its mouth to speak but Thomas was already running. His skin cried out, a million tiny bites, as he stretched his legs to leap over clumps of bluebells. The wooden gate was in front of him, filling the narrow gothic arch in the ivied wall. He reached in his pocket for the key and fumbled with the lock. The revenant was beside him again, the tumble of emerald leaves on the wall visible through her white dress.

'Wait, Thomas,' she whispered. 'Leave Maud. You have to face Karsch. You can defeat him here. This is your place, and I can help you.'

Thomas pushed the gate open, revealing the view of downlands and the sea. But he hesitated for a moment; was this the right path to take? Should he follow his grandmother's advice? But what if Karsch had come into Broceliande through Albion, as he suspected? He thought of Maud again, his strange little friend, perhaps gasping for breath, choking, waiting helplessly for rescue. Ignoring the ropes of pain around his limbs he stepped into the garden of Albion and drew a deep breath of clean, sea-swept air.

But where – where was Maud?

And how would he find her? The garden of Albion appeared so large, an expanse of hills and shoreline, of valleys where patches of woodland nestled, of sheep-grazed, windswept uplands, one topped by a stone circle. But Thomas knew this distance was illusory, that the garden was as large – and as small – as his own Broceliande. Unfortunately he was a stranger here. He didn't know the lie of the land and neither did the garden know him.

Thomas took a deep breath and began to run down the hill towards the shoreline. He comforted himself with the thought that while he didn't know where to go, the nature of the garden would still be the same – a place of dreams and desires where wishes might become manifest. Perhaps if he longed to see Maud, the garden would show him the way. He stepped onto a narrow white-chalk path and allowed gravity to draw him down and down, running to a cliff-top and a view through clouds of briars to the beautiful cobalt, creased-silk sea.

A cliff path parted the hedge of briars just to the right. Thomas began the descent, past tussocks of dry grass and trembling pink thrift. The way was narrow and stony, with occasional drops where he had to jump or steep slopes where he had to slide, sending dust and white rubble tumbling. Then at last he was on the pebbled beach itself. He rested for a moment, sweating and out of breath. He wiped his face with the palm of his hand and stared across the beach to the sea. How inviting it looked, small aquamarine waves turning over and over on a seam of sand beyond the maze of large, smooth pebbles, whale grey, chalk white, faded blue. He shaded his eyes and turned a circle on the spot, scanning the horizon. The sea one way, the cliffs and hills the other. Far away the stone circle was still visible. Is that where he should have gone? Where is Maud? he wondered. I have to find her. Take me to her.

No immediate answer leaped into his head. No helpful goat or revenant stepped up to show the way. Instead the waves continued their steady rise and retreat, the water curling again and again. Thomas sighed. He could waste no more time. Karsch would be after him soon enough, angry at his escape and eager to take his life so he could claim the garden. And Karsch would know where Maud was – where, perhaps, he had left her. Thomas looked to right and left. The beach was shaped like a quarter-moon, backed by the white cliffs, the sea filling its mouth. Which way to go? No one direction tugged his instinct. Neither direction offered any promise. Perhaps he was entirely wrong. What if she was elsewhere in the garden, or out of the garden altogether? Thomas hopped from one foot to another. He had been rash to come here. He should have attempted an escape from Broceliande as soon as he'd overcome Karsch's hungry plant. Then he would have found out what had happened to Lee and Miss Hudson, and they could have helped him confront Karsch. (But the thought flickered in his mind, these two had told him Karsch was dead and buried – they had lied to him. Who could he trust now, but Maud?)

'Maud!' he cried out, cupping his hands around his mouth to enhance the sound. 'Maud, where are you?' A seagull wheeled over his head. The sea shushed on its piece of sand. The blue sky burned over his head. With a sigh, Thomas made a random choice and set off to the left. He had to keep moving now. Karsch would be on his trail. It had been foolish to shout and draw attention to himself.

The beach was difficult to walk on at any speed. He hopped from pebble to pebble, keeping close to the foot of the cliff. The illusory sun beat down. Far away on the curved horizon the expanse of sea dissolved into a blue mist. He noticed strange plants growing on the pale soil that clung to nooks in the cliffs. Trailing flowers, stumpy shrubs with succulent leaves, dry stalks with fleshy pods. Presumably Blake cultivated these, plants for a Garden of Love.

To the east of the bay the pebbles gave way to smooth iron-grey slabs of rock with numerous rust-coloured pockmarks. Some of these depressions were only the size of a fingertip. Others formed large rock pools, lined with smaller pebbles, where gardens of sea plants flourished in the salty, sun-warmed water. Thomas hopped around them, careful not to slip on the rock. The rock gardens were beautiful – the underwater weeds burning with colour – russet, amber, jade – where miniature sea creatures swam or scurried over the sand as Thomas's shadow fell across their contained world. Despite his sense of urgency, Thomas slowed down and marvelled as a coral-coloured crab drew itself into the shelter of an ivory fossil shaped like a multi-fingered hand. This giant slab of iron-grey rock possessed many layers, variously eroded by millennia beneath the sea. Here and there Thomas had to step up or down, and one stratum had broken or buckled, revealing another layer underneath where gatherings of limpets were glued. It was like nothing Thomas, land boy, had ever seen before.

Then, suddenly, he skidded to a halt, all power melting from his muscles, the coordination of his movement coming apart at the seams. Shock washed over him. A host of words rose into his throat and choked there, jammed, impossible to move. He shook his head, trying to make sense of what he was seeing. He swallowed, hard, then croaked: 'Maud?'

At first all he recognised was the shape of her face, just below the surface of the water in one of the larger rock pools. She was lying in the rock pool, entirely submerged, her eyes open and staring. Her black hair floated like ink around her face. Her pale lips were closed, her white dress wrapped around with clinging weed – fine, tentacled straggles the colour of ox blood.

'Maud?' Thomas whispered. He was shaking now. Maud was so utterly still, except that stray fronds of hair slowly moved, disturbed by the stirring of the water. The scene rose up in his mind – Karsch holding her under, her fights and screams (for Maud would not have yielded easily, she would have kicked and bitten) and then her panicked struggles, choking, taking in the cold sea water till her life ebbed away. Till she was drowned.

Still Thomas stared. All will, all passion had fallen away. The desire to save this strange, precious girl had fuelled his escape, his flight from Broceliande into Albion. So what was left for him now? His gaze remained fixed on her face. How peaceful she looked, another jewel in the glittering treasure chest of the rock pool, among the lumps of pearl and lapis and beryl-coloured stones, the silk bladder-wrack and velvet anemones. She was pale as alabaster, the tracery of royal purple veins still visible through the translucent skin on her throat and temples. A drowned princess from a fairy tale. An enchanted mermaid . . .

Thomas looked away, to the horizon. He didn't feel anything yet – except a numb sense of breakage and a premonition of the grief and anger soon to come. Slowly sensation returned to his body and he moved himself, heavy and tired, to the side of the rock pool. He stepped into the water. Should he move her? She looked so calm and beautiful in the water, but he couldn't leave her body here. Would an illusory tide fetch her, conjured fishes nibble at her flesh? He had to take her from the garden to the real world, where she would be buried and mourned.

Thomas slid his arms under Maud's body. Cold water soaked through his clothes and chilled his skin. Sand swirled beneath his feet, so that clouds obscured the jewellery box perfection of the rock pool. Weighted with water, Maud was heavy. Thomas struggled to lift her, the trailing skirts and petticoats holding her fragile body in the pool. Clumsily he raised her head and shoulders clear of the water. Her black hair hung back in streaming clumps, as he cradled her face. He dragged her out and onto the side. Black as ebony, white as snow. Thomas leaned forward and wiped threads of hair from her face.

Bending over, his face close to hers, something stayed him. What was it he could smell? Amid the perfume of the sea, the odour of weed and stone, he detected something else. He moved his face again, breathing in, searching for this elusive scent. There it was – a thread of shrill citrus, an undertone of bitterness. Like burnt lemon rind, perhaps. Puzzled, Thomas put his finger on Maud's lower lip and drew her mouth open. He sniffed it. Yes, here the scent of citrus was strong. He studied her neck and wrists, her hands and fingernails. His earlier imagining of Maud's struggle with Karsch had not been correct. There were no bruises or scratches, no damage to her fingers, no blood under her nails. No, Maud hadn't drowned. Karsch had poisoned her. An image of the Poison Garden rose in his mind. He remembered the warning of the revenant, his grandmother also killed by poison – and his thoughts flew to Mrs Lawrence. Was she helping Karsch after all? But she loved Maud – why would she allow him to poison her?

Thinking of Karsch, Thomas remembered that he was also in danger. He scanned the beach, Maud still on his lap, but could see no pursuer as yet. What should he do now?

'She isn't dead, Master Reiter.' The words, out of nowhere, broke on the air like balls of glass. Thomas turned around, stunned. Fear crawled over him.

'Who's there? Who is it?' Fear made his voice loud and strange. He could see no-one but the voice was so close.

'This is my place now. I'm not some green boy from the country. I hold it, shape it. Do you think I need to plod its weary paths like you?'

Thomas seethed with fury. 'Karsch!' he shouted. 'Where are you? Show yourself!' He laid Maud gently on the rock and jumped to his feet. 'Why can't I see you? What do you mean she isn't dead?' Despite himself, despite his fear, a faint hope shone. Was Karsch telling the truth?

'You were a fool to come here, Thomas. You have only the smallest inkling of the potential within the creative spheres. Within this space I am master. I create and form it. I shape it around myself. You see, I claimed it a long time ago. Maud had no hope of making it her own. And the box was kept safely for me for four years while I waited and planned the retaking of the rest of my property.'

'Mrs Lawrence?' Thomas said. 'She's been helping you? But this was Maud's garden and Maud is her ward. Why would you kill her?'

'*Ach*, tut, Thomas. I told you. Maud isn't dead. She certainly looks dead – anyone would be fooled, even a fine chemist or a doctor. But that isn't truly the case.'

Thomas shivered. He stared at Maud. She wasn't moving, wasn't breathing. When she'd lain in his arms he'd detected no heartbeat. Could she truly be alive? Again hope quivered in his chest, but he tried not to acknowledge it. Surely Karsch was lying to him, adding to his torment.

'Where are you?' Thomas said again, his voice a little lower as he fought to regain control of himself. No use letting Karsch goad him into frightened rage. He had to keep his head clear.

He became aware of a tall shadow beside him, a dark shape seemingly drawn on the air. As the shadow became more distinct, the beach, the cliffs, became less so, fading away in a sudden twilight, sucked away like smoke, until Thomas and the shadow were standing instead in a soft, black space much like the dome at the centre of the gardens were the guild had met for tea. After a moment a new scene took shape, a narrow cloistered corridor with a stone floor and arches to one side overlooking a courtyard garden covered with snow. Thomas looked behind and ahead, to see the corridor ended in darkness in either direction. Maud had disappeared with the beach and the sea.

'Shall we walk?' Karsch was fully present now, dressed in a long white robe like a monk, appropriate to the cloister.

'You tried to kill me in Broceliande,' Thomas said. 'Why don't you kill me now? What are you waiting for?' His voice was fierce but the question frightened him. Karsch clearly had the power here.

'I am sorry, Thomas. I have no choice. While you are alive I cannot take control of your grandmother's garden. You were clever to escape the first time, but coming here was not an intelligent choice at all. It is a pleasure for me to kill the others, for what they did to me. But it isn't a pleasure to kill you. Only an unpleasant necessity.'

Karsch stopped walking. In his hand he held a short pistol, which even at this extreme moment struck Thomas as incongruous, since he was still dressed in his monk's outfit. A flicker of regret crossed Karsch's cold face as he raised the pistol and pointed it at Thomas's chest. Thomas closed his eyes. Blood roared in his ears and he sent out one last, desperate plea for salvation . . .

The moment stretched. The expected detonation, noise, impact didn't occur. Thomas kept his eyes squeezed shut, hanging in darkness, waiting, waiting for Karsch to act.

He opened his eyes. They were standing on the beach again. Maud lay on the rock slab at his feet.

Karsch was standing in front of him, but he wasn't moving. The pistol was still in his hand, aimed and ready to fire, but he couldn't pull the trigger because a thin silver blade was pressed to his throat, tight enough to break the skin. And holding the knife, elegant as always, was Karsch's one-time admirer. It was Rupert Hegel.

In a low voice, almost caressing, Hegel spoke to Karsch in German. Karsch's face tensed and his eyes blazed. Hegel pressed the blade closer and a bead of blood emerged from Karsch's throat. Karsch dropped the pistol.

Hegel sighed. He muttered something further in German and then said: 'Thomas, quick, pick it up and give it to me.'

Thomas hesitated for a moment. He felt detached from his body, a delay between the order of his mind and the obedience of his limbs.

'Quick!' Hegel repeated. So he stooped down, conscious of

Karsch's gaze boring into him, scooped up the pistol and handed it over. Hegel whipped the blade away from Karsch's throat and instead levelled the pistol at his captive.

A quick conversation followed, between Karsch and Hegel, which Thomas could not understand. Karsch was loud and venomous, seething with fury. Hegel's tone was more level but Thomas could see how he struggled with his emotions. The hand holding the pistol was shaking.

Karsch took several deep breaths and calmed himself. Then he began to speak again, his tone more soothing. Evidently he was extending some kind of appeal. But Hegel shook his head. Without taking his eyes from Karsch he said in English: 'Thomas, we must leave this place right away. There is a gateway that will take us to Nineveh.'

Karsch, his face tense with irritation, rattled out another stream of incomprehensible German. Hegel flinched, but he remained resolute. In English, in a voice as cold as ice, he said: 'Even you are not perfect, Wilhelm, and this is not a clockwork world, as you should know. Nehemiah Blake was our friend. His body may have died, but he is still a part of this world of Albion. He stands in opposition to you. He appeared to me, in the dome at the centre of the gardens, and unlocked the gateway into Albion so I could pass through.'

Hegel issued instructions to Karsch.

'What about Maud?' Thomas said. 'Karsch said she isn't dead. Is he telling the truth?'

Hegel nodded. 'He is. We have the means to revive her. Just leave her where she lies for now.'

A surge of relief flooded Thomas and he bent down to touch the side of Maud's face.

'But she's so cold. She isn't breathing.'

'Still, she is alive. Come now, we have to go.' Hegel didn't take his eyes from Karsch for a moment. He was afraid of him.

'Where is the gateway?' Thomas asked.

'The stone circle on the hill-top.' More orders in German. Karsch turned smartly and began to walk across the beach. Hegel kept close behind him. Thomas followed on, tired and aching. He kept looking back to where Maud lay by the pool, her hair fanned on the shining rock.

Three

They stood in Hegel's Perfume Garden, where the sound of falling water played and bloated roses blossomed. Karsch stood against the wall, his arms outstretched, bound against the brickwork. Cords from some vinous plant had thrust from the soil to pin and tie him. Once he was held tight, Hegel's paranoid vigilance relaxed a little. Still he was tense, unable to be entirely still, unwilling to take his eyes off the captive.

'What about Maud?' Thomas nagged. He was also afraid, not trusting the bonds restraining Karsch, fearing he might yet have another trick to play on them.

Hegel exclaimed in German. Then he said: 'Be quiet, Thomas! Do not think about Maud now.' Hegel paced up and down, as though unsure how to proceed. Thomas knew he should be silent so that Hegel could think but he couldn't contain himself.

'Where are the others?' he piped up. 'Lee and Miss Hudson. And what about Mrs Lawrence? Did you know she was helping Karsch? She gave him Blake's garden!'

Hegel stopped his pacing. Karsch didn't speak, only stared grimly.

'Mrs Lawrence is dead,' Hegel said. 'For all her helping him, he killed her too. Poison, of course. At her house – the servants called me. She was sitting in her parlour by the fire. There beside her, a cup and saucer, a pot of Bergamot tea. The servants told me a German had come to visit, and when they described him I realised who it must have been.' He looked at Karsch, into his eyes. 'How could it be? I wondered. How could it be Wilhelm Karsch? Karsch is dead. I played an elegy over his grave . . . I left the old woman in her armchair and ran home.' He was talking entirely to Karsch now, as though he had forgotten the question came from Thomas. 'I knew Lee and Miss Hudson were taking the children into the gardens, so they could claim them,' he said. 'So I found the gateway from Nineveh to Albion. It was locked of course, but as I stood before it the door swung open and standing there, Nehemiah Blake, as thin and transparent as a scarf of mist. Where is Karsch? I said. Where are the children? And Blake, a ghost in the material of his garden, swept me up and set me down, soundless . . . where I could take a blade to the murderer's throat.'

'Blake killed my son!' Karsch said. Thomas's mind flew back to the night in his grandmother's garden when Blake had wrestled with the young man in the bluebells . . . that was Karsch's son? Of course, of course. There was a family likeness, though Thomas had been thrown off the track by the young man's accent. His mother, presumably, had been English.

'Rupert, Thomas.' Lee emerged from the darkness, with Miss Hudson. She put her hand on Thomas's shoulder, in a gesture of affirmation and comfort though she didn't speak to him. Instead they stared, the last three guild members, at Karsch pinned against the wall. Lee shook his head, as though he couldn't credit what he was seeing. So who was lying? What was the truth?

'I saw you dead,' Lee said. 'I buried you, Karsch, with my own hands.'

Karsch stared coldly, his gaze moving from Lee to Rupert and to Miss Hudson. His face filled with anger.

'I wasn't dead,' he said. 'I wasn't *dead*. How could you have been so stupid? So cruel!'

Thomas's thoughts flew to Maud, lying under the salt water of the rock pool, without breath or heartbeat, and the odour of burnt lemon in her mouth. Was there a connection?

They were silent for a moment, the three. Then Hegel piped up.

'I went to see Mrs Lawrence. She has helped him. She gave him Blake's garden after his death four years ago.'

Still Miss Hudson and Lee continued to stare at Karsch. Hegel nodded.

'Go on,' Lee urged. 'Tell us what happened to you. Tell us what you did.' His voice was low and mellow, but beneath it Thomas sensed the big man's anger, barely under control.

Karsch waited a moment before replying, as though composing his thoughts. Then he said, very cool: 'There is a rare herb, once found in northern Europe, called Grace in Death. It is a very unassuming little plant, a low stem, flat, curved leaves, and a yellow flower. A perennial, which grows only on broken soil and only where the dead have been buried – humans or animals. It is thus a habitué of graveyards and necropolises. It was known and developed by the Guild of Medical Herbalists for its effects on the living body – bringing on a death-like stupor, suspending all the signs of life. No breath, no heat, no pulse. In fact, this isn't entirely true. There is still a pulse, but so slow, maybe only one beat in an hour, but of course this would be easy to overlook if you didn't know the truth.'

Miss Hudson and Lee looked at one another. A horrible truth was dawning.

'The poison in the coffin we opened,' Lee said. 'That was an extraction from this herb? That was Grace in Death.' He placed his hand on his forehead.

'My God, you were still alive,' he said. 'We buried you alive.'

Miss Hudson paled. They stared at him, Thomas and the three guild members. Karsch continued to speak.

'I was paralysed, utterly unable to speak or move, not even to blink. I was alive when you left me in the grave, lying on top of the broken coffin. Trapped inside the prison of my useless body, I was awake when you covered me in soil. I was conscious when you played an elegy over the grave.

'Yes, yes, I heard it, far away. The music you wrote for me, Rupert, because you were so fond of me. What a haunting piece! And yes, it did haunt me, for the years I lay underground in the dark, that piece of music embedded in my mind, playing over and over again.'

Thomas was shivering. Karsch's account filled him with horror. To be buried! To lie in the dark and cold unable to see or move, weighed down by earth for days and months and years! He could imagine nothing worse.

The others were quiet too, stunned and appalled at what they had done. Lee shook his head.

'How long?' he said.

'Eleven years.'

'How did you survive so long? With no nourishment. Did your body not decay? How did you get out?' Miss Hudson, tremulous with shock and emotion, bubbled over with questions.

Karsch grinned. Thomas noticed for the first time the glint of madness in his face, a thread no doubt embroidered in his mind during those long, unendurable years in the ground. Karsch tugged at his bonds, and then, strangely level, he told them what he had endured.

*

The poison worked through his brain and blood, inducing in him a condition similar to that of the Indian spiritual men who achieved remarkable control of their breathing and heart rates through long years of discipline and meditation. The state was similar to hibernation, when animals escape the privations of winter by sinking into a deep sleep, their metabolism slows, and they spend months in a trance, without need of food or water, every bodily function slowed to a low level. A hibernating creature doesn't decay as it sleeps, and neither did Karsch, lying under the ground. His stupor was deeper by far than a winter hibernation but his body ticked on, slowly, slowly. He lay in the dark, unable to open his eyes. He drifted off into long mental wanderings, interspersed by dreams. From time to time he rose to consciousness, like a swimmer reaching the surface of a bottomless black lake, when he would be overwhelmed by the horror of his situation and his inability to make so much as a move to alter it. Then the violin elegy would revolve in his head, the prologue to his long torment, until his mind, trapped and walled in, boiled over with rage and lust for revenge.

And so it went on, and on. Surely he couldn't survive for ever? Although his body was functioning at the lowest possible level, it would starve in the end. Or he would age – but so slowly – and die as any other mortal creature did. He longed for death, for an escape from his burial. It was beyond endurance. How could a human mind withstand this? But he had withstood it, somehow. Karsch had clung on, keeping an unbroken hold on his desire for life, and his need to exact revenge on the supposed friends stupid enough to bury and leave him.

Perhaps he would have spent decades underground. Perhaps he would have died, except that one of the guild members created a cemetery garden, where she cultivated many varieties of poison. And, one day, she discovered the herb called Grace in Death. It was Mrs Lawrence, of course. Always the most secretive member of the guild, she began her own private research, poring over books and manuscripts at the library on the uses of this particular poison. It was used as a medicine, when ancient Briton warriors were injured far from home, to relieve their agonies and preserve their bodies until healing could begin. Would-be magicians and witches had employed Grace in Death to create the illusion of resurrection. The ruthless had used it as a punishment, walling up their prisoners in the dark, just as Karsch had been unwittingly buried. But as the centuries passed, its use fell away. A changing climate halted its natural growth, and soon it would grow only in the protection of the guild's magical gardens.

Making her researches, learning of the herb's uses, Mrs Lawrence had a chilling insight. She recalled the story Lee and Blake had told, of the poison that had leaked from the grave and its lemon odour. What if the trap in the coffin contained a distillation of Grace in Death, held in a volatile liquid primed to evaporate and release its poison if the coffin was breached by thieves? What if Karsch were still alive, paralysed under the ground? The old records explained how to brew up an antidote, using the roots of the same herb, pulverised and boiled to a concentrate. So she cultivated Grace in Death in Arcadia, her necropolis garden, tested its efficacy on animals, and then, filled no doubt with a terrible dread, she returned to the churchyard where Karsch had been buried so long before.

Why didn't she tell the other guild members? Why not share the burden of this terrible secret? Perhaps even then she had an inkling how this might work to her advantage. Karsch was brilliant – the best of them all. There was potential for manipulation. How grateful he would be, to his saviour. Maybe there was some way this situation could be beneficial to her. So Mrs Lawrence acted alone. She made inquiries at the fringes of the London criminal underworld, the world to which she had belonged for much of her life, and hired two reliable, discreet assistants to open the grave.

Karsch, lying underground, felt the upheaval of turf and soil. His mind was in turmoil, rousing itself to consciousness after so long dreaming and drifting. Slowly, slowly, the weight of earth was lifted from his body. He heard voices. A man carefully lowered himself into the open grave and cautiously cleared away the final covering of dirt from Karsch's face and body. A rough hand tugged his mouth open and a searing liquid trickled over his cold tongue and down his throat.

The awakening wasn't instant. It took several hours for his comatose body to ingest and circulate the reviving liquor. As soon as they'd forced the curative down Karsch's throat, Mrs Lawrence's men half lifted, half dragged him out of the ground. This wasn't so difficult – he had wasted away, his body slowly feeding on itself, burning the very barest amount of energy to keep it alive. They laid him out on a horse blanket and Karsch finally opened his eyes to see a huge grey-and-white moon sailing over the horizon, in an ocean of stars. One of the hired men raised a lantern to see better how Karsch had fared. And they blenched, these hard men, used to shocking spectacles. How appalling a sight he presented them. His skin was dead white after so many years in the dark. His slowly disintegrating clothes had protected him somewhat but still his body had been damaged by the damp and the gnawing of soil dwelling creatures. He was marked with boils and infections, particularly on his face and hands. One of the men crossed himself. The other rolled

Karsch in the blanket. Together they dumped him in the back of a cart and trotted through the night to a remote cottage on the moors Mrs Lawrence had secured. She was waiting for him, her sleeves rolled up, prepared to clean and nurse and heal him after the long years of torment.

After a day and a night, the paralysis had left him but it took many weeks and months to repair his damaged body, to rebuild wasted muscles and regain strength and vigour. All the while Mrs Lawrence fed him poisonous stories about the other guild members, the swiftness of their forgetting Karsch, their failure to realise what they had done, their boasting of the guild's achievements with no mention of Karsch's pivotal role. And Karsch, always obsessive, and primed with the lust to punish those who had made him suffer so, needed little encouragement to plan out his long, careful campaign.

One day, six months after his rescue, Mrs Lawrence brought Karsch two unexpected visitors. One was his son George. Many years ago Karsch had kept an English actress as a mistress and George, now twenty-four, was the son of this union. George, tall and blond like his father, had long assumed Wilhelm to be dead. George had married four years before, but his young bride, who had hair the colour of a crow's wing, had died giving birth to a daughter – a pale, unpromising little creature called Maud.

So Wilhelm Karsch and his son George learned all they could of the guild and the gardens, using Mrs Lawrence's Arcadia to grow and nurture plants and poisons. Karsch was in no hurry now. He had time enough to study, to cultivate new herbs and fruits, to acquire mastery over them and the powers they conferred.

Augusta was his first victim – except that plans went awry

when George tried to take control of her garden and Karsch lost his son. He was devastated and withdrew once again into his studies. Periodically a paralysing illness came over him, the after-effects of Grace in Death and the years spent underground. But his ambition returned and spurred on by Mrs Lawrence, he resumed his campaign for them to gain control of all the gardens. It was Mrs Lawrence who organised Albert Constantine's murder, tugging again at her criminal connections for someone bold enough to carry out such a public assassination. And in the meantime, she kept her counsel, reported back to Karsch the guild's every deliberation, and allowed him to take control of Blake's garden, Albion. This was her mistake, of course. Once he had a garden of his own Karsch didn't need his protector any longer. His ambition was boundless and once Mrs Lawrence was dead he claimed Arcadia too, her Poison Garden.

Karsch grinned. They stared at him, Lee, Miss Hudson, Hegel and Thomas. Thomas interwove what Karsch had told them with what he already knew. Maud was Karsch's granddaughter. Did she realise this?

The others were silent. Miss Hudson staggered slightly, but Lee put out his arm to steady her. Hegel's gaze was fixed on Karsch but his lips trembled. He rubbed his hand nervously over the scars on his face.

'He is insane,' Lee said in a low voice.

'Who wouldn't be?' Miss Hudson answered. Her voice wavered. 'To endure what he endured. How could any of us emerge from that with a clear mind? And we did that to him. What worse could be imagined?'

'We didn't know,' Lee said. 'We had no idea. He was dead!

I saw it with my own eyes, I felt for his pulse and there was none.'

'You are right, Mr Lee, we didn't know, but still we are responsible,' Hegel stated. Although Karsch was just in front of them, they spoke to each other as though he couldn't hear them. The revelation had broken them – shattered them to pieces. How could they carry the burden of what they had done, however inadvertently?

'We were careless and afraid,' Miss Hudson said. 'We should have taken his body back to London, not hastily buried it to protect ourselves. Perhaps then his true condition would have become evident.'

Against the wall, Karsch observed them coldly. But Thomas strode up to him.

'Does Maud know she's your granddaughter?' he said.

Karsch didn't reply. He wouldn't even look at Thomas, instead keeping his attention on the last three guild members. Thomas looked over his shoulder towards them and said: 'He killed my grandmother and he colluded in the death of Mr Constantine. No matter what you did, he's a murderer.'

Still they stared. Like three broken toys, as though their joints had gone awry. Thomas felt his fury rising. He wanted to shake them, to wake them up.

'He poisoned my grandmother!' he shouted. 'And what about Maud? We have to get the medicine to wake her up again.' He ran to Lee, grabbed his arm and tried to drag him away from Karsch but the big American simply shook him off.

'What are we going to do?' Thomas yelled. 'What shall we do with him? I want you to take him to the police! I want him arrested!'

Miss Hudson shook her head then, a fragile old lady. 'Oh no, we can't do that,' she said. 'How would we explain it? How could the truth ever be told? The guild manages its own affairs. It has always done so, through all the centuries of its existence.'

Thomas stamped his foot in anger and frustration. He strode over to Karsch, still pinned against the wall.

'You tried to kill me,' he said, bunching and loosening his fists. Rage burned inside him, urging him to strike out. But Karsch, witnessing his fury, simply leaned his head back against the bricks and laughed.

'What a little firebrand,' he said. 'Just like Augusta! She was very fierce, you know.'

Thomas was provoked beyond endurance. He spun around and slammed his fist into Karsch's stomach. The German winced but continued to laugh.

'Thomas, Thomas!' At least this attack woke Lee to action. He stepped forward and pulled Thomas away. He kept a tight grip on the boy's shoulder.

'That isn't going to get us anywhere,' he said. 'We have to think about this – all of us. We have to work out the best thing to do.'

They unbound Karsch and together left the garden, to emerge in Hegel's London home. Once Karsch was locked in a secure upper room, Lee returned to Albion to fetch Maud. Miss Hudson and Thomas travelled through the city to Mrs Lawrence's house.

The ancient woman, Lucy, the quiet creature Thomas remembered from his first visit, ushered them into the house.

'You've come to see her,' she whispered. 'The coffin's in the parlour. It hasn't been closed yet, if you wish to pay your respects.'

Miss Hudson nodded. 'Show us, please,' she said. Lucy, Mrs Lawrence's sister, mumbled inconsequentially about funeral arrangements she had to sort out and a stream of incoherent worries about her own future.

'And there's our little girl, our Maud. You won't want to keep her; what shall I do? Where shall she go?' She gestured them to precede her into the parlour. The mahogany coffin lay on a polished table, like a boat on a dark lake. Thomas looked down at the widow in black, her old face collapsed against the skull. Was she truly dead? Or was she, also, paralysed by Grace in Death? He glanced up at Miss Hudson.

'How do we know?' he said.

'We need to find the antidote she created. Perhaps that is the only way to be certain.'

Thomas felt a sudden clutch of panic. 'My grandmother,' he said. 'Did he use it to poison her too?'

Miss Hudson pursed her lips. 'I think not. You saw the revenant, Thomas. It told you that she was dead and how she was killed. It is my suspicion that even Karsch couldn't sentence any one of us to the horror we inflicted on him.'

She asked the servant to take them to Mrs Lawrence's study, and there began the search for the remedy to Grace in Death. Ranks of thick glass bottles stood on the shelves lining the room. The shelves were closed behind glass doors. Stopped with glass or cork, labelled in the widow's looped handwriting, the bottles contained a multitude of colourful syrups and potions. Large jars held cargos of dried leaves, petals and seeds, or the lumpy stumps of roots. For Thomas it had the feel of a homecoming, as though he had stepped back into Constantine's shop.

'Help me, Thomas,' Miss Hudson urged, as she opened the doors and pushed among the bottles. He wasted no more time, putting his memories aside to rummage through Mrs Lawrence's feast of poisons for the liquid to wake the sleeping Maud. And he found it, at last, on a high shelf. The label read Grace in Death – the Recovery. The liquid was transparent but caught the winter sunlight as he lifted it down, so it flashed white. Without a word he held it out so Miss Hudson might see.

'We need the boxes too,' Miss Hudson said. 'See, on the table. There is Arcadia, the Poison Garden. Somewhere here we shall find Albert's box too. Now we know who was responsible for the burglary at his house.'

And so it proved. Miss Hudson found the ornate box tucked in the top drawer of a desk. The two visitors returned to the parlour.

'Give the bottle to me, Thomas. I'll do it,' she said. Miss Hudson used a pipette to suck a measure of the antidote from the bottle and squeezed it between the widow's thin, white lips. Thomas waited, appalled and intrigued in equal measure, but several minutes elapsed and the body didn't move.

'Karsch said it took time for the liquid to take effect,' he warned.

'You are quite right. But the funeral isn't for two days yet. That is time enough.' She frowned then, giving the body a look of hate. 'Evil old witch. Perhaps she deserves this, for betraying us. For killing Albert. When she realised what had happened she should have told us all. Perhaps we could have helped Karsch, instead of nurturing his anger.'

They looked at each other, Thomas and Miss Hudson. An evil act, however unintentionally done, had generated a long legacy of evil in return.

They hurried back to Hegel's house. Maud was lying on the sofa, beneath a blanket. Miss Hudson gave her the medicine and they all waited for her to wake up.

'Do you think she knew?' Thomas said. 'About Karsch? About Mrs Lawrence working with him for so long?'

'I don't think so,' Lee said. 'Why would Karsch have given her

269

Grace in Death otherwise? He didn't want to kill her or hurt her – she is his granddaughter after all. But he needed to keep her quiet for a time, to have her out of the way once she found out her garden had already been claimed.'

Thomas scowled. He was impatient for her to wake up, to know she would be well again. It didn't take so long. After twenty minutes her pulse began to quicken, and she took one short, convulsive gulp of air. She surfaced like a swimmer, her limbs thrashing, reaching out for light and safety.

'Maud! Oh Maud, I thought you were dead.' Thomas felt his eyes fill with tears, emotion overcoming him in a rising tide.

Maud looked right at him. Her face was full of mischief, laughter bubbling up.

'I know you did,' she said. 'I could hear you, you know. Wailing about my death by the side of the sea. I didn't know you cared for me so much.'

Thomas was taken aback. 'I . . . I wasn't. I don't, I mean, of course I care for you, Maud.'

She laughed again, an unexpected colour rising to her cheeks. Before he had a chance to retreat she threw her arms around his neck and gave him a hug.

They were sitting around the table in the dining room, the curtains drawn against the winter night. A fire burned in the hearth, spitting and cracking as stray drops of rain fell into the chimney. The room was warm and intimate as the five finished their meal and the desultory conversation lapsed into silence.

Louisa Hudson, Lee and Hegel were consumed by the knowledge of the suffering they had caused Karsch, inadvertent though it was. It ate at them, plagued their thoughts. And they would live with this for the rest of their lives. It would never go away.

Upstairs, locked away, Karsch waited. His imagined presence lingered among them, unspoken but on the minds of each one. What would they do with him?

Finally Lee stepped up, where the others waited and dithered. 'I could take him with me, back to America,' he said. 'We could let him free to make a new life. Don't we owe him something?'

'No!' Thomas jumped in. 'He's a killer! He's mad. You can't let him go. Think of what he has done! If you let him go, even in America, he'll kill again, I'm sure of it. Can't you see how insane he has become? And he will kill you.'

Hegel leaned back in his chair, pressing his fingertips into the surface of the table.

'The boy's right,' he said. 'We cannot risk letting him go. He is too dangerous. We could keep him locked up. Perhaps at Huntington Hall.'

Miss Hudson shuddered. 'It is possible,' she said. 'A prisoner for the rest of his life. That is a great responsibility. What if he should escape?'

'We could kill him,' Lee said. 'A poison – it wouldn't be difficult.'

'No!' Miss Hudson responded. 'There has been enough killing.'

Silence again. What should they do?

Maud, who had been sitting quietly, raised her head and said: 'I know what you should do.'

'What? What should we do?' Thomas demanded.

'You tell me he's my grandfather, yes? I don't want you to kill him. I don't think any one of us wants to be part of that. So he needs to be kept safe somewhere. A place he will never escape. Well, then, why don't we make the seven gardens whole again, send him inside, lock it in a box and hide it where no-one will ever, ever find it?'

They looked at one another, Lee, Hegel, Miss Hudson.

'But we shall lose our secret places,' Hegel said. 'We should lose the garden's powers – everything!'

They contemplated this loss, the three older guild members. Hegel looked stricken at the thought. Lee leaned his elbows on the table, his long hair falling forward over his shoulders.

'You are right, Rupert. But don't forget what's happened, and what we did. Perhaps we don't deserve them.'

Hegel looked at Miss Hudson. She was lost in thought. They waited for her to respond. At last, wrinkling her brow, she said: 'I think Maud is right. It is the best resolution. We will lose the garden, but we all have plants enough we have brought into the ordinary world. The gardens are powerful and dangerous. We took them on too lightly. I am also afraid Mrs Lawrence and Karsch corrupted the garden with their murderous ways. Perhaps it needs time to heal itself, to be balanced again. Perhaps it can heal Karsch too.'

Hegel paled, though a skim of sweat shined on his face. 'So, it is agreed?' His voice trembled. 'I know it is the right thing – but it is hard to do, to let them go.'

At midnight, London's churches tolled the hours, the iron tongues of numerous bells sounding out the end of one day, the beginning of another. The Guild of Medical Herbalists placed the seven boxes in a circle on the table. One by one, they opened them, these caskets of wonders. Albion, Broceliande, Arcadia, Nineveh, Tadmor, Xanadu and Acoma.

Lee sat at the head of the table, Karsch to his right. Then the others – Miss Hudson, Maud and Thomas. Maud kept staring at Karsch. It was as though she wanted to open him up and see what was inside. Her grandfather! Was there any family resemblance? Thomas searched for it in their faces.

Karsch was very still and self-contained. His hands lay calmly on the table, his body relaxed. He gave no impression of madness. The mania was a mask that might rise or subside at any given time, so Thomas was still wary. The sheer presence of the man generated shivers of anger which Thomas fought hard to suppress.

Candles burned on the long table, reflecting in the surfaces of the seven decorated boxes. Thomas sensed the power within them, the glass globes themselves like seeds capable of flowering with infinite worlds, worlds within worlds.

'You are in accord with the decision?' Hegel addressed Karsch. Hegel was nervous, though he tried to cover his feelings. Karsch raised his face and stared directly into Hegel's eyes.

'Yes,' Karsch said. 'It is entirely appropriate. It is what I always wanted. Yes, to possess the garden entirely. To be its master.' His eyes burned with a peculiar, intense light. No wonder Hegel was still afraid of him. Karsch possessed unshakeable self-belief – and this imbued him with extraordinary power.

'It will be forever,' Miss Hudson broke in. 'I don't know how long forever might be inside the glass seed – perhaps the length of your natural life, but it may be for much longer. Its generative powers are such that you may endure forever.'

Thomas shivered. Wasn't Karsch agreeing to, in effect, another live burial? Though his glass prison would offer endless opportunities to explore and create, an illusion of infinite space, and perhaps the company of its many previous visitors, in the form of revenants created by the hungry, fertile substance making up the mysterious dome. Then again, wasn't life itself – his own life – a burial if you were to look at it like that? Like Karsch in the dome, Thomas himself was trapped within the walls of his own mind, and the limits of the reality into which he was born. How could Thomas himself be sure he wasn't trapped in another, unseen glass bubble? Thinking this, Thomas felt a quiver of panic. What did it mean for a world to be real? The scene tumbled away from him: the London winter, Hegel's house, the table, the candles burning, the seven boxes. It all spun away, in this precipitous moment of doubt. A dream? An illusory world? How could he ever be certain? He closed his eyes.

'Thomas. Thomas!' Maud whispered across the table. She stretched out her foot and dug her sharp heel into the top of his foot. 'Wake up, silly. Pay attention!'

He opened his eyes. The scene was still intact, just as he'd left it. Maud was right of course. Wake up. Pay attention. It was the best he could do.

The boxes were unlocked, one by one. Lee opened Acoma, Miss Hudson, the forest world of Xanadu. Then it was time for Thomas and Broceliande, Hegel and Nineveh. Karsch was last – Albion, Arcadia and Tadmor; the three gardens he had brought under his control.

As each lid was raised, light streamed from the box and filled the room. Strange scenes rose all around them, light windows on other worlds. The walls seemed to melt, to reveal vistas across the desert, or temples on hilltops. The ceiling dissolved to reveal an azure kingdom where seagulls cried. Thomas gripped the table, afraid his mind would be torn to pieces, holding on tight as the glass seeds' fantasy worlds lured him, drew him in. How easily the mind latched on to these enticing realities.

Lee's voice rose above the assault of dream worlds.

'Take out the pieces from the boxes. Place them here, on the table,' he ordered. Thomas could barely master his hands but through a grand effort of will he plunged his unwilling fingers into the box. He couldn't see what it was his hands closed on, the light was too bright. But the piece of glass was warm and smooth, so heavy he struggled to raise it. Once clear of the box, the light vanished promptly, reversing into the material of its origin. Then Thomas could see it, black in the centre, a translucent grey at its outer edges, the surface tinged with mobile silver. And still it enticed, calling him to focus, to step inside. He snapped his gaze away and placed the glass on the table alongside the six other pieces.

'What do we do now?' Maud said. Her voice was clear and bright after the tumult of dreams, the storm in which the table and the six people were the still eye.

Karsch turned to look at her. 'We watch. We wait,' he said. They didn't have to wait long. The seven pieces, each of which seemed solid and immutable, began to soften and flow like huge globes of mercury. It was as though they sensed each other, yearned to be whole again. Uncanny, tremulous, the liquid pieces moved together and swallowed one another – creating again one large black globe in the centre of the table. The views of other worlds, like a trail of scarves pulled out of a hat by a magician, folded away and disappeared.

Candlelight and darkness. The fire burning. The distant sound of revellers in the street, the quiet clop of a horse's hooves in the road. London reality reasserted itself, humdrum and marvellous at once.

Thomas sighed. Miss Hudson laughed suddenly.

'You have the original box,' Lee said. Hegel nodded. 'Then there is only one thing remaining to do.'

They all looked at Karsch. He rose from his chair and stood up straight. One last glance at Maud.

'*Auf Wiedersehen*, granddaughter,' he said. 'Till we meet again.' Then a grin, in which the mad mask briefly shone through. He placed his hands tenderly on the glass globe and stared into its depths, like a fortune-teller straining to see a clouded future. A thin beam of light rose from the globe, and another shone from Karsch's chest. These two white paths met between them, and Karsch's corporeal self seemed to fade, drawn along the road of light into the glass world. His physical body dimmed and melted away. The beam of light disappeared into the glass and Karsch was gone.

EDEN

And the Lord God planted a garden,
eastward in Eden.

Genesis

The wind blew from the east, carrying the ship across the dark Atlantic waters. The huge iron steamship, itself a miniature world on the expanse of the salt ocean, grumbled through the night towards the coast of America.

Lee and Thomas stood on the deck. A slim moon kept pace with them, mile after mile. The wind was brisk, cutting through to the skin despite warm coats and fur-lined hats.

'We're about halfway,' Lee said. 'Another four days and we'll be there.'

Thomas felt a thrill of excitement. Never in his life had he imagined such a trip. 'I can't wait!' he said.

Lee laughed. 'Well, I hope it lives up to your expectations, Thomas. It's a great country, and I'm very happy you're coming with me.'

The last days before the departure had been tumultuous and difficult. First the funeral for Mrs Lawrence, which Thomas and Miss Hudson had attended with Maud, a gesture of support and solidarity. It had been a curiously vulgar affair – so many overdressed and tearful ruffians turning out to pay their last respects, a mountain of gaudy wreaths from unnamed mourners doubtless from the old woman's gangland past. The silver-haired vicar looked distinctly nervous, officiating at such a gathering. Maud wept a little at the graveside but her tears were dry by the time they left the cemetery for the wake. This took place in a smart hotel where the ruffians drank too much gin and grew maudlin and tearful themselves. At the end of the afternoon a fight broke out, which marked the end of the party, and soon everyone had gone home. Maud returned for a last night at Mrs Lawrence's home. The following morning she and her aunt Lucy would be travelling to Huntington Hall to live with Miss Hudson. It seemed to Thomas she would lead a closeted and quiet life there, but Maud seemed happy enough.

'There is still the library. Do you have any idea how much there is for me to learn? Miss Hudson has a huge garden at the house – a real garden. The Guild of Medical Herbalists won't vanish just because we don't have the magic garden any longer,' she told him. She seemed very different now. The façade of childishness had melted away. She had put this cloak to one side since the death of Mrs Lawrence.

'Mr Lee has asked me to go with him to New Mexico,' Thomas told her. 'When I return, I intend to finish my apprenticeship. I want to build on Mr Constantine's work and fulfil my grand-mother's legacy. Besides, my parents would lke me to have a proper trade.'

Maud had waved them off at the station, as Lee and Thomas began the journey to Liverpool where the steamship waited.

'Will you write?' she asked, her voice a little anxious. Thomas nodded.

They stood for a few moments, neither knowing what to say. Then Maud threw caution to the wind and hugged him, tight and tense.

*

'It is time,' Lee said. His voice was heavy. They were the only people on deck. A skim of rain was falling now. It was after midnight. The American bent down and picked up a wooden box. It was locked, the lid sealed with a thick layer of wax.

'Are you sure?' Thomas said.

Lee sighed. 'Nope. I'm not sure. There are no easy answers here. We throw this away? Conceivably the most marvellous thing mankind has yet encountered . . . it is a tough call, Thomas.'

They stood a few minutes more, reluctant to make the commitment. Thomas thought of Karsch, inside the dome. Where was he? What could he see and feel? What marvels was he conjuring? And he thought of Maud back at Huntington poring over books and papers, cultivating herbs and potions, appropriately witchlike with her black hair and the rooks circling over the house.

'It may be marvellous,' Lee ruminated, 'but I don't think we are wise enough to use it. Not yet.'

He lifted the box over the railing and held it for a moment or two more, suspended over the speeding sea. Another squall of rain wet their faces. The ship rose and plunged and the decision was made for them because the box was falling, down and down, into the tumult of the sea. It sank like lead, beneath the veil of foam and into the inky water.

Thomas tried to fix his eyes on the spot where it had fallen but the ship carried on and the heaving, rain-spotted surface of the ocean did not retain any sign of it. He imagined the box sinking down into the cold Atlantic water, deeper and deeper, into the lightless depths. Would it ever be recovered? Perhaps the garden drove its own destiny and one day it would be hefted from the water in a net of fish, or washed up on a beach in some distant century. Thomas stepped away from the railing. He didn't want to think about it any more. Lee was waiting for him, and America, and his own, bright marvellous life. Another squall blew across the deck, empty except for the two of them.

'Come inside,' Lee said.

'Yes,' Thomas said. 'It's cold out here, and I'd like something to eat.'

He turned away from the sea and the two of them left the deck and went inside to find warmth, food and company.

Eden . . . contains seven gardens:

Arcadia – the Poison Garden – Ernestina Lawrence
Acoma – the Garden of Journeys – Robert Lee
Albion – the Garden of Love – Nehemiah Blake
Broceliande – the Garden of Dreams – Augusta Williams
Tadmor – the Garden of Healing – Albert Constantine
Nineveh – the Perfume Garden – Rupert Hegel
Xanadu – the Garden of Time – Louisa Hudson

Acknowledgements

For information on the Guild of Funerary Violinists I am indebted to the learned Rohan Kriwaczek and his book *An Incomplete History of the Art of Funerary Violin*, published by Duckworth Overlook in 2006.

A Funerary Violinist himself, Mr Kriwaczek has since 1999 dedicated himself to promoting funeral violin, including the writing of his incomplete history. He is currently Acting President of the Guild of Funerary Violinists.

The characters in this novel are all invented, however, so any inaccuracies in the depiction of this historic guild remain entirely the fault of the author.